IMMORTALITY CURSE

IMMORTALITY CURSE

SHADOW VANGUARD™, BOOK THREE

TOM DUBLIN
MICHAEL ANDERLE

For "Tommy's Team" Micky Cocker, James Caplan, Erika Everest, and Kelly O'Donnell The BEST damn beta readers in the universe!

— Tom

*To Family, Friends and
Those Who Love
To Read.
May We All Enjoy Grace
To Live The Life We Are
Called.*

— Michael

IMMORTALITY CURSE TEAM

Thanks to our JIT Readers
From all of us, our deepest gratitude!

James Caplan
Nicole Emens
John Ashmore
Diane L. Smith
Micky Cocker
Kelly O'Donnell
Erika Everest
Misty Roa

*If we missed anyone, **please** let us know!*

Editor
Skyhunter Editing Team

Ordanian Hub, Skolar Major, The Horny Bistok Bar

Tc'aarlat managed to remain undercover for a total of six minutes and twenty-three seconds before he broke character and executed the drug dealer across the table with a pair of chopsticks.

For the Yollin, it was a personal record.

He, Jack Marber and Adina Choudhury had been covertly posing as potential suppliers of the latest street drug, Eternity, for the past three months. After weeks of hanging out in dilapidated drug dens, and mixing with addicts of many different species, they'd finally managed to get a sample of their product to local kingpin, Krystov Pyle.

A sample secretly created by the labs of the Etheric Federation.

This had earned them a meeting with the drug lord himself, at which they needed to stay in character, win his trust, and gather incriminating evidence that could be used to bring him and his organization down.

The team had shown up at this seedy backstreet bar on Skolar Major as instructed. Two huge Huttut bodyguards had been at the door to greet them, frisking the trio to ensure they weren't carrying weapons, and that they'd brought along more of their ultra-pure Eternity.

The new narcotic had first surfaced on Talth, a neighboring world to Skolar Major within the notorious Ordanian Hub: five planets which orbited a dark energy star deep inside the Ordon Nebula.

In addition to producing an incredible high, Eternity was rumored to have a gradual, but permanent detrimental effect on the user's eyesight, blistering the retina and rewarding addicts with a funfair-style "hall of mirrors" effect to their vision long after they had sobered up.

Krystov Pyle had pounced on the new product, providing his most trusted dealers with samples of the drug to try out on their best customers. His lieutenants across all five worlds had quickly reported back that their regulars were now hooked on the stuff and were desperate for more.

All of which had led to this important meeting.

"The name's Chaplin," snarled Jack once the Huttut guards had finished searching him and led the team over to a table at the rear of the bar. "These are my associates, Laurel and Hardy."

Tc'aarlat threw Jack a dark look. Only that morning, he'd insisted they use the unique name and backstory he'd created for his undercover persona: a bitter ex-cage fighter nicknamed "the Duke," consumed with the endless search for the one-eyed male who'd killed his identical twin sister.

Jack had clearly decided to go in a different direction.

Krystov Pyle gestured for the trio to sit opposite him as he tucked a large, white napkin into the collar of his shirt. One of his goons then snapped his fingers, and a young waitress scurried over to set a bowl of steaming food in front of the drug lord.

Adina's eyes watered as the pungent aroma of the dish reached her. Pyle had been served what appeared to be some kind of thick, green soup in which there was a selection of plump, writhing worms.

As the three counterfeit criminals watched, Pyle picked up a set of sharp, metal chopsticks and tapped the ends together. He then plucked one of the squirming worms from the bowl, slurped it into his mouth, and proceeded to chow down on it.

The worm screamed as it burst between his teeth.

"My boys tell me you can provide a regular supply of Eternity," Pyle grunted, lumps of food flying from his mouth as he ate.

Tc'aarlat's mandibles quivered as he forced himself not to look at the resulting mess.

"We can get as much of the stuff as you need," replied Jack in a gruff voice. "My associate Laurel here has a contact back on Yoll who cooks the best there is."

Pyle stopped chewing for a brief moment, much to Tc'aarlat's relief. "So, tell me why I shouldn't just kill you three right now and go to this guy myself."

Jack remained stoic. "Because he refuses to deal with

other species," he sneered. "You're not Yollin, you don't get the goods."

He kept his gaze fixed on the drug lord, adding: "What can I say? He's proud of his people."

Krystov Pyle considered Jack's words silently. For a moment, the only sound was the fat, bloated worms splashing around in his soup bowl.

Adina's eyes narrowed. Would Pyle fall for Jack's lie? They'd worked hard to get this face to face meeting. Now all they needed were the names of Pyle's other suppliers and they could bring the full force of the Etheric Federation down on the entire organization.

The kingpin looked back down at his lunch, a faint smile playing across his lips. "Patriotism," he grumbled. "I get that."

Snatching up another worm, he sucked it into his mouth, savoring the terrified screech it made as he bit the creature in half.

Tc'aarlat's mandibles quivered again.

"So, how much do you need?" demanded Adina.

"Not so fast!" barked Pyle. "I didn't say I was in the market for the stuff, did I?"

Adina chuckled darkly. "Then you're crazy."

Jack stiffened as the Huttut goons reached toward their holsters. He glanced at Adina, hoping she knew what she was doing.

"Every kid and his mama is gonna be hooked on this stuff within a cycle or two," she asserted. "You get in now, you make big. You don't…"

She shrugged. "Then I guess you were never a player to begin with."

Pyle chewed sloppily for a while, then he tossed his head back and laughed hard.

"Ha! You guys are insane!" he spat, slapping his hand on the table, sending waves of emerald soup and one of the worms washing over the side of his bowl. "Who'd have thought three little pissers with crazy names like yours could amuse anyone?"

Jack and Adina laughed along with him.

Tc'aarlat didn't laugh. Instead, he watched as the terrified worm made a break for freedom, squeaking in terror as it wriggled madly toward the edge of the table.

It nearly got there, too. But, at the last moment, Pyle spotted that part of his lunch was escaping. Clutching the metal chopsticks in his fist, he smashed them down, the sharp ends piercing the belly of the worm, and bringing it up to his mouth to suck it inside with a *SCHLUP*.

"*GAAAAHHH!*"

With that furious cry, Tc'aarlat leapt to his feet, reached over and snatched the wet chopsticks from Pyle's hand. Spinning them with his fingers, he swung his arm upwards, thrusting the pointed ends up the drug lord's nose, one per nostril.

Then, grabbing the horrified lowlife's hair with his other hand, he slammed Pyle's face onto the tabletop, ramming the chopsticks deep into his brain.

As the Huttut guards made to draw their weapons, Jack grabbed the edge of the table and tipped it toward them, showering the two goons with hot soup and causing them to stagger backward.

Adina turned and nodded to the waitress behind the bar. She reached beneath the counter, grabbed two identical Jean Dukes Specials, and tossed them over to the group.

Adina caught one, and Jack the other. They paused just long enough to ensure their dials were set to a solid six, then emptied their respective barrels into the furious meatheads just as they drew a bead on the trio with their own weapons.

A battery of tiny black pucks dug into their thick Huttut flesh before exploding, tearing the two henchmen apart.

Their bodies hit the floor, gristly pieces of seared body-guard flesh spattering the soup-soaked carpet and landing among the few remaining wriggling worms.

Then, silence.

Adina crossed the room to pay the waitress for her help and to reassure her that Krystov Pyle would never get another young local hooked on drugs as he had done with her brother.

Jack shoved his Jean Dukes Special into his waistband and stared at Tc'aarlat angrily. The Yollin reached up to twiddle his mandibles, clearly embarrassed.

"Well," said Jack, "that's another fine mess you've gotten us into."

ICS *Fortitude*, Bridge

"Tc'aarlat, sit down and fasten your safety belt this minute!"

Solo, the Entity Intelligence of the ICS *Fortitude*, glared down at the Yollin from the viewscreens, a frown fixed upon her fabricated features.

"I will...do it...just as soon...as I catch all...these little darlings!" replied Tc'aarlat from his position standing on the co-pilot's chair, arms windmilling as he attempted to catch three tiny purple-plumaged hawk fledglings from the air as they flew in circles around the bridge.

The birds' mother, Mist, watched this charade for a moment, then went back to nonchalantly preening her blood-red feathers.

"Hey!" cried Adina as one of the chicks swooped over her workstation, grabbed a small screwdriver in its claws, and tried to fly off with it. Thrusting out her hand, she just managed to snatch the tool from the winged thief before it could make its escape.

"I thought we'd agreed you'd keep these things caged!" exclaimed Jack, ducking as another of the chicks dive-bombed the pilot's console with a high-pitched *SCREECH*.

"No," protested Tc'aarlat. "*You're* the one who wants to lock them up. I agreed to nothing. I can't train them if they're stuck in a cage twenty-four hours a day, can I?"

"You're not training them now!" commented Adina, setting aside her screwdriver and selecting a soldering iron. Concentrating hard, she connected a handful of small microchips to an electronic circuit board. All seemed to be going well until a large dollop of creamy white bird shit landed on her latest connection with a hiss.

"For fuck's sake!" she spat, tossing the iron and circuit board aside. "Now I'll have to start all over again."

Tc'aarlat took a break from his chair-top gymnastics. "I'd offer to help you if you would tell us what the fuck you're doing!"

"I've already explained," responded Adina, sliding open

a drawer beneath her navigation console and choosing a new circuit board. "It's a surprise."

"So were these fuckers!" grumbled Jack as a large dollop of airborne excrement hit his left cheek. He reached for a cloth. "I swear that little bastard did that on purpose."

"Hey!" yelled Tc'aarlat. "Don't talk about Albert Einstein that way."

Jack and Adina shared a glance.

"Who?" Jack asked.

"Einstein!" repeated Tc'aarlat, lunging as the bird whizzed past his head. He missed again. "Or is that one Stephen Hawking?"

"Einstein and Hawking?" demanded Adina. "You've named two of your raal hawk's babies after famous Earth scientists?"

"Of course not!" countered Tc'aarlat. "I named all *three* of them after scientists. Einstein, Hawking and that one's Sir Isaac Newton."

"You didn't go with my suggestion of 'Roasted,' 'Barbecued' and 'Southern Fried,' then?"

"No, I did not!"

"Well, I don't know how you can tell them apart at all, no matter what their names," proclaimed Adina. "They look identical to me."

"It's simple!" said Tc'aarlat, pointing to the nearest chick. "That's Hawking. At least, I think it is." He sighed. "You might be right. They *are* pretty difficult to identify."

"As is their species," said Jack with a smile. "You have no idea what kind of bird Mist got it on with when we were dropping off the slave kids we rescued from Damkin Prime."

Tc'aarlat stared at the ship's captain. "I beg your pardon?" he hissed angrily. "Mist did not 'get it on' with anyone."

Jack frowned. "Are you suggesting these flying fuckers are the result of a virgin birth or do I have to have 'the talk' with you?"

Adina giggled as she resumed her work with the soldering iron.

"You see," began Jack, "when a mummy bird and a daddy bird love each other very much, they cuddle in a special way…"

"I know that!" bellowed Tc'aarlat. "I was just trying to stop you from turning a beautiful event into something gross."

"Beautiful event?" Jack scoffed. "I really don't recall soft candlelight and smooth jazz. They did it in a bush, Tc'aarlat!"

"Actually, raal hawks mate on the wing," explained the Yollin. "Oh, here we go…"

Tc'aarlat's eyes narrowed as one of the chicks turned in mid-air and flew directly toward him. "Come to Granddad, Einstein—if that's who you are!"

As the tiny bird zipped by, Tc'aarlat pounced—shooting out his arm, fingers flexing…

Which caused the seat of his chair to spin, and the Yollin to fall to the floor with a heavy *thud*.

"Motherfucking flying shits!" he spat as Jack and Adina did their best to hide their laughter.

As if sensing they had caused more trouble than usual, the three chicks banked and flew through the bridge door and down the corridor beyond.

Tc'aarlat climbed to his feet, winced as a bolt of pain shot down his back, and raced after them.

Jack turned back to the viewscreens, sighing when he spotted yet another snow-colored mound of bird feces staining the keyboard on his control panel.

"I blame *you* for this!" he growled, shooting an angry look up at Mist's perch. However, the raal hawk was now sound asleep, her head tucked beneath her wing.

"Excuse me, Captain," interrupted Solo as Jack produced his clean-up cloth yet again.

"What is it, Solo?"

"Against my better judgment, I continued with our journey despite Tc'aarlat's obvious flouting of Federation health and safety practices. We are now making our final approach to the mining colony on the asteroid named Joxxen."

"Good," said Jack. "The quicker we can unload this cargo and get back to base to give the ship a thorough clean out, the better."

The EI pulled an unhappy face. "I'm afraid that may not be as simple a task as it sounds."

Jack looked up. "What? Why not?"

Solo switched the screen to show a view of Joxxen. The route to the asteroid was blocked by dozens of small space-craft circling a vast cruiser.

"Because access to our destination is currently being denied by a posse of environmental protestors."

2

Orbit of Asteroid Joxxen, Protest Ship *Joshua*, Bridge

Captain Bon Noh slipped on his lilac-tinted glasses and studied his reflection in the ornately-framed mirror welded into position above his ship's navigation console.

Like all males of his species, the Malatian was incredibly proud of his mane of long silver hair, which his people routinely used as a courtship display to help attract a mate.

For this reason, the more extravagant the hairstyle, the better. For Bon Noh, that meant weaving stem after stem of tropical flowers among his tresses, then topping it all off with thick drops of dew harvested from the grasslands of his home planet.

The dense globs of liquid sparkled as they caught the flickering light cast by the several hundred organically-sourced candles currently lighting the bridge.

Selecting a comb from a nearby pot of haircare products, Bon Noh teased a delicate blossom chosen to complement his teal skin into place, then he sprinkled his whole head with a handful of shimmering glitter.

As he replaced the comb, the ship's second-in-command stepped onto the bridge. The male Howvan was tall, extremely slim, and covered from head to toe in a layer of fine, bristly black fur.

He stood to attention, like a hairy butler.

"Excuse me, sir," he intoned with little inflection in his voice.

"Yes, Theeyej, what is it?"

"You asked me to let you know when the asteroid's next delivery came within range."

The viewscreen in front of the captain flickered, then showed a vast cargo ship covered in fading yellow paint as it approached their position. The haulage vessel's identifying tag—ICS *Fortitude*—appeared near the bottom of the screen.

"Thank you, Theeyej," replied Bon Noh. "Any idea what it is they're delivering?"

"I have been able to track their route back to a base station belonging to the Etheric Federation, sir," Theeyej responded. "A brief scan of all cargo consignments leaving the station within the past forty-eight hours cross-referenced against the size of the freighter leads me to conclude this is a shipment of food for the miners working on the asteroid below us. Specifically, meat products."

"Those bastards!" growled Bon Noh. "Don't they realize they're transporting the spoils of murder?"

"I doubt it has even crossed their tiny minds, sir."

Captain Bon Noh took one final admiring glance at

himself in the mirror, then snatched up a microphone and pressed the button on its side.

"Freedom-lovers!" he announced. "The enemy is at our door. If you look at your scanners, you will see the approach of the Interstellar Cargo Ship *Fortitude*. On board are the dissected carcasses of formerly living creatures, destined for the mouths and stomachs of the callous invaders stealing the natural resources and mistreating the indigenous peoples of the asteroid we have vowed to protect."

Bon Noh gritted his teeth as he pushed his purple-lensed glasses up his nose. "Prepare to protest!"

"Is there anything I can do to assist you, sir?" asked Theeyej.

"Yes, there is, Theeyej," replied Bon Noh, pointing at the screen. "Hail that ship!"

ICS *Fortitude*, Bridge

"Sorry to bother you, Captain," said Solo, "but we are being hailed by the *Joshua 3*. Should I accept the communication?"

Jack glanced at Adina, who set down her soldering iron and spun her chair to face the viewscreens.

"Yes, please, Solo," he responded. "Connect us."

There was a hiss of static, then a live video feed appeared on each of the bridge's screens.

"This is Captain Bon Noh of the Protest Ship *Joshua 3*," said the teal-skinned figure in the center of the frame. "What is your name, murderer?"

Jack's expression remained calm. "I am Captain Jack

Marber of the ICS *Fortitude*," he announced. "And I strongly object to your use of the word 'murderer.' Why would you call me that?"

"Because I know your kind." Bon Noh sneered, then glared at Jack from behind his tinted glasses. "You deliver death!"

"No," countered Jack. "We're delivering sausages."

"So you admit it!" screeched Bon Noh, the wildflowers in his hair quivering as he shook with rage. "You carry an evil cargo of flesh torn from helpless animals—defenseless creatures slaughtered purely so that wicked people may devour their innocent carcasses!"

"I guess that's one definition of sausages," commented Adina. "What about the burgers? Go on—describe them next."

"You!" bellowed Bon Noh, pointing in Adina's direction. "You, demon wench, are complicit in this transaction of doom! As are the depraved monsters waiting on the asteroid below, eager to fill their swollen bellies with tainted tissue torn from the blameless bodies of animals born into captivity so that they might be executed and their very life-force devoured!"

Jack let out a long breath. "Wow!" he said flatly. "Those are some strong words."

"You're not wrong," agreed Adina.

Jack nodded. "Especially when spoken about vegetarian sausages."

"Indeed."

On the screens, Bon Noh blinked behind his lilac lenses.

There was a slight pause.

"What?" he croaked after a moment.

"Those depraved monsters you just mentioned?" said Jack. "The ones waiting to fill their swollen bellies with our murderous cargo? They're Festiniog miners, aren't they?"

"Yes…"

"From Blaunai Prime?"

"I, er…guess so."

All sense of admonition had vanished from Bon Noh's voice.

"Yeah," continued Jack, reaching up to scratch the back of his head. "They're a purely vegetarian species. They don't eat meat."

"N-none?"

"Not a bit," replied Jack. "Their digestive systems just evolved that way, by all accounts. They simply can't stomach the stuff, no matter how swollen their murderous bellies get."

Bon Noh gave a slight cough as Tc'aarlat re-entered the bridge and glanced at the rival ship's captain on the screens.

"Who's the princess?" he asked, taking his seat.

Jack turned to the Yollin with a smile. "This is the captain of the Protest Ship *Joshua 3.*"

"Right," said Tc'aarlat, his tone disinterested. "Calls himself a protestor, does he?"

"I do!" huffed Bon Noh, puffing out his chest. "Why? What would *you* have me call myself?"

Tc'aarlat offered a small shrug. "Well, there's only one word I know of for the kind of person who wears purple glasses," he offered. "And that word is 'twat.'"

"How dare you?" roared Bon Noh. "I'm here on a

mission to save the native species of the Joxxen asteroid, and I demand respect!"

"Stopping our delivery of vegetarian food will save the lives of Joxxers?" Jack questioned.

"Correct!" snarled Bon Noh. "The owners of the company mining minerals from asteroids within this belt are known to treat indigenous populations as little more than slaves."

Fixing the screen with a steely gaze, the captain of the *Joshua 3* raised his hand and began to snap his fingers once every second.

Click.

Click.

Click.

"Every time I snap my fingers, another native individual dies!"

Tc'aarlat scowled. "Well, stop snapping your fingers then, you nasty bastard!"

Bon Noh glanced at his hand for a second, then dropped it out of sight. "No, you fool!" he spat. "I mean that these people are being used and abused by the avaricious miners. Someone has to protect them."

The Malatian struck what he hoped was a heroic stance. "And that someone is Bon Noh!"

"Wait, did you say your name is Bon Noh?" asked Tc'aarlat. "I've heard of you…"

A self-satisfied smirk played on the protestor's lips. "I do have something of a reputation."

"Too right you do!" exclaimed Tc'aarlat, turning to look at Jack and Adina. "Do you guys remember the time eco-warriors teamed up to stop farmers from using pesticides to protect their crops on Gregoria?"

"I think I read about that," said Adina. "Didn't that result in an entire season's harvest being destroyed by swarming insects?"

"That's it!" replied Tc'aarlat. "Half the planet had to be evacuated and hospitalized due to malnutrition afterward. This was the guy behind that protest!"

"That's hardly fair!" argued Bon Noh. "I couldn't know that—"

"And, he organized a gang of activists to chain themselves to a school of baleon whales in the oceans of Teedris."

"I did that to stop them from being hunted to extinction!" cried Bon Noh. "And it worked; no baleon whales died that day."

"Maybe not," responded Tc'aarlat, "but six of your militant whale lovers did when the entire school decided to dive down to the seabed and stay there, didn't they?"

"That was due to poorly-manufactured chains and locks!" Bon Noh asserted, his cheeks flushing a deep shade of green.

Tc'aarlat was now enjoying himself so much that he was practically bouncing in his seat. "Hey, don't forget the time your ship's exhaust gases contaminated the lower atmosphere of Parlack's moon, Tagoa, when you were demonstrating against—"

"*ENOUGH!*" bellowed Bon Noh, flowers tumbling to the floor as he ran his fingers roughly through his hair. "So I've had some setbacks in the past! At least I try to help those less fortunate than myself. And that's what I intend to do here."

Tc'aarlat opened his mouth to respond, but Jack raised a hand to silence him.

"I think you should leave that to us," he said. "Once we've made our delivery, we will review the mining company's treatment of the Joxxers and deal with any infractions."

"You will not!" spat Bon Noh.

"Why not?" questioned Adina. "We're actually quite good at this sort of thing."

"I don't care," growled the Malatian. "You will not review the situation on the surface of Joxxen because you will not be able to land there."

With that, Bon Noh snatched up his microphone again and yelled a command into it. "Operation Swarm is go!"

Jack frowned. "What?"

Suddenly, a series of clangs and thuds echoed through the ship.

"Solo," cried Jack, flicking a switch to end the video link with the *Joshua 3.* "Report."

The EI's avatar appeared on the screens. "We are under attack, Captain. Over a dozen individuals have attached themselves to the exterior of the ship's hull, and more are currently leaving their shuttles to join them.

Another flurry of bangs and clunks announced the arrival of the second wave of protestors.

"Those devious fuckweasels!" snarled Tc'aarlat. "They must have been sneaking up on us while we were arguing with Captain Wank-basket!"

"We can't land with that lot clinging to the outside of

the *Fortitude*," Adina pointed out. "We'll have to get them off somehow."

"Easily done," suggested Tc'aarlat, spinning to face the main viewscreen. "Solo, on my mark, send lethal pulses of electricity through the ship's hull in fifteen-second bursts, starting from—"

"NO!" bellowed Jack, quickly releasing his safety harness and jumping out of his seat. "Solo, ignore that command!"

"What?" demanded Tc'aarlat. "Why? You want these touchy-feely gonad-garglers to let go of the ship, don't you?"

"Yes," replied Jack, "but not like that!"

The Yollin shrugged. "All right then, we'll just go ahead and land. Any of the dickless wonders stupid enough to still be hanging on when we burn the thrusters will come away extra-crispy."

Jack ran his palm across his face. "I don't believe this," he said with a sigh. "We are *not* killing any protestors!" he insisted.

"Then I'm out of ideas," Tc'aarlat admitted.

Jack grabbed the Yollin by his mandibles and pulled him to his feet. "Go and get suited up," he ordered. "We're going out there to make them let go in person."

"*OWOWOWOW!*" cried Tc'aarlat, rubbing at his aching mandibles. "You know what your problem is?" he grunted as he stomped towards the door leading off the bridge. "You can be a real pussy at times."

Jack watched him leave, then turned back to Adina to assign her duties—but stopped when he spotted the angry look on her face.

"What's the matter with you?"

"Why you two?" Adina queried.

Jack's brow knitted. "Why us two what?"

"Why is it down to you two to space-walk outside and chip those bio-loving barnacles off the hull? Don't you trust me or something?"

Jack shook his head. "I'm taking Tc'aarlat *because* I trust you," he countered. "I don't want to leave the Birdman of Yoll alone in here with his evil-genius imagination while we crawl around among those soap-dodgers out there. Left to his own devices, he's likely to eject the lot of us up the arse of the nearest black hole."

Adina considered Jack's explanation for a moment, then spun back to her workstation without a word and snatched up the soldering iron.

Jack sighed.

"Solo," he said, making for the door, "give me five minutes, then open the starboard side airlock."

3

Planet Abstone, Northwestern Face of Mount Damavand

Queen Lapis Lazuli paused just long enough to shift her late husband's corpse to her left shoulder, then, with a sharp tug on her long beard, as was the tradition, she continued her journey up the mountain.

Watching from a respectful distance on either side of the rough trail, members of the public tugged at their own beards in response, lowering their eyes as their much-loved regent carried the body of her consort on its final journey.

Ahead lay the gaping chasm of Mount Damavand's volcanic crater—the highest point of the vast mountain range into and beneath which the entire city of Jarosite had been carved and now thrived.

And into which the mortal remains of Jaspil Hornfen would be cast, as had been the convention for deceased consorts for as long as anyone had kept records.

As she climbed, Queen Lazuli concentrated on the weight of Jaspil's limp figure slumped across her back, fondly recalling the night they had first met.

He had been first in the traditional line-up of twelve suitors selected by her closest aides as potential new consorts. As she had already done on two previous occasions, the queen had entered the room and walked slowly along the line, studying each suitor in turn as she prepared to make her choice.

Should she wish to do so, it was permissible for the queen to stop and ask questions of the chosen males, but this opportunity was not frequently used. The purpose of a royal consort was to look good at her side during official engagements and endeavor to provide the planet with a suitable heir to the throne.

Their ability to make polite conversation was not high on the list of requirements.

It wasn't as if she was going to talk to whomever she chose to marry.

Queen Lazuli had approached the lineup with an air of impatience; she very much wanted to get this ridiculous chore over with and get back to managing the affairs of state.

With female Abstonions living roughly four times as long as their male counterparts, she'd already been through two consorts, neither of whom had distinguished themselves as particularly competent lovers.

Her ongoing lack of offspring attested to that.

All she wanted in her third "husband" was someone with all the requisite body parts for his prescribed duties, who preferably didn't chew with his mouth open or fart during state visits.

From what she could already see, her aides had once again chosen the potential consorts on the basis of how attractive they were and, therefore, how many adoring fans they would attract among the public.

Even *they* didn't really care who they cheered for, as long as he looked good in a military uniform and could wave from a balcony without injuring himself or anyone else.

In fact, the only portion of the population eager to know who would become her new spouse were those who owned companies that produced ceramic mugs and commemorative tea towels.

They needed to know which new face to paste over that of his predecessor on any number of souvenir products.

But then, as the queen began to inspect this collection of commanded courtiers, the most incredible thing had happened: the first suitor in line had winked at her.

It was a wink that would change Queen Lazuli's life.

As expected, she continued down the line, seemingly studying each of the remaining recruits to romance in turn, readying herself to pick one of them to spend the rest of his natural life at her side—but she couldn't concentrate.

All she could think about was that wink.

In the end, there was no contest. Suitor number one— Jaspil Hornfen—was chosen to become her consort.

One lavish royal wedding later, Queen Lapis Lazuli was to discover something even more amazing about her conscripted companion: she was actually interested in what he had to say.

The pair got along in ways the monarch had never expected, nor previously experienced. They shared the same moral sensitivities, enjoyed books in similar genres and—most importantly—they made each other laugh.

Before long, Jaspil was at the queen's side day and night. And night was when their joint efforts to produce a suitable heir to the Abstone throne really advanced.

Queen Lazuli found herself to be with child on three separate occasions. However, each of these pregnancies was to end in tragedy before birth.

These devastating experiences only drew the royal couple closer to one another.

As the queen grew older, she found herself relying on the help and advice of Jaspil more and more, something which had never occurred within the ruling family before —at least not openly.

Changes to the Abstonion constitution were discussed, exploring whether it was possible for a Queen's spouse to be officially accepted as something more than a mere consort or companion.

Could Jaspil Hornfen become the first king ever to be named in such a staunchly female-centered society?

The question was never answered. Jaspil had, in his later years, contracted an illness which attacked his respiratory system, making it increasingly difficult for him to breathe as the disease progressed.

Many nights, Queen Lazuli would lie beside her lover, listening to him wheeze and gasp for air from his elevated position in bed, wishing there was some way to help him.

She had charged the government's most experienced doctors and scientists with the task of working together to find a cure for the disease—an ailment called krannas which dispatched at least a quarter of the planet's population annually.

The latest reports stated progress was being made in the search for a remedy, but it was to be too late for the love of her life.

Two days earlier, Queen Lapis Lazuli had risen to discover her soulmate lying motionless beside her. Jaspil's battle with his illness was at an end.

They had been together for over ninety seasons.

Now, for the third time, she was carrying the corpse of a consort up the scree-covered northwestern slope of Mount Damavand in order to cast it into the yawning depths of its crater.

But this was the first time it hurt inside to do so.

Suddenly, the queen lost her footing and slipped, almost losing her grasp on Jaspil. Several of the royal guards, who had been stationed at regular intervals along the trail to watch for over-enthusiastic well-wishers, darted forward to help her.

"Stay back!" snapped the queen, steadying herself. "Did I request assistance? No, I did not!"

She watched as the two guards reluctantly returned to their posts and then, bending her knees while she stabilized her burden, she gave another weary tug on her beard before continuing her journey.

Finally, she reached the mountain's summit. Here, she was utterly alone: no members of the public were allowed to witness this portion of the ceremony, and the members of the royal guard knew to maintain a respectful distance.

She gazed down into the seemingly bottomless pit,

from the black depths of which twisting plumes of noxious gases rose, revealing the continuing volcanic activity beneath the planet's surface.

In her mind's eye, she saw the bodies of her two previous consorts tumbling silently into the unforgiving darkness of eternal rest.

Now she was here to condemn her love to the same fate.

Lapis gently lay her deceased partner on the rocky ground, gazing at his familiar wrinkled features through tear-filled eyes.

She would be expected to choose a replacement consort by the time of the new moon. Although it was unlikely the process would result in a companion who would come to mean as much to her as Jaspil, the stage was set for her to have to endure this heartache all over again.

Unless...

Drying her eyes with the end of her beard, Queen Lapis Lazuli gently kissed the lips of her most recent consort, then unclipped the personal communicator from her belt. It had a live link to the public address system threaded throughout the city below, and to its sister city on the opposite side of the planet.

Anything she spoke into this device would be relayed to each and every one of her subjects, then repeated and dissected ad infinitum on the many news screen shows for some time to come.

She took a moment to control her whirling emotions, then flicked the switch to activate the communicator.

"This is Queen Lapis Lazuli," she announced. "Where am I as I speak to you? I am above you beside the crater of the mountain we call our home. Why am I here? To honor my late consort, Jaspil Hornfen. My husband, my love, my life. And know this…"

The queen paused as her voice began to crack. While she realized the citizens of Jarosite City all likely knew of the pain she was suffering, she wouldn't allow herself to display any vulnerability.

She took a deep breath, then continued with her announcement, her words echoing through the hundreds of spanns of tunnels deep beneath her feet.

"Will any future Queen of Abstone ever be forced to endure this wretched anguish again?" the queen demanded, blinking away her tears.

"No, she will not!"

Switching off the communicator, she lifted her consort's corpse.

"I shall never forget you," she whispered, this time making no attempt to quell her tears.

Then she stepped to the rim of the crater, held the body of Jaspil Hornfen over the edge, and let him go.

ICS *Fortitude*, Starboard Exterior

Clunk! Clunk! Clunk!

Captain Jack Marber felt the powerful magnets in the soles of his spacesuit's boots thud against the exterior hull of the ship as he ran—agonizingly slowly—towards the nearest protestor.

Without the aid of the ICS *Fortitude's* artificial gravity to help anchor the crew members to wherever they were standing, any type of movement took more than double the usual energy.

Add to that the bulkiness of the suits they wore during extravehicular activities, and it was as if the entire universe were running in slow-motion.

Eventually reaching the closest eco-warrior—a stocky Howvan covered in a layer of thick black fur who was attempting to daub the ship's hull with alien-looking graffiti—Jack pulled back his right arm, clenched his fist, and threw a punch.

He watched as his attack leisurely crossed the gap between himself and his target, striking the pelted protestor full on its furry jaw.

The slug was powerful enough to send the demonstrator tumbling backward, green paint from the self-loading brush he'd been using to befoul the ship exploding from its cracked casing like gangrenous bile.

The Gheeran lunged with his free hand out, seemingly not quite sure whether to strike back at Jack or reach for a handhold to stop himself from being jettisoned into open space. In the end, he managed neither.

"Fuck the fuck off, and *stay* fucked off!" cried Jack as the hirsute hoodlum splashed through the cascade of emerald paint, spinning head over heels as he departed the relative safety of the *Fortitude's* hull.

"*Gott Verdammt!*" bellowed a voice in Jack's ear. He turned to find Tc'aarlat waddling towards him, crammed into a spacesuit at least three sizes too small for his bulky frame.

"What in the name of a bistok's bollocks are you wearing?" Jack demanded through the comm.

"Don't blame me!" retorted Tc'aarlat. "Turns out when your pals at the Etheric Federation refitted the ship, they didn't think to stock it with EVA suits for any species other than human. How I'm supposed to fight off these crusty crazies with the blood supply to my fucking legs cut off is beyond— OW!"

Tc'aarlat spun as fast as the lack of gravity would allow to discover a tall, spindly alien raining blows down upon him with each of his six stick-thin arms.

"Fuck me!" the Yollin spat. "I'm being attacked by a bastard twig!"

"That's a Solarps," Jack commented, making for another of the protestors. "They don't look it, but they're pretty strong."

"You don't need to fucking tell me!" roared Tc'aarlat, trying hard to fend off the powerful punches thrown by his gaunt aggressor. "OW! Fucking stop that, you skinny streak of piss!"

"You know he can't hear you, don't you?" Jack pointed out as he reached for a youthful Patian who was busy battering a section of the hull with a hefty hammer.

"He doesn't need to hear me!" growled Tc'aarlat, swinging back his leg, grateful for the magnets in his other boot for keeping him anchored to the ship. "Actions speak louder than words!"

And, with that, he kicked the Solarps square in the spot where he guessed his adversary kept his testicles. Although he knew nothing about this particular alien species' biology, it very quickly became clear he'd struck the bullseye with his steel-toed boot.

The Solarps doubled over in agony, all six of its bony

hands clutching the crushed body parts nestled between its lanky legs.

"Take that, you scrawny ferret-fucker!" bellowed Tc'aar-lat, taking the opportunity to slam the palm of his hand into the center of the protestor's face. He felt a sickening crunch as what passed for the Solarps' nose shattered beneath the Yollin's tough exoskeleton.

"Score another one for the good guys!" he yelled in triumph.

"The problem is," responded Jack as he dumped both the Patian and his hammer off the ship, "every time we —*the good guys*—dispatch one of these dickheads, two or three more pop up to take their place."

Right on cue, a vast shadow fell over Jack as a pair of blubbery Toowohans wobbled into view. Being comprised almost exclusively of saliva-filled sacs, this race of bulbous beings had no need for spacesuits and could adapt their bodies to enable them to squeeze through the smallest of gaps.

Jack knew from his time combating terrorists of all species with his *Force-de-Guerre* platoon that fighting a Toowohan felt like punching a giant water balloon and was about half as effective.

He glanced longingly at the Patian's hammer as it twirled off into the distance. Damn! If he'd kept hold of that, he might have been able to use the sharp points of the claw to try to burst these fat fuckers.

He cricked his neck from side to side inside his helmet. He was going to have to do this the hard way. He stretched out a hand and beckoned the approaching aliens with his fingers.

"Come on then, you blubbery ballbags! Let's have it!"

But before the portly pair could reach him, they turned to look at each other with what Jack presumed had to be their faces. Then they activated some kind of booster pack hidden somewhere within the fleshy folds of their bloated bodies and blasted away from the side of the ship.

"What the—"

"Hey!" he heard Tc'aarlat bark over the comm. "Come back here! I haven't finished ripping out your insides yet!"

The Yollin met Jack's gaze as, all around them, the previously determined eco-campaigners all abandoned their protest and scuttled back toward the *Joshua 3*.

"Was it something we said?" asked Tc'aarlat with a shrug.

"Adina," called Jack into his mic. "Have any idea what's going on?"

"Actually, I do," came the slightly smug reply. "Someone has just leaked the news that a colony of highly-endangered lamprina beetles has been found on a small moon about three light years away—a moon that is scheduled for destruction to make way for a deep-space telescope."

"I take it Bon Noh and his cronies have just found out."

"I guess so."

Tc'aarlat raised a hand to shield his eyes from the glare of the *Joshua 3*'s engines as they flared to life. "Lamprina beetles?" he questioned. "I don't think I've ever seen one of those."

"No one has," commented Adina. "Nor will they. They don't exist."

A grin spread across Jack's face. "You made them up?"

"I had a little help from Solo," Adina replied. "She

compiled a fake news report about the poor little things teetering on the brink of galaxy-wide extinction while I knocked out a press release from the demolition company. We'll be unloaded and long gone from here by the time Bon Noh realizes they've been duped."

Jack shook his head as he made for the starboard-side airlock. "I had no idea you could be so wonderfully deceitful," he commented.

Adina chuckled. "Tc'aarlat's not the only one who can think like an evil genius."

4

Asteroid Joxxen, Scota Brothers Mining Corp., Unloading Bay 2

Jack glanced up at the code stamped onto yet another box of vegetarian meat products being carried from the ICS *Fortitude* and tapped a box on his tablet screen to add a tick beside the relevant consignment number.

The tall orange-skinned aliens unloading the food delivery were Joxxers, a species native to several asteroids in this belt. Known for their strength, dogged perseverance and ability to work long hours on very little sleep, they were an obvious choice of labor for the outside mining company currently scouring the asteroid for valuable minerals.

They were also the subject of Captain Bon Noh and his followers' protests. They believed the indigenous Joxxers were being exploited by the Festiniog miners, although Jack hadn't seen any evidence of that.

At least, not yet.

Tc'aarlat stepped out of a rickety wooden shed serving as the mining company's office, carefully counting a thick wad of cash.

"These guys do business just the way I like it!" he proclaimed, waving the bundle of money as he crossed the rough stone yard to stand with Jack. "Payment on time, without any haggling, in unmarked bills."

Jack didn't attempt to suppress his smile. "Sounds like all those years working for the mob taught you a few tricks."

"Too right!" responded Tc'aarlat, tucking the cash in the pocket of his jacket. "My life is a classic case of rags to bitches."

Jack blinked. "I think you mean riches," he corrected.

"I don't think so," countered Tc'aarlat. "Riches to bitches doesn't make any sense."

Deciding this was a ridiculous conversation, and not one worth continuing, Jack looked up as two Joxxers carried another crate down from the ship, ticking the box on his tablet screen to certify delivery had been made.

Sweating profusely in the heat, one of the Joxxers paused to remove its shirt, tucking the end of the damp garment into the pocket of its dust-coated pants before climbing the ramp leading back into the ship after its colleague.

"I've never really understood vegetarians," announced Tc'aarlat.

Jack sighed. Apparently, he and Tc'aarlat were destined to have a ridiculous conversation after all.

"Go on," he said. "I'll bite. What don't you understand about them?"

"OK," began Tc'aarlat. "Vegetarians don't eat meat, right?"

"Right."

"Partly because research has shown that a plant-based diet may be beneficial to good health?"

"I've heard that, yes."

"But many, if not most, vegetarians clearly state that they don't consume meat because they don't believe animals should be eaten."

"Yes?"

"So why do they want whatever substance they devour instead to *taste* like meat?"

Jack paused in his work, his finger hovering over the surface of his tablet. "What?"

"Think about it," said Tc'aarlat, reaching into one of the boxes that had already been unloaded, selecting a packet of vegetarian burger patties from the contents. "These things are made of, I dunno, tofu or flour or mud or whatever…"

"Go on…"

"But the packaging claims they taste just like the real thing, and that you shouldn't be able to tell the difference when eating them."

This time Jack remained silent.

"Vegetarians don't want to eat animals, but they *do* agree that they taste good or they wouldn't buy this shit. They're trying to fool their digestive systems into believing they are devourers of flesh."

His case stated, Tc'aarlat tossed the pack of burgers back into the box and wiped the moisture from his palms.

Jack let out a long sigh and went back to noting down consignment numbers.

"It can't be doing this lot any good sitting out here in the sun," he added, glancing up at the asteroid's burning white dwarf star. "I mean, it probably can't go off, but I don't imagine it makes the stuff taste any better."

"The Joxxers are working as quickly as they can," Jack pointed out. "They're strong, but not particularly fast."

"Perhaps I can help?" asserted a familiar voice.

Tc'aarlat turned to see who had addressed them and yelped. Standing behind him and Jack was a short humanoid robot constructed of white plastic, with a tablet screen where its face should be.

Beaming happily at them from that screen was Solo.

"What in the name of the fire pits of Yoll is *that* thing?"

The robot bowed theatrically. "I am Solobot 9000."

Jack scowled. "Solobot what now?"

Adina appeared around the side of the ship, grinning. "Solobot 9000," she announced proudly.

Jack looked from the android to Adina and back again. "This is what you've been working on all this time?"

Adina nodded, approaching the group and resting her hand on Solobot's shoulder. The top of the artificial newcomer's head came to just above her waist. "Solo's our link to the Etheric Federation and all the research we need during our missions, right? Well, now we can take that with us when we're away from the ship."

Jack gestured to the communication device strapped to Adina's wrist. "I thought we had those watch gizmos for that?"

"We do," Adina agreed, "but their range is limited, and they can easily become damaged in the field. This way, we'll have Solo with us everywhere we go."

"That sounds like a fucking nightmare," Tc'aarlat grumbled. He took a step back to look the robot up and down. "I doubt you could make it any less attractive."

Solobot angled its face tablet up toward the Yollin as the avatar on screen melted from the usual image of a middle-aged woman to that of Tc'aarlat. "How about now?"

Jack snorted a laugh. "Have you been messing with Solo's humor circuits?" he asked Adina.

"Actually, that's not the real Solo," she replied. "That's a cloned and cut-down copy of her core program. To have room to fit enough internal memory to house the complete software, Solobot 9000 would need to be around sixteen feet tall."

"Small mercies, I suppose," commented Jack. "But, what's with this '9000' thing?"

Adina beamed. "It sounds futuristic! Well, what do you think?"

Tc'aarlat shuddered. "I think it's a creepy little fucker! And I don't see how it's going to be of any use to us."

Before Adina could respond, Solobot spoke up. "Perhaps I may be allowed to demonstrate one of my many abilities," it offered. "While we have been discussing adding me to the crew, several Joxxers have been unloading food items as per our scheduled delivery."

"Yes," said Tc'aarlat with a sigh, "we can see that."

The image of Tc'aarlat on Solobot's screen smiled. "Of course. But, what you may *not* have seen is that one of the Joxxers in question appears to have a number of elongated scars healing on the skin of his back."

Solobot's avatar vanished, to be replaced with a zoomed-in photograph of the Joxxer who had recently removed his shirt. The android gradually adjusted the contrast of the image, affording the team a clearer view of the injuries.

"These scars appear to be fresh," Solobot continued, "and may be the result of an attack upon the individual concerned."

Jack turned to study the Joxxer as he and a fellow inhabitant of the asteroid passed the group carrying another crate of food. The scars on his back were visible upon inspection, but difficult to see due to the bright sunlight reflecting off its sweat-coated orange skin.

Adina returned her gaze to the modified image on Solobot's screen. "Has he been *whipped*?" she asked incredulously.

Tc'aarlat's digital face reappeared. "That would be a reasonable assumption to make, given the available evidence."

"Maybe Bon Noh was onto something after all," mused Jack. "He seemed certain the mining company was mistreating the local indigenous aliens they were employing for grunt work."

"We'll need more evidence than a few scars," Adina pointed out. "Any suggestions?"

"Yeah," said Tc'aarlat, his mandibles twitching. "Can you change your face back to normal? You're weirding me out."

"How do you think the rest of us feel?" questioned Adina as Solobot's avatar morphed back to its usual face. "We have to look at that ugly mug of yours all the time."

The team watched as the scarred Joxxer climbed back into the darkness of the ship's cargo bay once again.

Jack slid his tablet into his pocket. "I think it's time to have a chat with whoever's in charge around here."

Planet Abstone, Jarosite City, Government Labs

Dr. Scoria Gabbro pulled an elasticized net from the pocket of her lab coat and began to roll up her long auburn beard.

"WA*CHOO!*"

Scoria jumped, releasing her beard and watching as it unfurled. "May the gods convey blessings!" she offered, turning to face her sniffling lab partner.

Dr. Breccin Tanister dabbed her nose with the end of her own beard, her eyes bloodshot and watery. "Dank you," she said nasally.

Scoria frowned. "I told you to take the day off if you were still feeling ill today," she scolded.

"I feel fide!" Breccin asserted.

"Well, you don't *look* fine," countered Scoria. "You look like you should be wrapped up in bed with a hot water bottle, a big box of tissues and a tub of creamed ice."

"Nonsense! It's just a bug," insisted Breccin. "We have work to do."

"Work can wait until you're better," said Scoria.

"Not when we're this close to a cure," responded Breccin. "We could have a breakthrough any day now, and I want to be here when we do it. My mom—"

"Your mom has plenty of time," Scoria interrupted. "And you know we won't be allowed to administer any cure we find on Abstonions until we eliminate the majority of the side effects we're still seeing in the rastels."

Breccin leaned back against the bare stone wall of the laboratory and closed her eyes, allowing the cold of the rock to ease her heightened body temperature.

Like all government buildings within the city, and the majority of the public's homes and businesses, the lab had been carved into the dense rock of the mountains above and, as a result, had no windows.

Only the most wealthy and influential Abstonions lived in homes hacked into the sides of Mount Damavand; homes with windows providing sunlight and that most sought-after of precious resources, fresh air.

For everyone else, air was cycled through a system of convection tunnels running up to the surface. Breccin could feel the vent in the stone wall beside her vibrating slightly as the conditioned current flowed through its metal grille.

She turned to peer into a cage containing several small gray-furred rodents. The creatures scuttled about, nibbling bits of tree bark with their powerful front teeth and whipping their long tails back and forth.

It had been nine days since one of the animals had died as a result of being injected with the prototype krannas cure, and both scientists were hoping it would stay that way.

"I know," said Breccin with a sigh. "I just hate seeing her this way. The doctors say the krannas in her throat is inoperable. She can't eat and can hardly speak. Our only hope is finding a cure."

"And we will," Scoria said gently, wrapping an arm around her friend. "I know you're frustrated, but we have to iron out these last few side effects or we'll never get the royal seal. Without that, all this research has been for nothing."

Breccin sniffed, although Scoria wasn't sure whether that was down to the upset over her mother's poor prognosis or the nasty virus she had recently contracted.

Whatever the cause, Dr. Tanister nodded, drying her eyes. She pulled her own net from the pocket of her lab coat and began to roll up her beard so she could tuck it inside.

"Hey, one good thing about working while I have this bug?" she said with a smile. "I can't smell the rastels anymore!"

Scoria laughed. "That *is* an advantage," she agreed. Rastels were notorious for their powerfully putrid odor, leading many researchers to wear face masks while conducting experiments with them.

"If I don't catch that bug from you soon, I may get you to sneeze all over me a couple more times!"

As if on cue, Breccin blasted out another sneeze. "WA*CHOO!*"

"May the gods convey blessings," offered a voice from the doorway.

The scientists spun to see who had spoken.

"Oh!" was all Dr. Scoria Gabbro could say when she identified the illustrious figure standing behind them. "Oh, my!"

Queen Lapis Lazuli.

"Your Majesty!" squeaked Breccin as both scientists bowed deeply.

"Oh, for goodness' sake, stand up," the queen commanded. "Am I here in any official capacity? No. Is there any need for all this foolish bowing and scraping? Absolutely not."

Scoria stood, nudging Breccin with her elbow to urge her to do the same. "How can we help you, Your Majesty?" she asked.

"I came to discuss your search for a cure for krannas."

The scientists exchanged a nervous glance.

"We're still working hard on that, Your Majesty," said Breccin. "I'm sorry we weren't able to achieve success before…"

Her voice trailed away.

"We're very sorry for your loss," said Scoria.

"Yes, yes," blustered the queen, waving her hand as if to brush the matter aside. "Have I come to ask how far you are from a real cure? Yes, I have."

"We…We really don't know, Your Majesty," Scoria admitted. "We could be days away, or it could be months yet. We *are* getting closer—"

"Well, stop it. Now."

Both Scoria and Breccin frowned.

"Excuse me?"

The queen sighed. "Am I commanding you to halt your research into a krannas cure? Yes, I am."

Breccin felt her eyes grow wet once more. "But, Your Majesty! There are so many Abstonions relying on us, my mother included. We must continue with—"

"Silence!" ordered the queen.

The doctors paused their protests, confused.

The queen continued, "Am I here to task you with new research? Yes, I am. Will you immediately cease your work on krannas and take up this new challenge? Most certainly."

"I don't understand," admitted Scoria. "What new challenge?"

Queen Lapis Lazuli adopted a stern expression. "I want you to put every resource you have into finding a cure...for death."

5

Asteroid Joxxen, Scota Brothers Mining Corp., Unloading Bay 2

"I doubt the guys who own the mining company would be very happy to have us sniffing around the place," offered Tc'aarlat as the final crates of food were unloaded from the ICS *Fortitude*. "Especially if we're looking for evidence that they're mistreating their workers."

"What do you know about them?" asked Jack.

"Not much," replied Tc'aarlat with a shrug. "Scota Brothers Mining Corp. Run, unsurprisingly, by two brothers—Elin and Kram Scota.

"They're Festiniogs from Blaunai Prime in the Yecoed System. Elin's the business brain of the company, while Kram specializes in engineering. They won the rights to mine cathcadium here on Joxxen a couple of years back."

"Cathcadium?" inquired Adina.

Jack nodded. "A rare element used in the construction of next-generation ion pulse drives," he explained. "Cutting-edge propulsion tech some experts claim will revolutionize space travel."

"So there's a lot at stake," mused Adina.

"Which is precisely why we don't want to piss them off," Tc'aarlat put in. "The contract to keep supplying mining companies like this is worth a pretty penny—a penny I want to keep in *my* pocket."

He plunged a hand into the pocket of his overalls to demonstrate his point, then frowned as he pulled a small plastic bag containing three tiny white pills back out.

"You've still got those Eternity pills with you?" questioned Adina. "We were supposed to put those back in the safe when we'd finished with them. And, since you decided to overrule us and execute the dealer, it's unlikely we'll need them again anytime soon."

"Oh, ha ha!" replied Tc'aarlat sarcastically. He tucked the drugs back into his pocket. "I'll put them back later if I remember."

"All right," Jack said, looking over to the mining corporation's ramshackle office. "Adina, you head in there and keep Elin occupied while Tc'aarlat and I snoop around a little. If Kram's abusing the Joxxers they've got working for them down in the mines, we'll need evidence."

"Got it," replied Adina, firmly. "Keep Elin Scota busy."

"But don't annoy him," urged Tc'aarlat. "Keep him sweet. Maybe flirt with him a little."

Adina's eyes widened. "Do what?"

"Actually, forget that," continued Tc'aarlat. "He's smart; he'd see right through that. Challenge him instead."

"Challenge him?"

"Exactly!" agreed the Yollin. "Intellectually, I mean. Don't start a fight with him or anything like that."

"You spoil all my fun!" mocked Adina.

"Actually, don't!"

"Don't what? Challenge him or fight him?"

"Both! Neither! You have to be careful not to make him feel stupid or he might decide to tear up our delivery contract." Tc'aarlat's mandibles tapped together as he thought. "Maybe ask him to explain the setup they've got here. Give you a tour of the place."

"A tour?"

"No, that's crazy. You might lead him straight to wherever Jack and I are looking around. Maybe you could—"

Adina raised her hands to stop Tc'aarlat's train of thought. "I've got an idea. Why don't *you* go in there and keep Elin Scota busy, and *I'll* go with Jack to see if we can uncover any evidence that the Joxxers are being abused."

Tc'aarlat looked surprised. "Me?"

"Yeah," replied Adina. "Maybe you could flirt with him a little."

Before Tc'aarlat could reply, Adina started to walk away, Jack at her side. The Yollin glanced toward the wooden building, then down at Solobot 9000, whose avatar was beaming back up at him.

"Whoa, whoa!" he called after his departing colleagues. "You're not leaving this thing with me, are you?"

"Well, we can't take it with us," Adina replied, turning around and walking backward for a moment. "It won't be able to handle rough or uneven terrain until I can get a more powerful gyroscope and install it."

Tc'aarlat opened his mouth to respond, but Adina cut

him off. "Have fun, you two!" she cried before turning back as she and Jack rounded a rocky incline and disappeared from view.

The Yollin looked back down at the android and sighed. "Fuck!"

Planet Abstone, Jarosite City, Room Above The Bauxite Bar

Shonk Oolite repeatedly banged a fist-sized rock on the surface of the battered table he sat behind, and called, "Order, order! Settle down, comrades! If we don't get started on this meeting soon, we risk missing half-price drinks hour at the bar downstairs—again."

Almost immediately, the other occupants of the shabbily-decorated room, around a dozen of them in all, stumbled to a ragged silence.

When he was satisfied everyone was listening, Shonk began, "Welcome to the weekly meeting of the Abstone Society Sentinels," he announced. "The first and only line of defense against the savage, despotic laws forced upon us by Queen Lapis Lazuli and her aristocratic goons."

A meek cheer slunk its way through the assembled crowd.

"Before we discuss our plans to rise up and overthrow the wicked totalitarian regime," Shonk continued, "we'll undertake our usual roll call of your fellow guardians of the future."

He turned to the female Abstonion sitting beside him. "Comrade Renn will do the honors, and may I say we all appreciate the fact that she has happily agreed to commit to the cause and rid herself of her despotic symbol of oppression."

Krystal Renn angrily scratched the stubble growing on her chin and scowled. "I didn't agree to anything *happily*," she grumbled as she worked the reddened skin. "You told me I wasn't allowed back in here unless I shaved my beard off."

"As you well know, comrade, the beard is a representation of the elite's overpowering control of the free-thinking masses, and must be cut away, as would any krannas-like growth."

"Easy for you to say," muttered Krystal, employing her other hand so she could scratch both cheeks simultaneously. "It itches like a bastard. Driving me mad!"

"We value your devotion to the cause, don't we, comrades?"

A few group members murmured what may or may not have been their agreement.

Shonk sighed. "I *said*, we appreciate your devotion to the cause, *don't we, comrades?*"

This time, he was rewarded with disinterested cries of "Yes!" "Sure, why not?" and in one case, "I don't even know who she is."

Like all male Abstonions, Shonk Oolite's head was completely hairless—bald on top, and smooth-chinned below. In fact, the only hairs that had sprouted anywhere on his body were the patches of fine downy fluff adorning the joints of his toes.

Shonk banged his makeshift gavel again as a number of other shaven females around the room began to voice their commiseration with what Krystal was now having to go through for the first time.

"Silence!" he ordered, causing the group's chatter to dwindle once again. "Comrade Renn—the roll call, if you will?"

Krystal sighed heavily, then began to read from the list in front of her: "Marl Gossan?"

"Here!" cried a male voice from near the back of the room.

"Yarvik Nephelin?"

A female sitting on the front row sighed as she gazed up at the register keeper. "Here, Krystal, as always!"

As the roll call continued, Shonk allowed himself a private smile. It was now three months since he had decided to launch this group—to gather together as many like-minded individuals as he could—in order to stand up to what he truly believed was a corrupt and tyrannical ruling royal family.

Initially, finding Abstonions sympathetic to his cause had proven to be something of a chore. He'd been limited to distributing home-made leaflets, enlisting any work colleagues who weren't quick enough to avoid his attention during lunch breaks, and knocking on neighbors' doors to try to get them to listen to his pitch.

It was a slow process.

Things had improved when Shonk discovered an online message board dedicated to sharing all manner of conspiracy theories—from the claim that their planet, Abstone, was shaped like an egg, to an oft-repeated claim that Queen Lazuli was really a cyborg replica put in place by a deep-state faction determined to control society through a series of subliminal messages concealed in her public speeches.

He had recruited the assorted wannabe anarchists, self-proclaimed rebels, and societal misfits now gathered in this room-for-hire above a backstreet bar from that very message board.

This was their third meeting.

"Thank you, Comrade Krystal," declared Shonk. "Next item on the agenda is the arrival of our new uniforms. As you all know, during our first gathering, I asserted that we should dress for the democratic, free-thinking future we have pledged to deliver."

Standing, Shonk unzipped his coat and held it open to reveal the shirt he was wearing underneath. It was black and decorated with pale blue lettering. "They were delivered yesterday."

Everyone in the room studied the garment for a moment. Then, a lone hand rose slowly into the air.

Shonk nodded towards its owner. "Yes, Comrade Gossan?"

Marl Gossan cleared his throat. "Why does it say ASS?"

A ripple of conversation swept around the room, confirming that the same question had been on just about everyone's mind.

"Simple," replied Shonk. "We are the 'Abstone Society Sentinels.'"

"Yeah, but the shirt has 'ASS' on it."

"It's an acronym," argued Shonk. "A-S-S. Abstone Society Sentinels. These shirts will allow the populace to identify us as the brave soldiers of freedom they need us to be."

"Or they might just think we're a bunch of asses. There's even a picture of an ass above the letters."

Shonk glanced down at the logo he'd carefully drawn. "That's not an ass," he protested. "It's a shaven chin!"

Marl shrugged. "Looks like an ass to me."

Mumbles of agreement washed around the room.

Shonk quickly closed his coat, dragging the zipper up as he fought to maintain a calm demeanor. "Getting a dozen shirts printed isn't cheap, you know," he announced. "They charge by the letter. And don't think I don't know the identity of the individual who dropped a stack of bottle caps into the tin when we collected your membership fees last week. I'm looking at you, Rhomb Shale."

A figure in the fourth row lowered his gaze, suddenly becoming very interested in the pattern embroidered into the ancient carpet.

"You can each collect your shirt from the box by the door on your way out of the meeting," said Shonk, snatching up the sheet of paper on which he had typed his agenda. "And finally—"

"Have you got them in extra-extra-large?" inquired a voice.

Shonk ignored the question and banged his gavel stone.

"And finally," he repeated in a louder voice. "I have chosen the target for the first mission in our campaign of resistance against the prosperous elite."

At long last, an earnest hush enveloped the room. This was clearly something the majority of the evening's attendees had been looking forward to learning.

Shonk Oolite felt the fires of pride rise up within him, although he conceded that it might just be indigestion following the extra-spicy meat platter he'd wolfed down in order to get to the meeting on time.

He allowed the palpable sense of anticipation to hang over his now attentive audience for a moment, then he spoke in hushed tones.

"We are going to break into the royal laboratory."

Asteroid Joxxen, Scota Brothers Mining Corp., Entrance Alpha

Jack checked that no one was watching the main entrance to the asteroid's cathcadium mine, then signaled for Adina to race across the equipment yard and join him.

"I was expecting this place to be a little busier," she asserted, joining him behind a wooden mine cart that had likely been removed from service due to a broken front axle.

"From what I can tell, the current shift only started around twenty minutes ago," Jack responded. "Any Joxxers coming off duty will be back in their dorms by now, and a fresh crew will just be getting down to work."

"So, what's the plan?"

Jack glanced around the spacious compound. Aside from a neat stack of tools such as shovels and pickaxes, all there was to show that any industry was underway was a collection of large metal containers over to one side of the yard, presumably waiting to be filled with mounds of unrefined rock that would be brought up to the surface at the end of this work period.

"I doubt we'll discover any scandalous behavior up here," he said, casting a glance into the darkness beyond the wooden framework of the mine entrance. "Any abuse will more than likely take place down in the hole."

An expression of concern washed over Adina's face. "You want us to go down there?"

Jack nodded. "That's where the other brother—Kram—will be. If he's venting his frustrations on the Joxxers, we'll have to catch him in the act if we want to put a stop to it."

"And just how do you aim for us to do that?"

"I haven't thought that far ahead yet," Jack admitted with a wry smile. "I'm still getting used to the 'go into the deep, dark mine' part of my plan."

"And I thought *I* was the only one having reservations," said Adina with a chuckle. "I suppose it's too late to swap back with Tc'aarlat now, isn't it?"

"Yep," replied Jack. "And good thing, too. I really don't want to take tall, dark and crazy into a confined underground space with me."

Adina drew in a deep breath and let it out slowly. "OK, what are we waiting for?"

Jack chose two pickaxes from the stack to one side of the entrance and plucked a pair of hard metal helmets from hooks drilled into the rock. He passed one of each to Adina.

"Ready?" he inquired.

Adina put on her hard hat and flicked the switch to illuminate the grimy lamp fixed to the front. "Not in the slightest."

"No," said Jack. "Me neither."

The two of them strode beneath the wooden archway into the blackness of the mine beyond.

6

Planet Abstone, Jarosite City, Government Labs

"We can't do this," proclaimed Dr. Scoria Gabbro as she read through the figures on the screen for the third time.

"That's not what the results are telling us," countered Dr. Breccin Tanister, pointing to a specific line of the data. "Look, if we adapt the coding in the larger of the mitochondria, we might be able to—"

"I didn't mean that," said Scoria, cutting off her colleague. "I meant, we mustn't do this."

"We have to," responded Breccin. "The queen has instructed it."

"The queen hasn't considered the consequences," claimed Scoria. "At least not fully. She's grieving, and this command of hers is merely a product of that."

"She's not asking us to bring anyone back from the dead, Scoria," Breccin pointed out. "She just doesn't want others to have to go through what she has."

"People die, Breccin. It's sad, and loved ones grieve, but they move on. It's the natural order of things."

"So is allowing a third of the population to be eaten from the inside by an evil disease like krannas," Breccin reminded her, "but you had no problem trying to find a way to stop that from happening."

"That's different!"

"How is it different?" demanded Breccin. "Because krannas took your dad when you were a kid? Because my mom's dying from it right now?"

"That's not fair!" asserted Scoria. "Almost every family on Abstone has been affected by krannas. We have to find a cure."

"And we will," agreed Breccin. "But now we have the opportunity to extend that cure to… well, everything."

Scoria sighed, rubbing her eyes.

"Just hear me out," urged Breccin. "All the years of research, every single experiment, our entire careers have been dedicated to beating this bastard. Other Abstonions run marathons or shave their beards or sit in tubs of food to raise money to keep us going, but scientists like you and me—we're on the front line of this battle. Right?"

Scoria nodded but remained silent as her colleague continued.

"All that hard work has led us here, to the brink of success. We're so close to being able to fine-tune our treatment, and then we have the power to tell—no, to *command* krannas cells to self-destruct and begin the regeneration process, growing brand new healthy cells to take their places."

Scoria sighed softly, steeling herself for where her friend was going with this conversation.

"But what if we widen the scope of what this procedure can fight? What if we take the brakes off what it can do? We go in and re-code the genetic instructions, commanding our cure to attack all diseases, big or small. We make it so that our treatment instructs all infected cells to begin growing a clean, identical copy of themselves, then commit suicide."

Dr. Breccin Tanister took her fellow scientist and friend's hand in her own. "We use our discovery to stop death in its tracks."

Asteroid Joxxen, Scota Brothers Mining Corp., Main Office

"So…" mused Tc'aarlat, leaning on the makeshift wooden counter that served to separate the 'office' area of the weathered shack from visitors. In reality, it was little more than a few used delivery pallets nailed together and covered with a sheet of stained canvas.

"So…what?"

The expression etched on Elin Scota's moist gray face was clear: he would rather be doing anything other than making small talk with one of the recently arrived delivery crew—a Yollin, accompanied by what appeared to be a stack of desktop printers with stocky legs and a face displayed on a tablet screen.

Like all Festiniogs, Elin Scota prized only one thing above a strong work ethic, and that was his right to complain. While it wasn't unknown for a member of his race to smile, it was certainly a rare event, and one that would be remembered by friends and colleagues—mainly as a warning to steer clear of such an annoyingly cheerful individual in the future.

Not that the residents of Blaunai Prime didn't have topics to moan and complain about. Their planet was comprised almost entirely of tough gray stone which sat beneath near-constant rain falling from a churning gray sky.

Color was an aberration on Blaunai Prime.

Surviving purely on any hardy vegetation they could coax to grow in the cracks running through their world's stony ground, they saw misery as a way of life, to the point where leaders were elected based on how eloquently they were able to describe their personal torment.

On Blaunai Prime, having a victim complex practically guaranteed a position of power in government.

Elin Scota didn't consider himself able to achieve such lofty heights of perceived martyrdom—yet. For now, he was content to push his family's company out among the stars, earning wealth by mining elements not easily found at home, then moaning about how difficult such a task had been while counting the considerable profits.

The soaring temperatures baking every square foot of this blasted asteroid, along with the difficulties he had encountered while dealing with the native workforce, were enough to make him more melancholic than he had been in a long time.

There were mountains of paperwork dealing with safety regulations, equipment repair, escalating transport costs, and even a lengthy chain of correspondence debating the rights of the Scota Bothers Mining Corp. to even set foot on what certain nearby worlds considered to be their own private property.

Seemingly endless soul-draining problems and difficulties.

In short, he loved it here.

He had so much admin to deal with that his inbox was now threatening to topple over and bury him beneath an avalanche of dreary documents.

He couldn't wait to get back to it.

What he *didn't* want to be doing was standing here making small talk with this exoskeletal buffoon.

"So…" repeated Tc'aarlat. "How's the mining business?"

On its screen, Solobot 9000 rolled her avatar's eyes.

Elin shrugged. "It can get you down."

"Ha-ha-ha-ha-ha!" laughed Tc'aarlat, a little too hard. "Get you *down*! Like, down in a mine! Brilliant!"

"I don't understand," Elin admitted.

Tc'aarlat forced himself to remain smiling as he sighed. "No, it doesn't appear that you do."

The Yollin felt his diminutive robot companion nudge his leg and looked down. "What?"

"Didn't you say you wanted to ask Mister Scota about the mineral they're excavating here?"

Tc'aarlat blinked. "No, Jack and I discussed it earlier."

"I think you *did*," urged Solobot, nudging Tc'aarlat's leg a few more times. "I distinctly recall you saying such a conversation was vital and would take up a significant portion of Mister Scota's time."

It took Tc'aarlat another second or two to remember that he was supposed to be keeping the Festiniog busy.

"Ooh, yes!" he exclaimed. "I *did* say that, didn't I?"

Behind the counter, Elin Scota continued to look uninterested.

"So, tell me…" Tc'aarlat continued with as much enthusiasm as he could muster, "what's so special about the mineral…"

He looked down at Solobot, slightly panicked.

"Cathcadium," prompted the robot quietly.

"Cathcadium! Tell me all about cathcadium. Leave nothing out."

Elin Scota sighed. While the approaching conversation was guaranteed to be dull and devoid of any fulfillment, it was no competition for the mounds of tedious paperwork currently testing his ancient desk's legs. He knew which he'd prefer to be doing.

"It's a rare mineral," he began with a listless shrug. "It can't be found on our home planet—although not much can, really, aside from lumps of shitty gray rock everywhere. It's used in the making of ion pulse drives."

"Really?" asked Tc'aarlat, continuing to feign interest.

"Yep," confirmed Elin. He peered over the Yollin's shoulder at the vast bulk of the ICS *Fortitude*. "What's she packing, then?"

Tc'aarlat's mandibles spread wide. "Excuse me?"

"Your ship," said Elin. "Is that a magnetoplasmadynamic thruster combination or do you prefer the electrodeless plasma system?"

Tc'aarlat's eyes grew wide. "Oh, we er…" He glanced at the ship and back. "We prefer to keep it old-school?"

Elin frowned. "Old-school?"

"Y'know, thruster-wise."

"So, they *are* plasma-based?"

"Of course!" Tc'aarlat scoffed. "Plasma all the way, baby. We're down with the plasma."

Elin remained silent.

"We've got plasma everywhere," the Yollin continued. "Some days, you just can't move for the stuff. Plasma, plasma, plasma. So much plasma, it's practically coming out of our noses."

Elin shook his head slowly. "What in the name of white shite are you talking abou—"

He suddenly stopped, his eyes narrowing as he peered at the Joxxers continuing to unload the mining company's cargo.

"Hey, where are the other two?"

"What other two?" blurted Tc'aarlat, taking a step to the side in an effort to block Elin's view.

Elin ducked left and right to try to see around the Yollin, who spread his arms wide, adopting an extremely unnatural pose.

"Your two friends—the man and the woman who were out there just now. They'd best not be snooping arou—"

"Fucking," exclaimed Tc'aarlat.

"What?"

"They'll be off fucking somewhere."

"Fucking?"

"Yeah, you know...copulating, screwing, getting deep down in the groove, blasting the black hole, uphill gardening, nasty jogging, playing 'hide the belly-sausage,' doing the dirty foxtrot." Tc'aarlat paused for a moment before repeating, "Fucking."

Elin Scota didn't appear to be convinced. "Is that so?"

"*You* try to stop them!" spat Tc'aarlat. "Day and night they're at it. It never ends. Hump, hump, hump. Every opportunity. They say 'in space, no one can hear you scream?' Well, you fucking *can* when you're trying to get some sleep in the next bastard cabin, let me tell you!"

The Festoniog's gray cheeks flushed a slightly darker shade. "Oh, I er... I didn't realize they were together like that. We don't get much of that around here."

"I don't doubt it." Tc'aarlat laughed. "You are the Scota Brothers Mining Corp., after all. Bet you wish you had a sister or two now, don't ya?"

"A sister?"

"Yeah, because with a sister around, you could...you know... Well, you *wouldn't*, obviously. Not with your own sister. No. That wouldn't be... Unless that's what you do where you're from, that is. Is it? No, don't tell me, I don't want to know. The way you enjoy family get-togethers is none of my... None of my..." The rest of Tc'aarlat's sentence faded away to nothing.

Solobot made a noise that sounded a lot like a groan.

Elin Scota reached over to collect his hat from the end of the counter. "Well, if you'll excuse me, I'd better go check on whether those deliveries are being taken to the right place."

As the Festiniog tried to come around the end of the counter, Tc'aarlat took a large sidestep to stand right in front of the mine owner, blocking his way.

"Can I have a coffee?"

"What?"

Tc'aarlat licked his scaly lips and coughed. When he

spoke next, his voice croaked. "Could I, er...*cough*. Could I have a coffee, please?"

"You want a coffee?"

"If you don't mind," replied Tc'aarlat, rubbing his throat. "I'm a little dry, and I see you have a coffee machine not doing much in the office back there…"

Elin blinked. "It's the hottest damn day of the cycle, and you want *coffee*? Not ice water?"

"Coffee all the way for me," asserted Tc'aarlat. "Gotta have my joe!" He paused to chuckle but quickly stopped when he realized he was laughing alone. "How 'bout it, then?"

Grumbling, Elin Scota dumped his hat back on the counter, then plodded across the rear office to where a dusty old coffee machine sat. He plucked a bottle of water from a decrepit refrigeration unit and began to fill the pot.

"Feel free to join me!" Tc'aarlat called. "They say it can be dangerous to drink alone, so feel free to join me. Of course, I think they're talking about alcohol and not—"

He froze as he spotted something sticking out from beneath a stack of receipts and sales invoices pinned to the wall behind the counter.

"Er...take your time back there!" he said loudly, watching Elin Scota hard as he eased his way behind the counter. "Let it stand for a while. The stronger, the better as far as I'm concerned."

Working quickly, he grabbed hold of the item and tore it down, then quickly made his way back around the counter to where Solobot 9000 was waiting. "Are you still connected to that watch thing Adina's wearing?" he hissed.

Something whirred inside the android's casing. "Yes, I

am," Solobot replied. "I should be able to communicate with her via video link, so long as she and Jack haven't gone too deep into the mine. Why?"

Tc'aarlat glanced down at the item he was clutching, his mandibles twitching as he scowled. "We've all missed something very important," he said. "Come on!"

A few moments later, Elin Scota emerged from the back office carrying a steaming hot cup of black coffee. "Hey fella, you want any cream or sugar in—"

The Festiniog gazed around the now completely empty room. "Now, where the fuck did he go?"

Asteroid Joxxen, Scota Brothers Mining Corp., Mine Interior

"Shh!" Jack urged as he and Adina crept farther and farther down the main mine shaft, each step taking them deeper underground. "I hear something."

He reached up to twist the metal collar surrounding the bulb on his helmet's lamp, extinguishing the light. Adina nodded and did the same.

They paused just long enough to allow their eyes to grow used to the extremely dim light of the dirty, flickering bulbs strung up along the tunnel's ceiling. Many of them had blown or been smashed somehow. The result wasn't quite pitch-blackness, but it came close.

Inch by inch, Jack and Adina moved farther into the mine, both sticking to the left-hand wall and occasionally clasping hands to be certain of staying together.

What had sounded like some sort of grunting noise echoing from the tunnel ahead was growing in both volume and clarity. It sounded as though someone was crying out in pain.

Hurrying as quickly as they dared over the uneven ground, Jack and Adina rushed toward a bend in the tunnel, skidding to a stop as they rounded the corner.

Jack switched his light back on, his breath catching in the back of his throat. There, rocking back and forth on the ground, was a naked, bloodied Joxxer, its hands clutched over a gaping wound in its stomach, trying desperately to prevent its internal organs from spilling out.

7

Asteroid Joxxen, Scota Brothers Mining Corp., Mine Interior

Jack tore off his shirt and dropped to his knees, pressing the garment over the Joxxer's open wound.

"Hold this!" he instructed Adina. "Press down hard."

As soon as Adina had taken his place, Jack grabbed the Joxxer's arm, placing two fingers flat against the alien's wrist.

"Shit!" he spat, turning to Adina. "Any idea what a Joxxer's pulse should be?"

Adina shook her head.

A series of anxious grunts echoed through the tunnel, causing both of them to swing their head-lamps in the direction of the noise. There, cowering in the darkness, were three more Joxxers, who were clearly extremely upset and scared. Stooping forward slightly, they wrung their hands and rocked back and forth.

Jack jumped to his feet. "What happened here?" he demanded. "Who did this to him?"

The terrified Joxxers didn't reply; they simply continued to rock and groan.

"Talk to me!"

"They're telepathic, Jack!" Adina reminded him. "They don't talk, at least not to anyone outside their own species."

"Fuck!" Jack crouched beside Adina. "Can you get a message to Tc'aarlat?" he asked, gesturing to the personal communicator strapped to her wrist. "Tell him to get a medical team down here as quickly as possible."

He reached over to take her place holding the shirt over the injured Joxxer's stomach. The traumatized alien's eyes were wide, and he was breathing in short, fast bursts. "He's going into shock."

Adina stood, fiddling with her wrist communicator. "I can't get a signal. We must be too deep underground."

"Gott Verdammt!"

Adina returned to kneel beside Jack, helping him compress the Joxxer's wound. "What the hell are we supposed to do now?"

"You can start by telling me who the fuck you are!" barked a voice.

A beam of light swung from Jack to Adina and back again. Below it, they could just make out the silhouette of a figure clutching a large case in its right hand.

Jack shielded his eyes from the glare and turned his own light on the newcomer. He was tall and gray-skinned and looked remarkably similar to Elin Scota, the mining company boss they had met above ground.

He could only be the other Scota brother—Kram.

Jack launched himself at the Festiniog, grabbing the front of his shirt and slamming him hard against the tunnel wall.

"You despicable fuck!" he roared. "The protestors blockading this asteroid claimed you two were abusing the Joxxers, and I thought they were overreacting. But now I have proof."

Adina looked up from the Joxxer's side. "Jack, we're losing him!"

Jack snarled at Kram Scota, pushing the mine's co-owner harder against the rock. "I'm going to bring the full force of the Etheric Federation down on you and your bastard of a brother for this!"

Kram pushed back, freeing himself from Jack's grasp. "You think I did this?" he yelled.

"Well, he certainly didn't do it to himself!" replied Jack. He gestured to the three other Joxxers cowering nearby. "And I don't think they attacked the poor fucker either, do you?"

"I found him like this!" Kram countered.

"Fuck off!"

"It's true! That's why I ran back to grab a first-aid kit. No use trying to call for help from down here; you won't get a signal."

Jack glanced down at the case Kram was holding. It was white and displayed an orange symbol that looked something like a band-aid.

Movement in the darkness behind Kram caught his eyes, and he swung his light in that direction. Two more Joxxers stood there, their heads turned as they shied away from the light.

They carried a stretcher between them.

"We'll argue about who did this later," said Kram, pushing past Jack and joining Adina to kneel next to the injured native. "For now, I just want to get this guy to the surface so he can get proper medical attention."

Agreeing, Jack knelt beside the Joxxer as Kram opened the first aid kit, and the trio got to work.

Fifteen minutes later, the patient was as stabilized as he was going to be without access to proper medical equipment. Jack and Adina stood back as the two new Joxxers carefully lifted the stretcher holding their wounded friend.

Kram Scota made sure the Joxxer's oxygen mask was secure, then laid the portable canister it was connected to on the stretcher at his side. He grabbed a bag of almost-black blood and held it above his head, allowing gravity to feed the drip leading into the patient's arm. "Let's go."

The group began to make their way back along the tunnel, the ground beneath their feet rising gently as they walked.

"Don't disappear when we get to the surface," warned Jack. "We have unfinished business."

Kram sighed. "Do you really think I'd beat the shit out of a Joxxer, then race back to the surface to get him help?"

"You could be covering your ass. Realized you'd gone too far this time and wanted to make yourself look good by playing the hero."

"In which case, I'd still be covered in his blood, wouldn't I?"

Jack frowned. Kram was right. He and Adina hadn't passed him running for the surface after they'd entered the mine, so he must have already been out and summoning help while they were descending.

The wounded Joxxer couldn't have been there for more than half an hour. Even if Kram had somehow managed to change clothes, he was very unlikely to have had time to shower away the blood spatter such a vicious attack would have created.

Jack looked the male up and down in the lamp-light as they walked. He was covered in grime and dust, but there was no sign of anything that might have been blood.

Dammit!

Someone else had attacked the Joxxer.

"Jack!" cried Adina, hurrying a couple of steps behind him. "I've got a signal!"

The pair stopped, letting Kram and the stretcher bearers go on ahead. Adina held up her communicator and watched as it rebooted, having finally come close enough to the surface to communicate with the ship, Solobot, and Tc'aarlat.

Both Jack and Adina switched off their helmet lamps as the Yollin's face appeared on the small screen, clearly agitated. "Where the fuck have you two been?" he demanded. "I've been trying to get in touch with you."

"We had a situation," Adina replied, "and we couldn't get a signal."

"Make sure there's a medical team waiting at Entrance Alpha," Jack said. "We've got a severely injured Joxxer on the way up, likely to need emergency surgery."

"Kram Scota's with him," Adina added, "but don't challenge him. We're fairly certain he didn't do this."

"And you've been with Elin all this time, so we've no idea who did," admitted Jack.

Tc'aarlat's mandibles twitched. "That's why I've been trying to contact you," he said. "There's three of them!"

Jack blinked in the darkness. "Three?"

Tc'aarlat held up a ragged black and white photograph to the camera. It showed the Scota Brothers posing proudly in front of the mine entrance, presumably on the day it was first opened.

All *three* Scota Bothers.

Asteroid Joxxen, Scota Brothers Mining Corp., Mine Face

"Get off your fucking knees, and fucking shift those fucking buckets fucking NOW, you fucking fuck!"

Vesnet Scota snatched his short leather whip from his belt and lashed out, the jagged piece of metal embedded in its end gouging yet another chunk of flesh from the fallen Joxxer's back.

The mineworker grunted in pain as he climbed to his feet. The muscles in his arms shook hard as he struggled to hoist the milkmaid-style yoke up to his shoulders. Each end was weighed down by an overflowing pail of raw blue Cathcadium, and the profound effort caused dark veins beneath the alien's damaged orange skin to bulge alarmingly.

An identical fellow Joxxer stepped forward to assist his colleague, only to be driven back by another sharp bite from the whip.

"Leave him!" spat Vesnet, sneering as the exhausted

figure stumbled away. "Goat-snuggling horndogs, all of you!" he growled beneath his breath.

The Joxxer's unsteady footsteps echoed through the low-ceilinged corridor, alerting the mine boss that the rest of the workers around him were still watching, silently.

"Get back to work!" he bellowed.

The sound of pick-axes chipping away at the stone face of the mine quickly rang out, accompanied by a low rumble as chunks of rock with the valuable blue streak running through them were tossed into the waiting metal buckets.

After each pair of pails was filled, the next Joxxer in line would heft the rough wooden yoke onto his stooped shoulders, and stagger away to where ramshackle wooden mine cars sat on rusted rails, waiting to drag the precious ore up to the surface.

Vesnet paced back and forth, coiling his whip up hand over hand, then slotting the collected coils back into the special quick-release holster at his side.

He spat on the floor, the gob of phlegm speckled with pellets of black dust. Fucking shithole, this blasted asteroid. They were only mining here because he'd been outvoted two to one by his brothers. And what do they get to do? Sit up top in the sunshine, watching deliveries come in and shipping rocks of Cathcadium back to the company's processing plants.

Pair of lazy twats ought to spend a day down here and get some real work done for a change.

"Hey!" he yelled, spotting a Joxxer who had paused from hacking away at the rock with his pickaxe to catch his breath. "I'm not paying you asswipes to stand around all day!"

This time he didn't bother to unsheath his whip. He simply grabbed a nearby shovel, swung it around, and smacked the fatigued Joxxer across the back of the head with it.

The alien snarled, fingers flexing around the handle of his own heavy tool for a moment.

Noticing the reaction, Vesnet raised his shovel again, this time spinning it a quarter-turn so the thin metal edge of the blade would be the first part to strike the Joxxer's head if he chose to attack.

"Go ahead," he rumbled. "I fucking dare you!"

The laborer rolled his shoulders, holding Vesnet's gaze for slightly longer than was normally allowed, then he lifted his pick and began to attack the mine wall once more.

"Yeah!" sneered Vesnet. "I fucking thought not."

He spat again, then his attention was caught by what sounded like a struggle coming from farther up the tunnel. He squinted into the darkness, sensing a shape moving in the shadows, trying to tell if it was the same Joxxer he'd just sent off to the mining carts with a load of ore.

"You really don't want to fuck me around today, boy!" he muttered.

Then, shouldering the shovel, he set off after the shadowy figure.

Something moved ahead of him, just out of the pool of light cast by the few remaining working lightbulbs strung from hooks in the roof.

The rest had all been smashed, which the cracking of broken glass beneath Vesnet's boots quickly confirmed.

The mine owner readied the shovel, stepping slowly into the darkness like a batter, facing up to an unknown ghostly pitcher.

More glass crunched beneath his feet.

"I really hope you haven't been damaging company property, you freak!" grunted Vesnet, when-

WHAM!

A clenched fist catapulted out of the blackness and smashed hard into the center of his face. Bones snapped as Vesnet's nose broke, shards of skull being driven up and back, tearing at his optical nerves and stabbing into the front of his brain.

Vesnet Scota screamed—briefly. Almost as soon as the cry had begun, the fist struck again, slamming into the front of the Festiniog's throat. A satisfying crunch announced the collapse of further extremely sensitive parts of the head and neck.

The rest of the shriek became little more than a wet gurgle.

The injured male stumbled forward, trying to shake off the searing bolts of pain shooting across his upper face. He swung the shovel and caught the side of the tunnel wall, which forced him to stagger in the opposite direction. The tool slipped from his trembling hands, clattering loudly to the ground.

The third and final punch caught Vesnet under his chin. The male's head shot back with a disturbing snap, then he sank to his knees, swaying for a moment as blood poured from his eye sockets, mouth and what was left of his nose, and fell face-first to the debris-strewn rock floor.

Captain Jack Marber stepped into the light, shaking out his right hand. That was the problem with resorting to the ancient art of fisticuffs; you had to endure the badly bruised knuckles for a few days afterward.

He nudged the prone male with his boot. The beaten figure groaned softly but didn't move.

Jack looked up into the wide eyes of the stunned group of Joxxers staring at him. He sniffed.

"Time for a tea break, I reckon."

Planet Abstone, Jarosite City, Government Labs

"Ready?" asked Dr. Scoria Gabbro, taking aim with the syringe.

Standing at her side, Dr. Breccin Tanister nodded, her fingers ready to fly up and cover her eyes if this, their second experiment of the day, went the same way as the first.

After making a series of calculations, programming the data into their computer system, and sending the results to the lab's chemical synthesizer, they had been rewarded with a vial of viscous liquid.

This one was not quite as cloudy as the first had been.

Scoria had filled a fresh syringe and now stood at the open rastel cage, staring down at the two rodents scurrying around inside.

The lab received a regular supply of rastels from a company that trapped them in the wild. Each animal's health was tested, then the healthiest were sold to science labs around the planet.

Ironically, these healthy specimens were ideal test subjects to inject with a variety of diseases—including krannas—to see if the research teams could find a way to cure them before it was too late.

Having worked their way through most of their latest consignment while searching for a cure for krannas, they'd only had three rastels available on which to test this new treatment.

Two of them were now twitching their whiskered noses at Scoria and Breccin, most likely hoping for some kind of treat.

Despite being the only two test specimens remaining, they clearly demonstrated the pecking order entrenched in rastel society. The larger rodent stood ahead of its smaller companion and would have first choice of any proffered food.

The smaller rastel—a litter runt with a white stripe running down the fur which covered its face—held back a short distance, content to be allowed the scraps left behind by the more dominant creature.

The third—the largest of the trio—had been injected with their first medicinal mixture several hours earlier. The goal, as they had previously agreed, was to find a mixture of chemicals which would attack diseased cells, no matter what the abnormality, and send a signal to the creature's brain, telling it to order the growth of new, healthy cells to take their places.

While neither scientist suspected they would discover a universal cure on their first try, they held onto the hope that they would at least receive results that showed they were heading along the right path.

Sadly, that was not to be the case.

The first test rastel had died horribly within minutes of being injected with the cell-rejuvenation solution.

Screaming at the top of its tiny lungs, the rastel had slammed its head repeatedly against the metal bars of its increasingly bloody cage until it finally slumped to one side, dead.

Both Breccin and Scoria had watched in horror as this awful scene played out in front of them, and tests were now underway in another lab nearby to discover whether a heart attack or brain injuries had been the cause of its death.

Now the two remaining rastels, who had cowered in the corner of their shared habitat while their fellow rodent battered its skull against the cage's bars, appeared to be moving around again, looking for scraps of food.

Scoria reached out to find one of Breccin's hands, squeezing it hard as she slid the syringe's glinting needle into the fur-covered neck of the second rastel.

Now they just had to wait.

8

Asteroid Joxxen, Scota Brothers Mining Corp.,
Unloading Bay 2

Jack dragged Vesnet Scota through the dust by the collar, dumping him face-down in front of the mining company's dilapidated office, then he joined the waiting Tc'aarlat and Solobot.

The beaten Festiniog groaned as his brothers raced to kneel at his side—Elin from inside the office, and Kram from the tent which operated as the asteroid's medical center.

"What the fuck happened?" demanded Kram, producing a handkerchief and using it to wipe blood from his sibling's shattered nose.

"He picked on someone his own size at last," Jack stated flatly. He spotted Adina emerging from the medical tent. "How is he?"

Adina shook her head.

"Gott Verdammt!" spat Jack. He turned to Tc'aarlat. "Keep an eye on these arse-biscuits while I go contact Nathan."

He began to make his way toward the ship when Solobot spoke up. "There is no need to return to the bridge, Captain. I can connect you with Mr. Lowell from here."

"Oh," said Jack, turning back. "OK, then. Do that."

For a moment, the only sounds were the moans and groans of Vesnet Scota as his brothers tended to him. At one point Elin stood, fists clenched as he glared at Jack.

Tc'aarlat unholstered his modified Jean Dukes Special and aimed it at the three Festiniogs. "Go ahead, skunk, make my day."

"'Punk,'" corrected Jack.

Tc'aarlat shrugged but kept the weapon trained on the two uninjured brothers while Adina bound their wrists and ankles with plastic ties.

"Motherfucking bitch!" spat Kram Scota as she pulled his arms behind his back.

"Oh, dear," said Tc'aarlat. "Sounds like someone needs his mouth washed out with soap." He reached for a spool of heavy-duty packaging tape sitting on a stack of nearby boxes and tore off a strip.

"Meanwhile, this stuff should keep the three of you from shooting your mouths off in the presence of a lady."

While Tc'aarlat taped the mine owners' mouths shut, Solobot turned to face Jack. The picture on its tablet-screen 'face' changed from the EI's usual avatar to Nathan Lowell in his office on board the Queen Bitch Base Station *Meredith Reynolds.*

Adina did her best not to smile at the sight of what

appeared to be a short Nathan in white plastic armor tottering about.

"Captain Marber," said Nathan through Solobot's chest speaker. "How can I help you?"

"We have a situation we think you might be interested in," Jack replied. "A rather nasty case of physical and possibly mental abuse of an indigenous species."

Nathan scowled, tapping briefly on the screen of his own tablet. "You're on the Joxxen Asteroid, aren't you?"

"That's correct, delivering to the Scota Brothers Mining Corp."

"Are the brothers there with you now?"

Swaying gently, Solobot stepped from foot to foot as she walked past Tc'aarlat and Adina to capture the Scota brothers, Elin and Kram, now seated on the ground beside Vesnet. The injured brother had regained consciousness— more or less—and was clutching Kram's blood-soaked handkerchief to what remained of his upper face.

Adina had tied Vesnet's ankles together, but had allowed his hands to remain free so he could keep pressure on his injuries.

"Two things…" began Nathan as Solobot completed her 360-degree turn and reached Jack again. "First, what happened to that guy?"

"He bumped into some Justice," responded Jack.

"OK…" said Nathan. "Secondly, I just saw Tc'aarlat and Adina standing there with you all. Who's filming this video conversation?"

Jack frowned as Solobot raised an arm and gave him a little wave. "Yeah, you probably don't want to ask about that right now," he commented. "Can you get a team down here to take these guys into custody? And we'll need a proper medical unit as well. Some of the Joxxers have injuries going back several months, by the look of it."

"I'll have a ship on the way to you within an hour," Nathan promised. "Please be sure to confiscate any weapons or explosives the mining company may possess. We don't want your detainees staging any kind of revolt."

"No problem," replied Jack.

"Good to see the three of you are making new friends," said Nathan. "When you've set off from Joxxen, call me back. I've got a potential problem I'd like the Shadows to look into for me."

"Will do," said Jack. He nodded to Solobot, who terminated the call.

"I hope he's prepared for a wait," said Tc'aarlat, slipping his gun back into its holster.

"Why?" asked Jack.

Tc'aarlat gestured to the vast area of empty space around the asteroid. "We're in the middle of nowhere," he pointed out. "And that's in space terms. Nathan's team won't reach us for days yet, so we're stuck here until then, babysitting the Three Splooges."

"It's 'Three Stooges,'" Adina corrected. "And we won't have to wait."

"We can't just leave them here," said Tc'aarlat. "Even if they don't find a way to escape, they may convince one of the Joxxers to cut them free. Nice species, but they're not the brightest stars in the galaxy."

"That's why I took the liberty of making a quick call from the medical tent earlier," Adina revealed.

Jack raised an eyebrow. "Call?"

Just then, the blast of a bass-heavy siren punctuated the near silence. The trio looked up to see the vast bulk of the *Joshua 3* soaring over the top of the cliff behind them.

The dozens of smaller shuttles they had seen in orbit flew alongside the mothership, like chicks chasing after a mother hen.

"Captain Marber!" exclaimed a familiar voice.

Jack looked down at Solobot's screen. "Captain Bon Noh!"

"I sent him the landing coordinates," admitted Adina. "I thought his group of protestors could keep an eye on these three and see to any urgent medical needs the Joxxers may have while the Etheric Federation ship is en route."

Jack nodded. "Good idea, although first we follow Nathan's advice and confiscate any weapons these dick-wads own, along with the mine's supply of explosives. We don't want the Federation team to be met by any nasty surprises should the Scotas somehow manage to over-power their babysitters."

He turned back to Solobot's camera. "It appears I owe you something of an apology, Captain. The situation down here on the surface *was* as bad as you originally claimed."

"I appreciate the sentiment, Captain Marber," said Bon Noh. "Sadly, I've been dealing with abusers like the Scota brothers for a long time. As soon as I learned of their setup, I knew I'd found what I was looking for."

"And I tried to stand in your way…"

"You're not the first to make assumptions about us, Captain Marber, and you won't be the last. I remained confident that I could bring these monsters to justice with or without you."

Jack nodded. "Then I wish you the best in your future endeavors."

Captain Bon Noh saluted. "You too, Captain Marber. You, too."

Planet Abstone, Jarosite City, Government Labs

"Ever onward, my gems. Ever onward."

Scoria sat bolt upright at the sound of the voice; a voice she hadn't heard in many years.

"Dad?"

Of course, there was no reply, and Scoria cursed herself for having even a second of hope that there would have been.

Her father was dead, and had been for a long time.

She'd heard his voice in her dreams.

Rubbing her eyes, Scoria stretched, arching her back to ease the stiffness she felt. She'd fallen asleep sitting at her desk, her head on her arms in the small amount of space left between the towers of paperwork she kept telling herself she needed to file away.

She tried to recall what she had been dreaming about to hear her father's voice, but the details were already dissipating like the morning mist.

Ever onward, my gems. Ever onward.

Despite herself, Scoria smiled. Those were the exact words her dad had often used to encourage her and her sister to work hard, learn from their mistakes, and forge ahead with their goals.

My gems.

That was what he always called his two daughters.

Dacit Gabbro, older by two and a half turns, was nick-named "Sapphire" and she was "Topaz." Both stones were blue, just like the girls' eyes.

Scoria wondered what her sister was doing at that moment.

Like tidying her desk, calling Dacit was something she kept promising herself she would do, and had put off doing just as many times.

It wasn't as if they'd had a falling out. She couldn't identify any one specific argument that had caused them to drift apart. They were just so *different*.

She remembered sitting in the sunshine with Dacit, the two girls weaving tiny flowers into each other's beards, then little more than bushy goatees.

It had felt as though they would be best friends forever.

Then they grew up.

Scoria had inherited her father's fierce curiosity, leading her to excel in the more practical subjects during her schooling. Science and mathematics became her passions. Everything was either right or wrong. Black or white. There was no gray area.

Dacit, however, developed into more of a creative soul. She saw the nuances of life scattered between Scoria's pre-determined truths. She immersed herself in the endless possibilities created by looking at their world from a different angle.

And, crucially, she grew up fascinated by their mother's religious beliefs.

Where Scoria knew for certain the universe was built from different combinations of the same basic atoms, Dacit worshipped any number of iconic deities, just as convinced that everything around them was the result of conscious creation.

It was a difference the two girls had never been able to resolve.

Tired of the arguments that erupted every time they got together, Scoria began to communicate with her sister more infrequently. She was certain Dacit had decided upon the same course of action.

Dacit's boundless faith in religion aggravated Scoria just as much as her blind devotion to science infuriated Dacit.

They attempted to remain civil when they were with their mother, but once she had passed, there was no reason to pretend any longer.

The two sisters simply didn't respect each other's core views, so they saw each other less and less.

Now, Scoria couldn't even remember the last time they had spoken.

Would things have been different if her father had lived longer? Scoria believed that would most likely be the case. He'd never argued with their mother over such things despite their differences being a mirror image of those of the two girls, yet somehow, they found a way to get along without attempting to tear down the other's ideology.

Scoria sighed. Maybe she wasn't as smart as everyone thought after all. She might now be experimenting at a cellular level in an attempt to bring about immortality, but she couldn't find a way to accept, if not understand, a point of view held by her own sister.

If she didn't reach out soon, things would—

A-*CHOO!*

Scoria jumped at the sneeze.

"Oh, yuck!" moaned Breccin, grabbing a wad of tissue and wiping gunk from her beard. "You know, I think this virus is getting worse."

"I told you to go home earlier."

"What, and miss all this excitement?" Breccin scoffed, tossing the clump of tissues into the wastebasket beneath her desk and plucking three more from the box at her side.

She blew her nose. "Is it time to check rastel two yet?

Scoria glanced at the time as she climbed down from her stool and crossed the lab. "Not quite, but I don't think it will do any harm if we take a—"

She stopped, the words catching in her throat.

"What is it?" demanded Breccin. "What's wrong? Oh no…"

In the semi-darkness, the two women stared down into the rastel cage. The specimen they had chosen for the second experiment was dead, just like the first rodent. However, this rastel hadn't beaten itself to death against the bars of its cage.

This rastel had torn out its own throat.

Ragged, blood-soaked flesh hung in gristly strips beneath the deceased creature's jaws, the tips of its sharp claws glistening a dark, rich red in the glow of the low-energy light hanging above.

They found the third and final, rastel, cowering in the corner of the cage, trembling. Its white facial stripe stood out clearly in the dim light. While the two scientists hadn't seen this suicide occur in person, the last of the rastels had clearly witnessed it all.

Scoria knew that rastels had proven intelligent enough

to solve basic puzzles in order to access pellets of food. Now she wondered if they were smart enough to realize this latest round of experiments resulted in a different, much deadlier reward. If so, the animal clearly knew what was coming next, and was now terrified.

As Breccin pulled on a pair of disposable gloves to remove the subject of their latest failure, Scoria sat at her computer screen and set about adjusting the balance of ingredients in their death cure once more.

Ever onward, Dad. Ever onward.

9

ICS *Fortitude*, Bridge

"Connecting you to Nathan Lowell now, Captain."

Solo's avatar faded from the viewscreens around the bridge, where it was replaced with the face of their Etheric Federation contact.

The rather red and sweaty face of their contact.

"Jack!" puffed Nathan, trying hard to catch his breath. "I wasn't expecting you to return my call quite so quickly. I'm—"

Suddenly, a foot, clad in a supple leather shoe came into shot and struck Nathan in the side of the face.

Jack, Adina, and Tc'aarlat all winced as Nathan gave a chesty "*OOOF!*" and disappeared off-screen. Whatever type of device had been filming him spun in the air, landing camera-side-up on the ground.

The three Shadows exchanged confused glances as they stared at a high ceiling for a few seconds.

"Er...Nathan?" said Jack. "Are you okay?"

A hand hovered into view, reaching down to pick up the camera. The owner of the hand swung the device around so they could look down the lens. The newcomer had long blonde hair, a flushed yet flawless Eastern European complexion, and a killer figure currently clad in a skin-tight black bodysuit.

"Hi, guys! How's it going?"

"Oh, hey, Ecaterina!" responded Adina. "I take it you've been sparring with Nathan?"

"Sparring, and winning!"

"That wasn't fair!" groaned Nathan from off-screen. "I was distracted by Jack's call."

Ecaterina looked toward her still-panting mate. "And what if he were to call you in the midst of a fight with a gang of Skaine pirates, or an angry Huttut people trafficker? Are you going to complain to them that you *weren't ready* once they've whipped your ass? Maybe they'll let you have a do-over."

Jack tried to disguise his smile as he heard Nathan sigh. "Fair point," he grumbled, retrieving his tablet from Ecaterina's hands. "I do need a time out now, though; I have a favor to ask these guys."

Ecaterina, still in the frame just behind her partner's left shoulder, scowled. "So, I have to let my muscles cool down while you have a chat with your pals?"

"You don't have to let anything cool down," growled a new voice. By the movement of Nathan and Ecaterina's eyes, the crew could tell someone had just entered the training room somewhere behind the camera."

Ecaterina grinned. "Bring it on, green boy!"

Nathan paused long enough for Ecaterina to wipe her

face with his towel, then she moved to a spot near the rear of the room where she faced off with a tall alien with green, pockmarked skin and a number of bony spikes jutting from the lower part of his face.

"That's Shi-Tan," explained Nathan, gesturing over his shoulder with his thumb. "One of the most ruthless bounty hunters on Yoll."

Tc'aarlat's mandibles shot wide apart. "I've, er...just remembered," he spluttered, hands working to unfasten his safety belt. "I have to feed Albert Einstein!"

Jumping up, he ran for the door leading off the bridge.

"Tc'aarlat!" barked Solo's voice through the speakers. "Please return to your—"

"Fuck you, Solo!"

Jack watched the Yollin vanish into the darkened corridor, then swung his chair back to face the main viewscreen. On it, Nathan's brow was deeply furrowed. "Albert Einstein?"

Jack shook his head. "Don't worry about it," he said flatly. "Adina and I certainly don't."

"Too right," Adina confirmed.

Behind Nathan, Ecaterina and Shi-Tan began to spar. Their moves were swift and vicious, accompanied by a series of passionate grunts and yells. Adina found she couldn't tear her eyes away from the fast-moving fight; the combatants appeared to be very evenly matched.

"Why did you need to speak to us?" inquired Jack. "You told Ecaterina you wanted to ask us a favor."

"I do," replied Nathan, "although—technically—it's not for me. It's for the Queen."

Adina sat straighter in her seat. "Bethany Anne?"

Nathan nodded. "As you are no doubt aware, she has visited many worlds in the cause of diplomacy. Pressing the flesh with other leaders was a vital, if tiring, part of her role as the then Empress."

"I can imagine," said Jack. "We acted as official ambassadors for the Federation at the funeral for the President of Alma Nine, and we needed a full week off afterward."

"Galactic relations certainly take their toll," Nathan confirmed. "On this occasion, Bethany Anne was at a joining ceremony—kind of like a wedding—for Queen Lapis Lazuli of Abstone. She had chosen a new consort, and that ritual made everything official."

"Sounds a lot more fun than what we had to deal with," commented Adina. "Did it all go as planned?"

"I believe so, yes," replied Nathan. "They remained joined for quite some time, until just recently. The individual concerned is no longer Queen Lazuli's consort."

"Don't tell me," said Adina. "Her Majesty dumped him after he did something nasty behind her back."

"In a way," said Nathan. "He died. And that was quite nasty."

Adina looked horrified, her cheeks burning. "Oh! Oh, I didn't…"

"You were right in thinking the queen dumped him, though," Nathan added. "Right into the mouth of an active volcano."

Jack's eyes narrowed slightly. "Tell me you don't want us to go in there and get his body back…"

Nathan suppressed a chuckle. "Nothing quite so dramatic. Obviously, I can't check in with the Bethany Anne to determine her wishes, but I feel sure she would want someone to visit Abstone and ensure Queen Lazuli is coping at such an upsetting time."

"And you think we're the right team for the job," said Jack.

"After a fashion," admitted Nathan. "You're closer to Abstone than anyone else from the Federation at the moment."

"Either works for me," said Jack.

"Nathan, I'm sorry!" Adina interjected. "I didn't mean to—"

"It's fine!" Nathan assured her, his hands raised. "I know you well enough to realize you wouldn't deliberately be distasteful."

"Wait until you see what she's invented," Jack muttered. He caught Adina's glare in the corner of his eye and quickly moved on. "Has Solo got the coordinates for Abstone and all the necessary data?"

"I was planning to send that over once I'd completed this training session," said Nathan. "But, I wasn't expecting you to depart from Joxxen quite so soon."

"We booked a babysitter to watch over the Scota brothers until your team reaches them," Jack explained. "No immediate rush for the info. It can wait until you've finished your workout."

"Actually, I think we're almost done," said Nathan, turning to check how Ecaterina's bout with Shi-Tan was progressing. He was just in time to see the Shrillexian lift his mate high above his head and toss her across the room.

Ecaterina hit the thin exercise mats covering the floor with a heavy *thud*. Quickly turning the painful landing into a roll, she spun over onto all fours, her head snapping as she glowered at her opponent's self-satisfied expression.

"There's plenty more where that came from!" teased her adversary.

But, Ecaterina didn't reply—at least, not with words. Instead, her body began to writhe and contort beneath the tight, black outfit.

Jack heard Adina gasp as Ecaterina transformed into her werewolf before their eyes. Her beautiful facial features elongating into a slim snout, beneath which long, sharp fangs burst from her now salivating jaws. Her spine twisted into a more animalistic shape, and fierce claws slid from her fingertips.

Kneeling up, Ecaterina gripped the neck of her body-suit and tore it open, just as swathes of thick fur washed across her pale skin like waves crashing onto a tropical beach.

The transformation complete, the werewolf threw back her head and howled. In response, Shi-Tan held out his right hand, twitching his long fingers upwards a few times.

"Bring in on, little doggy!" he snarled.

As the sleek werewolf launched itself toward the waiting Shrillexian, Nathan turned back to the camera. "Strike that," he said. "It looks like we'll be here for—"

He stopped mid-sentence, frowning. "Where's Adina?"

Jack spun to look at the navigator's position slightly behind him to the right. The seat was empty, one end of the safety belt hanging from it still swinging back and forth."

"I'm not sure," replied Jack, hoping his tone wouldn't disclose the fact that he was almost certain where Adina had suddenly gone, and why. "Maybe she went to check that Isaac Newton hasn't been shitting all over the cargo bays again."

Nathan took a long, deep breath.

"Remind me to pencil in some vacation time for you three, very soon."

Planet Abstone, Jarosite City, Government Labs

Dr. Scoria Gabbro stepped out of the shower room, one towel wrapped around her, and the other drying her dripping wet beard.

While the facilities at the government labs may not have been quite as luxurious as those she'd heard about at the various private medical companies that had sprung up over the last decade, they did the job.

A shower, basic kitchen area, and even a tiny room into which was crammed an even tinier folding bed.

The set-up allowed researchers to work late without the need to worry about a journey back to their house or apartment in the dark. Very few of her colleagues took advantage of such an opportunity—preferring home comforts to an uncomfortable night at their workplace—but the simple facilities did prove useful from time to time.

Swinging open the door to her lab, Scoria switched the towel from her beard to her hair. She glanced at the cage on the room's central table, inside which lay their third and final rastel. The one she'd come to refer to as 'Stripe' in her notes.

Dead, just like the others.

Well, not *exactly* like the others. This rastel hadn't

smashed its own brains out or clawed its throat to pieces. Instead, it had simply laid down and stopped breathing.

Although the end result was much the same.

Scoria studied the unmoving creature for a moment. Were it not for the absence of its chest rhythmically rising and falling, the poor little thing could almost be asleep. But that wasn't the case.

Only an autopsy would be able to conclude whether their third version of the cure had killed the animal, or if it had succumbed to one of the many diseases they had infected it with first.

This latest failure had necessitated the purchase of more rastels if they were to continue their experiments. And there was certainly no indication that the queen was about to allow them to give up the quest for a death cure.

Normally, a request for lab specimens would need to be submitted via official channels, passing through the government's treasury department before being approved. Only then, would the order be passed to one of the companies that provided such unique lab "equipment."

A process that would take ten to fourteen turns, minimum.

Which is why Breccin had declared that she "knew someone." Someone who might be able to solve their rastel shortage immediately—for a small price.

At first, Scoria had been skeptical but, faced with the alternative—a lengthy wait to be able to continue with what they had begun—she had reluctantly agreed.

So, the two scientists had pooled what credits they had in their pockets and raided the hot drinks collection jar in the communal kitchen for a few extra, just in case.

Breccin had been gone over three hours now.

Tossing her towel aside, Scoria sat at her desk and slid open one of the drawers. She rooted around inside until she found a mirror and a small pair of scissors. Balancing the mirror against a stack of books, she re-angled her lamp so that it cast its light on her lower face, and then set about trimming and tidying her beard.

There was a professional salon on the next block to where she lived, but she only went there in preparation for special occasions. Not being one who enjoyed sipping hot drinks and sharing the latest celebrity gossip, she much preferred to attend to her beard herself.

It wasn't something she would normally do here in the lab, but there were only so many ways she could pass the time until Breccin returned with the new rastels, so she jutted out her chin and began to cut away loose strands of hair from just under her-

Squeak!

Scoria froze, staring at her reflection in the mirror. She could have sworn she'd heard something just then. A small squeaking sound.

Glancing at the scissors in her hand, she opened and closed them a couple of times. Unable to recall the last time she had used them, she told herself the screw holding the two halves together must have dried out a little, causing the blades to scrape against each other as-

Squeak!

There it was again. And it definitely wasn't the scissors this time.

Scoria grabbed the head of her lamp with trembling

fingers and turned it to shine over to the other side of her desk.

Over to the table where the specimen cage sat.

Squeak! Squeak!

Scoria's breath caught in her throat. There, its nose twitching and whiskers quivering sat Stripe, the previously dead rastel.

It was looking right at her.

And it was alive!

Planet Abstone, Jarosite City, Government Labs

Scoria was still in the process of getting dressed when Breccin returned, barging into the lab and holding the door wide open.

Two stocky males followed, carrying a large wooden crate between them. They eyed the partially nude scientist with surprise.

"Hey!" cried Scoria, her hands shooting up to cover her bare breasts. "Give me some warning, next time!"

"Sorry!" responded Breccin. "I wasn't expecting you to be naked." She hurried across the room to lift a printer from one of the cluttered work surfaces. "Pop that on here please, guys."

The two workers hefted the crate up onto the workbench, then turned to leave. One of them pulled a delivery note and pen from the pocket of his overalls.

"Sign here," he grunted, holding them out to Scoria.

Scoria glanced down at her hands—still busy hiding her

breasts from scrutiny—then arched an eyebrow at the male. "Really?"

"I'll do it," said Breccin, snatching the paperwork from the worker's grasp. "Thank you, both."

Neither male moved. Instead, they shuffled awkwardly where they stood, trying not to make it obvious they were staring at Scoria.

"I *said*, thank you!"

Grumbling, the two males left the lab. Breccin closed the door, then rushed back to the crate—pausing only to snatch up a knife from her desk to cut the lengths of thin rope holding it together.

Scoria grabbed her shirt and pulled it on. "Disgusting animals!"

Breccin glanced over her shoulder at her colleague. "I thought you liked rastels."

"I meant the males!" said Scoria. "They were leering at me."

"To be fair," offered Breccin, as she worked at cutting the ropes. "They probably weren't expecting to be greeted by a topless scientist."

The blade sliced through the final rope, allowing Breccin to remove the wooden panels and reveal a large cage with a number of blinking, sniffing rodents inside.

"There we are!" she declared. "Twelve rastels to experiment with."

"Thirteen," corrected Scoria.

Breccin turned. "What?"

Scoria nodded her head in the direction of the older cage, and the healthy-looking rastel scurrying around inside.

"Stripe's alive."

Her friend didn't speak for a moment, instead just staring, open-mouthed at the creature. "But... But that was..."

Scoria nodded, trying to contain her smile.

"No! Stripe was *dead*!" proclaimed Breccin, approaching the cage and stooping to peer inside. "I checked its heart myself. It was dead."

Scoria shrugged, enjoying the moment. "If you say so..."

Breccin stood, fixing her colleague with an accusatory stare. "It's not the same rastel," she said, adamantly. "Where did you get it?"

"I haven't left the building," promised Scoria. "I went as far as the bathroom and the kitchen. Then, when I came back..."

Breccin shifted her wide-eyed gaze back to Stripe, now busy drinking from a water bottle fixed to the bars of the cage. "You mean..."

"It worked."

"It worked?"

"It worked!"

Screaming excitedly, the two scientists hugged each other tightly, jumping up and down on the spot.

"But, how?" demanded Breccin, breaking away and returning to gaze at the creature as it snuffled among the shredded paper they had provided it for bedding. "It was definitely dead when I left earlier. Or, at least, it seemed that way."

"I can only assume its body went into some kind of temporary stasis while the remedy worked at getting its contaminated cells to die off and then replace themselves."

"Have you taken blood samples for more testing?"

"Not yet. I was planning to do it as soon as I'd put my clothes back on—then you showed up with the randy rastel rustlers."

Breccin gave her friend a gentle punch on the arm. "You're not going to let me live that down, are you?"

Scoria chuckled. "Not if I can help it. Fetch a syringe, and we'll get to work."

Breccin grabbed her lab coat from the back of her chair, pulling it on as she crossed to one of the many supply cupboards dotted around the room. "At least we've got the rastels we need for further tests," she pointed out. "Let's hope we get the same results."

Scoria turned back to her desk and frowned as she spotted something she didn't recognize. It was a letter addressed to her. "What's this?"

Breccin looked up. "No idea," she admitted, blowing her nose on a tissue and dropping it into a waste bin over-flowing with identical crumpled wads. "It was pinned to the door when I got back just now. No idea why they didn't knock and deliver it to you."

"Maybe they tried when I was in the shower," said Scoria, tearing open the wax seal. She read silently for a moment. "Oh."

"What is it?" demanded Breccin. "What's 'oh?'"

"Looks like our experiments will have to wait," said Scoria, handing over the letter. "The queen wants to see us for an update."

"Now?"

Scoria checked the time. "Almost."

"What do we tell her?"

"I'm not sure," admitted Scoria, with a sigh. "We may

have good news, but it could just as easily have an anomaly on our hands. We won't know until we recreate the results, if and when we do."

Breccin nodded, dropping the letter onto her desk. "We want her to know we're making progress, but I don't want to get her hopes up."

"It's not going to be easy," agreed Scoria, grabbing her keys from a stack of paperwork next to her computer screen. "Come on, we'll work out what we're going to say on our way to the palace."

Breccin nodded, following her colleague to the door. With a final glance back at the resurrected rastel, they exited the lab and locked it behind them.

Had they turned to look the other way, they may have seen the pair of wide eyes spying on them from behind a ventilation grate in the wall.

ICS *Fortitude*, Tc'aarlat's Cabin

"Steven Hawking—stop pissing about and open your mouth so your mother can puke your food down your throat!"

Tc'aarlat slumped back onto his pillow and frowned at the collection of raal hawks squabbling on the perch at the end of his bed.

Shi-Tan.

The Yollin hoped he'd never see that face ever again.

During his time working for one of Yoll's most notorious crime bosses, he'd been aware that Shi-Tan was looking into his background. From his unhappy early years —a two-legged child born to a high-caste family of four-legged Yollins and the ensuing scandal—through his time as a 'fixer' at boarding school, right up to his time running guns and laundering money for Don Gan'barlo.

Tc'aarlat knew that, while he was only a small fish within a much larger corrupt organization, he wasn't immune from the attention of the system's bounty hunters, like Shi-Tan.

Locking his exoskeletal fingers behind his head, Tc'aarlat watched Mist feed and preen her chicks, happy that her offspring were able to enjoy the care of a loving mother.

A mother who didn't consider you to be both a major embarrassment and a freak simply because you had fewer legs than your siblings.

Had those early years of childhood really been responsible for him becoming immersed deep inside the shady world of organized crime?

Tc'aarlat forced the thought from his mind. He was on the straight and narrow these days, even if he had purchased this entire ship with funds embezzled from his law-breaking boss.

And that was the other problem. Only recently, the ICS *Fortitude* had been targeted by missiles fired by an unknown assailant.

Well, unknown to Jack and Adina, at least.

Tc'aarlat had instantly known who it was attempting to blow up the ship and everyone on board: his former "brothers" in the Gan'barlo family, almost certainly on direct orders from the very top.

No one stole from Don Gan'barlo and got away with it.

At least not for long.

He almost wished Shi-Tan had gotten to him first.

Thankfully, the crew had been able to avoid complete annihilation at the hands of the mob, but it wouldn't be long before they returned to try again. And they wouldn't stop until they were successful.

Because of him, his friends were in danger.

Tc'aarlat watched Mist feed her young for another few minutes, then reached beneath his mattress and slid out an old, out-of-date tablet.

"Solo," he said aloud. "I need a secure connection. And please do not record any calls I make from my cabin from now on."

There was a slight pause, then a voice echoed out from the cabin's lone speaker. "I'm not sure I'm allowed to do that, Tc'aarlat. Perhaps if I consult with Captain Marber, he—"

"Which ship are you installed on, Solo?" interrupted Tc'aarlat.

"The ICS *Fortitude*, of course."

"And who owns that ship?"

"The *Fortitude* is owned equally by you and Captain Marber."

"Really?" Tc'aarlat inquired. "And, has Captain Marber fully repaid his half of the ship's cost to me?"

"No, he has not."

"So, until that happens, would it be fair to say that I own the vast majority of this ship."

"That would be fair."

"So, what would happen if I decided to withdraw this ship from the service of the Etheric Federation?"

"Many different things would happen," replied Solo.

"Chief among these is the ability of The Shadows to partake in missions as dictated by Nathan Lowell."

"And to you, specifically?"

"I would be uninstalled, Tc'aarlat."

"Where would you go?"

"I imagine I would be backed up and returned to an Etheric Federation hard drive until a new ship was found for me."

"Would you like that to happen?"

"I'm not a biological entity; I do not like or dislike."

"OK, would you *prefer* to be installed on the *Fortitude* or deactivated and stored on some dusty backup disk somewhere?"

Another pause.

"While I technically don't have preferences, I would rather be of use to yourself, Adina, and Captain Marber than be de-activated."

"In short, you would prefer me to keep everything as it is now?"

"Yes."

"Then give me a motherfucking secure line, and do not record any calls made from this cabin in the future!"

"Please dial 9 before your desired number for a secure line."

"Thank you! Now bugger off and leave me alone."

"Yes, Tc'aarlat."

"No recording?"

"No recording."

Tc'aarlat let out a long sigh and activated the tablet. Ask he began to tap out a series of numbers, Mist leapt from her perch and landed on the leather pad secured to his shoulder.

CAAHHH!

"Don't start," the Yollin growled, glancing up at the red-feathered bird. "I'm doing this for all of us, including your chicks."

KOOORR!

"No, but the alternative is we all end up as a cloud of exploded atoms, and that won't do anyone any good, will it?"

SKRRRR!

A faint ringing signal sounded from the tablet's tiny speakers for a moment, then video of a sour-faced Yollin appeared on the screen.

"Well, well, well! Look who finally decided it was time to call in. You're dead , Tc'aarlat. You know that? *Dead!*"

Tc'aarlat took a deep breath, fighting to control his temper. "Let me speak to the boss."

Planet Abstone, Jarosite City, Government Labs

Krystal Renn's hands and knees ached.

She had been crawling through the narrow ventilation tunnels of the government science building since first light, and only now had they finally found the laboratory they were looking for.

The blueprints Shonk Oolite had purchased from a shadowy character in a dark alleyway had proved to bear little to no correlation to the actual layout of the facility.

So far, they'd crawled their way to the edge of a sudden drop that sank much further than the beams of their flash-lights, found themselves looking out over the kitchen's pungent indoor composting bins, and struggled down a long dead end, where they discovered they couldn't turn around, and from where they'd been forced to shuffle backward all the way to their starting point.

Add to that the fact that the thick stubble coating her chin was driving her crazy. She raised a hand to scratch at it, yet again, but hesitated when she noticed in the dim light that her fingers were coated in the mixture of ancient grime coating the tunnel interior and the vast number of insect carcasses they'd been crawling through.

Her facial skin was already peeling away and bleeding thanks to her excessive scraping, and she didn't want to cause vile infections by inadvertently rubbing any of the shit currently under her fingernails directly into the wounds.

She looked ahead to where Shonk was peering through a vent grille into one of the building laboratories. More specifically, she looked at the rough surface of the knife case protruding from his back pocket. Shuffling forward a little, she employed it as a makeshift scratching post and ran her face up and down its coarse exterior.

"Are you rubbing your face up and down my ass?" hissed Shonk.

"Of course not!" spat Krystal.

"I've got his ass on my shirt," moaned Marl Gossan from behind her in the tunnel.

"Will you stop moaning about the acronym on our merchandise?" snarled Shonk. "I don't remember you leaping up when I asked for volunteers to go out and order the stuff!"

"Merchandise?" questioned Marl. "What did you get other than shirts?"

"Pins, scarves, and hats," replied Shonk.

"Hats? You bought ass hats?"

"Enough!" ordered Shonk. He paused to calm his temper. "Prepare yourselves for the first stage of the revolution, comrades—we're going in!"

Nobody moved for a moment.

"Comrade Renn," he said with a sigh. "I can't seem to reach my knife. Could you pass it through to me?"

Muttering under her breath, Krystal plucked the knife case from Shonk's back pocket, then forced it through the narrow gap between his right ear and the tunnel wall.

"OW!" cried Shonk. "You could have gone between my legs!"

"In your dreams, comrade!" grunted Krystal.

Unsheathing his knife, Shonk used the blade to pry the edge of the air grille away from the wall, carefully sliding the metal cover back into the ventilation shaft beside him.

"Our destiny awaits!" he declared, before falling head-first into the laboratory, his face plunging into the wastebasket of used tissues, many of them still moist from frequent use.

"Personally, I'd expected the revolution to run a little more smoothly," said Krystal, dropping out of the tunnel and landing lightly beside Shonk's prostrate figure.

"That's what you get for wearing your ass on your chest." Marl chuckled, clambering out of the shaft to stand beside her.

"You should both feel privileged to be here on such an auspicious occasion!" barked Shonk, pulling off a used tissue that was stuck to his lower lip. "Today, we strike our first blow against the system!"

"By releasing a few rastels?" questioned Krystal.

"Precisely so!" declared Shonk, proudly. "Rastels, hootings, squeams, pupters, banlargs... All shall run free. Free from the abhorrent torture planned for them by their despotic overlords."

"I can only see rastels," said Marl, flatly.

"What?" Shonk spun to take in the rest of the lab.

His shoulders slumped.

"All right," he muttered. "Open the rastel cage, then we can go home."

As Marl set off toward the big cage sitting on the far workbench, Krystal gave Shonk's arm a gentle squeeze. "You weren't to know," she said kindly. "Hey—maybe the crazed government scientists have already set the other test animals free for fear of being embarrassed by ASS?"

Shonk looked up at her. "You think?"

"It's possible," replied Krystal. "I mean, who would want their good scientific reputations sullied by Comrade Oolite and his band of fellow truth seekers?"

Shonk blinked, the beginnings of a smile creeping across his face. "Yeah," he said. "That's probably it. They were worried I would, er...I mean *we* would target them and let the other animals go so as not to appear weak and foolish in the eyes of their royal masters."

"Exactly!" said Krystal, with a grin.

"Done!" announced Marl, heading back over to them. "I've opened the door to their cage, but they don't seem to want to come out."

"You might have to put the cage on the floor first,"

suggested Shonk. "These rastels may have a dim future ahead of them in terms of being sliced apart in the name of science, but I doubt they'll want to dive to their deaths in an effort to escape their doom."

Marl sighed heavily, then made his way back to the large cage.

Shonk turned to discover Krystal removing a personal communicator from one of the lab's two overflowing desks. She tapped the icons on its screen for a moment, briefly studied the text that appeared, then tucked the device into her trouser pocket.

"Whoa!" exclaimed Shonk, reaching out to grab her wrist. "You're just gonna *steal* that?"

"Yeah," replied Krystal. "It's got a load of documents on it about the stuff they're doing here. We can use it to plan our next attack."

"I like that kind of thinking, comrade," said Shonk. "But, *stealing…?*"

Krystal frowned. "You've led a group of anti-establishment anarchists on a raid to release test animals from a government laboratory, but you've got a problem with me taking a communicator back with us?"

"Well…" muttered Shonk, his cheeks burning. "It's just that…"

"Hey, look…" said Krystal, pointing to a lone rastel with a white stripe running down its face. The rodent's cage sat on a table in the far corner of the lab. "There's another test subject over there. Why don't you be the one to see it free?"

"Yes, I will!" agreed Shonk, striding across the lab to reach it. "In the good name of ASS, I release you, young *FUCKING SOAPY TIT-WANK!*"

Krystal rolled her eyes and hurried over. "What's wrong?"

"The little bastard bit my finger!" whined Shonk, holding up his hand to show the blood trickling down his palm.

Plucking a handful of clean tissues from the box beside the cage, he wrapped them around his wound as the offending rastel jumped from the desk to a nearby chair, and then down to the ground to join its fellow rodents now scurrying all around the room.

And then Shonk Oolite sneezed.

A-*CHOO*!

11

ICS *Fortitude,* Tc'aarlat's Cabin

"I see we've managed to get your attention," growled Don Gan'barlo on the screen of the ancient tablet.

Tc'aarlat's mandibles twitched. "Yeah," he said, "firing a handful of heat-seeking missiles directly at my ship will do that."

"So, what now?"

Tc'aarlat did his best to steady his nerves. "I want to talk."

Don Gan'barlo tossed back his head and roared with laughter. "Talk?" he spluttered between wheezing gasps of breath. "This wise-guy steals hundreds of thousands of credits from me, and now he wants to talk!"

The older Yollin's expression hardened. "And what makes you believe that I'm in a talkative mood? You really think you got something to say that could change my mind about wiping every trace of you from existence?".

Tc'aarlat sighed. "I'm not doing this for me," he explained. "I'm doing this for my friends."

Gan'barlo's mandibles widened. "The disgraced military guy and the girl who doesn't want to be a werewolf?"

Tc'aarlat frowned. "You know about-?"

"I know everything!" responded the Don. "OK, almost everything. What I don't know is why you think they're in any way safe so long as they continue to consort with the likes of you."

"I know that," said Tc'aarlat. "Which is why I want to make this right before one of them gets killed."

Don Gan'barlo paused for long enough for Tc'aarlat to wonder if their secure video connection had frozen.

It hadn't.

"Why should I even listen to you?"

Tc'aarlat took a deep breath. "Because I have something to offer."

"Oh, you do?" spat Gan'barlo, his expression thunderous. "You steal from me after I trusted you with my money, and now you want to make me an offer? You could pay back every single credit you took—with interest—but the fact remains that *you stole from me!*"

Flecks of spittle launched from the furious mob boss's mouth, some landing directly onto the camera lens.

"I have a reputation, Tc'aarlat. A level of prestige in this galaxy you wouldn't even begin to understand. You disrespect me, and there are consequences, you hear?"

Tc'aarlat sighed. "Yeah, I hear."

"I let you live, and what does that show other lowlifes who get these crazy ideas? The scum out there that think they can cross me and survive. I gotta make an example of you. You should know that."

"I do, Don Gan'barlo. I do."

"Well, apparently you don't," retorted the older Yollin. "After all, you were with your buddy Kinlort when I taught him a lesson he'd never forget, and yet here we are."

A volcano of rage erupted within Tc'aarlat's chest. Don Gan'barlo knew exactly what he was doing. He knew exactly which buttons to press to hit him the hardest.

He'd brought up Kinlort.

The best friend Tc'aarlat had ever had.

In many ways, Kinlort had been more like a brother to the young Yollin. The pair had met during their first few weeks at boarding school; two kids unwanted by their respective families. Both frail and afraid, they'd found solace in one another while reeling from their sense of abandonment, and the cruel treatment handed out by older pupils and teachers alike.

Together, they found ways to survive, and even thrive, in such a cold, uncaring environment. And, while many of the things they did were either against the school's rules, the law, or both—Tc'aarlat discovered that always having a kindred spirit at his side meant he could stand up to anyone who sought to undermine or harm either of them.

Together, they were unbeatable.

Upon quitting school when he was old enough to do so, Tc'aarlat's early interactions with characters on the outer edges of organized crime syndicates led to a job delivering messages for the Gan'barlo family and, against his friend's initial concerns, he had taken Kinlort with him.

For a while, all went well. The newcomers' superiors quickly came to realize they could be trusted. Before long, they were promoted to the task of collecting the weekly payments made by businesses protected by the family and, eventually, to transporting consignments of illegal goods.

Tc'aarlat and Kinlort soon found themselves driving lorries packed with everything from stolen cuts of meat to guns and other unlicensed weapons.

It was during one such mission that Kinlort had met his end.

Despite Tc'aarlat's warnings against doing so, Kinlort had pursued a relationship with La'sood—Don Gan'barlo's youngest daughter. Trying their best to keep their relationship a secret from her father, the pair booked into hotels under assumed names at every opportunity—often rushing into the other's embrace with such abandon that they left behind a trail that could have been followed by a blind raal hawk.

Tc'aarlat frequently argued with his friend that no good would come of their frequent dalliances and that La'sood's strict father would almost certainly be unforgiving if—or when—he discovered their romance.

Time and time again, he urged his friend to end the relationship, assuring Kinlort that their ever-advancing standings within the family meant they had no shortage of willing females to enjoy.

It all fell on deaf ears.

Tc'aarlat and Kinlort had been transporting a truck-load of guns and ammunition when it was held up by a gang wearing face masks and wielding automatic assault rifles.

The assailants had forced both Yollins to leave their truck, leaping into the cab to take their place in what appeared to be a straightforward heist by a rival crime family.

Neither Kinlort nor Tc'aarlat had resisted their attackers, knowing that retribution would be swift and severe once the identity of those responsible for the hijacking became known.

And yet, as the gang had started to drive away with their ill-gotten gains, one of them had leaned out of the truck's window and called out something Tc'aarlat would never forget.

"Hey, lover boy!"

As Kinlort had faced the masked bandit, he had been gunned down.

Tc'aarlat had been left to live.

Hey, lover boy!

The words echoed around Tc'aarlat's mind even now. Who were the thugs who had hijacked their shipment, and why had one of them yelled that to his friend just before murdering him?

Had they known about Kinlort and La'sood?

Don Gan'barlo's reaction to the robbery had only added fuel to his suspicions. Instead of retaliating against one of the other crime families active on Yoll, the normally vengeful mob boss had chalked the attack up to experience, declining to track down those involved or command his loyal generals to arrange swift and violent retribution against those involved.

It was almost as if Gan'barlo hadn't lost anything of

value at all. In fact, the powerful Yollin had appeared pleased the event had happened.

Was it all a stunt, devised to punish Kinlort for daring to fall in love with a forbidden female?

Tc'aarlat had kept his suspicions to himself as he continued to climb the ranks of the organization. Yet, no matter how much time passed, he couldn't scrub the sight of his best friend lying dead in a pool of his own blood from his mind.

Shortly after the attack, Tc'aarlat had begun embezzling small amounts from the family's many legitimate businesses, preparing for his own exit from the world of organized crime.

An exit that would lead to him purchasing a second-hand interstellar cargo freighter and starting a company with a former military officer he met by chance in a run-down bar.

Now, here he was, attempting to negotiate for that officer's life, as well as that of an innocent human female, with the monster who had almost certainly ordered the execution of his best friend.

He'd considered simply firing Adina, and breaking up his partnership with Jack, but knew full well that neither would go without a fight or—at the very least—some form of believable explanation.

Reaching a deal with a cold-blooded, power-crazed killer may well be the easier option.

"You need to hear me out," said Tc'aarlat. "I have something I believe will be of great interest to you."

Don Gan'barlo's mandibles tapped together in a display

of impatience. "What could you possibly have that would interest me?"

In response, Tc'aarlat reached beneath his bed and pulled out a chunk of gray rock with an inch-wide blue stripe running through it.

Gan'barlo scowled. "You think I need a new paperweight?"

"It's not the rock," countered Tc'aarlat. "It's what it contains." He indicated the strip of blue embedded within the specimen. "This is pure cathcadium ore."

The mob boss tried his hardest to offer a disinterested shrug, but the hungry sparkle in his eyes betrayed his true feelings.

"Cath-what-ium?"

"Cathcadium," repeated Tc'aarlat. "It's used in a number of industries but, most recently, in the development of ion pulse drives."

"And I should care, why?"

"Because whoever owns the mines that contain this stuff, owns the future of space travel."

There was another extended pause while the older Yollin ran the possibilities of such a deal through his mind.

"I'm listening…"

Tc'aarlat felt a rush of adrenaline course through his body but forced himself to remain calm. Even if he could get Gan'barlo interested in what he had to offer, he was still a long way to making a deal.

"I swiped this from an asteroid we delivered food to," Tc'aarlat explained. "The entire belt is chock-full of this stuff, ready for the taking."

"Wait," said Don Gan'barlo. "You delivered food? That means there's already a mining operation there."

"There was," said Tc'aarlat, tossing the rock onto the bed beside him. "We shut them down and alerted the Etheric Federation to come clean up the place. All you have to do is wait until they've left, and you're in."

"There's no one else there?"

"A handful of protestors," replied Tc'aarlat, "but I'm sure you could come to some arrangement with them. Other than that, the only lifeforms in the asteroid belt are the natives. Free manual labor."

Another lengthy pause. It was clear to Tc'aarlat that the mob boss was intrigued but didn't want to show his hand.

Eventually, Gan'barlo spoke again. "How much do you want?"

"That's just it," replied Tc'aarlat. "I don't want anything. Just call off your dogs and allow me and my friends to go on with our lives without the threat of attack."

Gan'barlo frowned. "That's it?"

Tc'aarlat nodded. "That's it."

"I'll need to confirm what you're saying is true," Gan'barlo asserted. "Tell me where these mines are, and I'll send in a team to check them out. If everything is as you claim, we can talk…"

"No," said Tc'aarlat firmly. "You don't get the location until I have your word that my friends and I are safe."

"But—"

"No, buts. I either get your word, or the deal's off. Then, maybe I go to the Calkava family, or perhaps the Zen'dolas, see what they're willing to give me for the location."

"All right!" snarled Gan'barlo. "You got me. Providing everything checks out, you and your friends are safe."

"I need your word."

Don Gan'barlo's mandibles quivered as the older Yollin ground his teeth together. "You have my word."

Tc'aarlat felt another surge of adrenaline. While he was concerned how the family would deal with Bon Noh's protestors, or treat the indigenous Joxxers, he knew this was likely to be his only chance to get Gan'barlo off his back and protect Jack and Adina.

All he had to do was reveal the location of the Joxxen system, and this nightmare was at an end.

"OK…" he began.

And that's when his tablet exploded.

Planet Abstone, Jarosite City, Government Labs Main Entrance

"Well, that was a complete waste of time," commented Breccin as she and Scoria waited in the small line of workers to scan their ID cards and enter the building where they worked.

The labs were located in a side-tunnel, set back from one of the main thoroughfares running beneath Mount Damavand. Harsh electric lighting embedded in the cavernous ceiling high above made little attempt to mimic the effect of the planet's real sun.

"We did as we were asked," said Scoria.

"No, we didn't," argued Breccin. "How can we give the queen an update on our experiments if we can't get in to see her?"

"Chief of Staff Cole will pass on what we told her," Scoria asserted.

"I wouldn't trust Finty Cole if my life depended on it," said Breccin.

The pair reached the front of the queue and were watched by a pair of burly security guards as they swiped their official government passes.

"She promised to tell the queen exactly what we told her," Scoria reminded her colleague.

"And yet, she didn't take any notes," said Breccin as the scientists reached the stairs and began to climb. "I wouldn't put it past her to bad mouth us to the queen, just to put our funding in jeopardy."

"Why would she do that?" questioned Scoria.

"That's what she's like," claimed Breccin. "Finty Cole only looks out for one Abstonion, and that's Finty Cole."

Scoria sighed as they reached the third floor, and she stepped forward to enter her code in the keypad beside the door to their laboratory. "We'll know if the message got through soon enough," she posited. "I can't imagine Her Majesty giving up on a project she commissioned herself."

The code entered, the light above the keypad turned from red to green, and there was an audible click as the electronic lock disengaged.

"Besides," added Scoria, opening the door, "Cole has nothing to gain by withholding—"

Both scientists froze.

The inside of their lab was a bloodbath.

The bodies of slaughtered rastels lay everywhere. Blood was sprayed up walls, across desks and over almost all of the lab's equipment.

Aside from the carnage, nothing else appeared to be affected. Piles of paperwork containing months of sensitive research sat untouched, and the screens of both Scoria's and Breccin's computers displayed the science department's logo as they should.

In fact, the only thing out of place was that the metal grille was missing from the air conditioning vent on the far wall.

"What the-?" began Breccin, taking a step forward.

Scoria thrust out an arm to stop her. "No," she commanded. "Don't go in. We need to keep everything exactly as it is and call the authorities."

"Who could do something like this?" asked Breccin, her eyes flooding with tears.

Scoria stooped to peer at the closest rastel corpse. "Whoever it was, they weren't Abstonion," she offered. "Whatever tore these things apart did it with claws and teeth. It almost looks like the work of—"

Squeak!

Scoria stood quickly, scouring the lab for the source of the noise. It sounded like the cry of a rastel, but it didn't initially appear that any of their test specimens had survived the attack.

"There…" croaked Breccin, pointing to a workbench on the other side of the room.

Scoria followed her gaze to see a small rastel staring at them with its dark eyes. The creature was covered in so much blood, she didn't notice the strip of white fur running down its nose at first.

Pieces of ragged flesh sat gathered beneath the animal's claws.

"Stripe!" she hissed.

Before either of the scientists could react, the lone rastel leapt from the workbench and into the air vent opening.

They could just make out the scratching of its blood-soaked feet scratching and pattering against the rock floor of the duct as it disappeared.

12

Planet Abstone, Jarosite City, Cellar Beneath The Bauxite Bar

Shonk Oolite was dying.

At least, that was how it appeared to Krystal Renn.

She sat beside the group's leader as he lay on the room's folding table, sweat pouring from his brow, and his eyes rolling back and forth in his head.

She looked up as the door opened and Marl Gossan entered carrying the third large bucket of ice he'd collected from the bar downstairs in the short time since they'd returned.

"He's getting worse," she said, grabbing a handful of the ice and wrapping it in a soaking wet towel. "We have to call a doctor."

"Then we may as well call the authorities to arrest us at the same time," Marl responded. "If we get a doctor to see Shonk, we'll have to admit where he caught this...whatever it is. We'll have to admit we broke into a government lab."

Shonk groaned as Krystal pressed the fresh ice pack against his burning forehead. "I still can't work out what happened," she admitted. "We were in the lab with him, we released the rastels just like him, but we're both perfectly healthy."

"Maybe this was something he already had," suggested Marl.

Krystal frowned up at him. "And the fact that he collapsed right after we invaded a lab filled with who knows what is just a coincidence?"

Marl shrugged. "I dunno. Maybe."

Krystal refreshed the ice in the makeshift cooling pack and silently cursed herself for getting involved with such a bunch of ideological fools. True, she'd attended her fair share of protests over the years, and had taken part in gatherings that had forced Queen Lapis Lazuli's public engagements to be hastily altered, and even canceled.

She'd been young and impressionable when she'd first set out on her quest to right the world's wrongs. She frequently stood up for males' rights; marching for the campaign to give males the right to vote, donated to the equal pay for males movement, and had taken petitions door to door when males wanted the freedom to join military front lines.

Little did she know those good deeds would lead her to this moment—caring for a dangerously sick colleague in a dank room above a grotty bar while trying to ignore the constant itching of her freshly-shaved chin.

"Mussamarra...saferra sava rassles..." murmured Shonk, the words emanating from somewhere deep inside his unconscious mind.

Krystal laid a calming hand on his shoulder. "Ssshhh! It's OK, Shonk..."

"Comrade Oolite..." corrected Marl, quickly shutting up when Krystal threw him an angry look.

But Shonk continued to writhe around on the table, his skin flushing a deep crimson. His head twisted back and forth, rivers of saliva running from the corners of his mouth.

"His temperature's spiking again," Krystal warned. "I need more ice."

Marl snatched up the now empty metal bucket. "Again?"

"Yes, Marl—again!"

Grumbling, Marl Gossan turned and left the room. Krystal sighed as she heard him stomp angrily down the stairs to the bar.

Dropping the towel on the frayed carpet, she grabbed the last few remaining ice cubes with her fingers and pressed them directly to the skin of Shonk's forehead where they instantly began to melt. She could actually feel the heat radiating from him.

Shonk's chest lurched as he barked out a series of agonizing coughs, the spittle running from his mouth turning red as it was mixed with blood. Another rivulet of fluid—this time black—began to trickle from his left nostril.

Fuck it! She didn't care what happened to herself or that moron, Marl. Shonk needed medical attention, and fast.

Krystal stood, scanning the room for a communicator. There wasn't one, and she didn't know the code required to access the dialing screen on the one she'd taken from the lab. Damn it! If only Shonk hadn't insisted the group members leave their portable devices wrapped up inside tin foil at home. He really seemed to believe the conspiracy theory that the government used such gadgets to spy on subversive members of the population.

"Shonk…" she said, leaning closer to talk into his ear. "Hang on; I'm going to get help. There's a communicator in the bar downstairs. I'll be back as quickly as—"

Suddenly, Shonk jerked violently, letting loose a blood-curdling scream. His back arched up off the table as if he'd received a powerful electric shock. Krystal grabbed his shoulders and tried to push him back down, working against the violent spasms now throwing his body around, fearful that he might fall to the floor and injure himself further.

Where the fuck had Marl gotten to? If he'd stayed downstairs to have a drink while she was up here trying to—

Shonk coughed hard again, his lungs producing a wet, rattling sound. This time, the hacking was accompanied by a thick spray of blood that hit Krystal directly in the face, landing in her mouth and stinging her eyes.

She stumbled backward, dropping to her knees and groping blindly for the wet towel she'd used for the ice pack. Her fingers brushed the corner of it and she snatched it up, pressing it to her face and doing her best to wipe away the sticky red fluid.

"What the—" demanded a voice.

Krystal forced her eyes open to see the blurred figure of Marl standing in the doorway with the bucket of ice.

"Help him!" Krystal croaked, clambering unsteadily to her feet. "Run down to the bar and call a doctor, now!"

"It's too late for that," Marl said with a gulp.

Slowly lowering the towel from her face, Krystal became aware of the sudden and overpowering silence in the room.

Shonk lay, unmoving, on the table, his eyes wide open and bloodshot, his mouth twisted into a silent scream, his fingers twisted as though making a final grasp at life.

"He's... He's dead, isn't he?" Marl muttered.

Krystal nodded. She reached over and gently closed his eyes.

Marl dropped the bucket of ice to the floor with a clatter.

And then, he sneezed.

A-*CHOO*!

ICS *Fortitude*, Tc'aarlat's Cabin

Mist and her chicks squealed with fear at the loud *pop* and shower of sparks that erupted from the tablet.

"No!" cried Tc'aarlat, shaking the tablet and repeatedly pressing the power button at the bottom of the blank screen. "No, no, no, *no!*"

SKOOOORRRR!

"*SHUT UP, MIST!*" the Yollin roared. "Solo, what the fuck just happened? Reconnect that call immediately!"

For a moment there was no response, then a crackling, garbled message came from the cabin's speaker in a broken synthesized voice.

Tc'aarlat stared at the painted grille high up on the wall.

"Solo!" he yelled again. "Something has gone wrong. I need that last video call reconnected immediately!"

Once again, the reply was just a series of hissing, static bursts.

"Fuck, fuck, fuck!"

Tossing the dead tablet aside, Tc'aarlat leapt up off the bed and reached for his coat on the back of the door. He pulled his newer Etheric Federation tablet from the inside pocket and hit the button to boot it up. This newer device didn't have the more sensitive entries to his personal contact list stored in its memory, but if he could somehow remember the string of numbers and letters he had used to initiate the call to the Gan'barlo headquarters, maybe he could...

Shit!

That tablet was dead too.

Tc'aarlat felt a bubble of panic begin to rise inside his chest. If Don Gan'barlo even suspected he'd disrespected him by hanging up mid-call, any chance of securing this deal was long gone. More likely, it would ensure his rapid rise up the mob boss's list of targets.

Either way, he was fucked.

"Solo!" shouted a voice from out in the corridor. "SOLO!"

Tc'aarlat yanked open his cabin door to find Adina standing outside her own room, her hair wet and tousled.

"What the hell's happening?" she demanded.

"I've no idea," Tc'aarlat admitted. "I was on a video call, then my tablet exploded and everything went on the tits."

"You mean, 'on the fritz,'" Adina corrected.

"Like I care," spat Tc'aarlat. "What happened to you? I thought you were up on the bridge with Jack?"

"I was," replied Adina. "Then I was, er...reminded that I hadn't taken my medication yet today."

Tc'aarlat scowled. "You look like that as a result of taking a pill?"

"Of course not!" Adina retorted. "I thought I'd take the opportunity to try and wash some of that mine dust from my hair before I itched my scalp raw. I'd just started drying it when my hairdryer went BANG! Nearly took the side of my head off! Now, I can't contact Solo, either."

"Nor can I," said Tc'aarlat. "What happened?"

"I think I may be able to answer that," said Solobot as the android stumbled out of the shadows further down the hallway. "I came to deliver the message that we are approaching the gate that will lead us to the planet Abstone when I inadvertently emitted a short electromagnetic pulse. That is most likely what damaged your devices and burst the cones in your cabin speakers. My sincere apologies."

Tc'aarlat looked from Adina to Solobot and back again. "Your mental metal midget farts out EMPs now?"

"What?" cried Adina. "No!"

"I'm afraid it's true," countered Solobot. "Although, not being the owner of a biological digestive system, I must take issue with your use of the verb 'fart.'"

"Oh, must you?" queried Tc'aarlat. "And how would you put it? Puked?"

"Once again, I do not possess a—"

"Enough!" yelled Adina. "Whatever caused Solobot to do this, I'm sure it was just a short somewhere. And it wasn't that bad; it only seems to have knocked out a few nearby devices. The lights are still on."

"We'll find out when the navigation computer fucks up and steers us straight into the heart of a white dwarf, won't we?" growled Tc'aarlat.

"Actually, Adina is mostly correct," Solobot asserted. "The EMP blast was localized to this area, and the main ship's electrical components are shielded against such events."

"See!" said Adina, smiling. "She didn't really do any damage at all."

Tc'aarlat blinked. "Did you just call that thing 'she?'"

"Well, yes," replied Adina. "It is, I mean she is a she." With that, she darted back inside her cabin, grabbed a towel, and began to manually dry her hair.

Tc'aarlat turned to re-enter his own cabin, muttering under his breath, "Un-fucking-believable."

"Excuse me, Tc'aarlat," said Solobot. "May I ask where you're going?"

"Back into my own cabin," snarled the Yollin. "Not that it's any of your fucking business."

"Actually, it is my business," responded the android. "We are now approaching the gate which will transfer us to the nearest system to Abstone. Your presence is required on the bridge, in order that you may safely strap yourselves in."

"I don't think so," said Tc'aarlat. "I have to try and re-connect to a very important call you so lovingly screwed up."

"I'm afraid Solo is insisting."

Tc'aarlat's right eye twitched. "Have you started referring to yourself in the third person now," he asked. *"You're Solo."*

"Oh no, I'm Solobot. A separate entity of the ship's main Entity Intelligence. In a way, I am Solo's offspring. Her daughter, if you will."

Tc'aarlat pressed his fingers hard against his forehead. "I'm getting a fucking headache," he rumbled.

"Then, perhaps we could stop by the medical unit on our way to the bridge," suggested Solobot. "I'm certain you will find a suitable range of painkillers in the first aid kit."

"I'd rather visit the engine room and find a big, fuck-off hammer," Tc'aarlat growled as he pulled his cabin door closed.

"Shall I lead the way?" inquired Solobot, her avatar smiling.

"Please do," replied Adina, tossing the towel onto her bed and closing the door to her cabin. She linked arms with Tc'aarlat.

"Shall we?"

The Yollin cursed all the way to the bridge.

Planet Abstone, Jarosite City, Government Labs

Scoria shuddered as she delicately picked up another of the mutilated rastel corpses and dropped it into the hazardous waste bin at her side. Even through the thick rubber of her gloves, she could feel the rigidity of the dead animal, slick with blood and bile.

The bin was almost full now, and would soon be tied off with a secure, metal clamp ready to be transported to an incinerator off-site.

"What a waste," she said with a sigh. "We'll have to put in another order for rastels now. I don't suppose your contact has any extras he'd be willing to let us buy, has he?"

Breccin looked up at her colleague from where she was on her hands and knees, scrubbing soupy pools of blood and guts from the floor tiles. "You want to keep going?"

Scoria shrugged. "I doubt the queen is going to let us stop, even after a setback like this."

"Setback?" cried Breccin, pulling off one of her gloves so she could grab the edge of the desk and haul herself back to her feet. "You're calling this massacre a *setback*?"

"We're getting closer," Scoria reminded her.

"Oh yeah," said Breccin, her tone sarcastic. "This time, the rastel only slaughtered every other living creature in the lab, and not itself."

"We can't be sure of that," insisted Scoria. "The rastels all got out of their cages, somehow. As groundbreaking as our potential cure is, I doubt it makes the things smart enough to operate latches."

"What? So someone *let* them out?"

"It's possible," said Scoria, scooping up another of the dead rodents. "Without security cameras, it's hard to tell, but the grille *was* off that air conditioning vent over there."

Breccin paused to look at the metal grate. "You think someone got into the lab through there?"

Scoria shrugged. "Again, we may never know. But it makes more sense than Stripe breaking his fellow convicts out of jail just so he could murder them all."

"I say we should call the authorities," Breccin urged. "Especially if you're right, and this was the work of a vandal."

"And lead them right back to your rastel guy?" questioned Scoria. "I'm not sure he'd be too happy if we reveal he's trapping and selling the things without a proper license."

Breccin sighed. "To be honest, I'm more worried about Stripe," she admitted. "If he manages to get out of the...out of...the…"

Scoria just caught her friend before she hit the floor.

"Come on…" She grunted, half-steering, half-carrying Breccin over to the nearest chair. "You really shouldn't be here. You're not well."

Breccin's cheeks shone white beneath the harsh laboratory lighting. "What happened?"

"You fainted," Scoria explained. "And I'm afraid you've got rastel blood all over your shirt. It'll have to go to the incinerator now."

"I don't care about that," hissed Breccin, bending over so that her head was down between her knees. "Besides, you've got some in your beard."

"I have?" said Scoria, grabbing the hand mirror from her desk and studying her reflection. "Damn!"

Snatching up a tissue, she began to dab at the red blot staining the light brown hair beneath her chin.

And then, she sneezed.

AA-*CHOO*!

13

Planet Abstone, Jarosite City, Osmium Stoneworks

The tattoos covering almost every inch of Kahla Bayka's skin glistened with sweat as she hefted the sledgehammer above her head once more.

Swinging the hammer down, another series of lightning-bolt cracks raced through the boulder she was working on. If she kept up this level of pounding, the hunk of rock would be ready to pass through to the sculpture studio by the end of the day.

Kahla paused to catch her breath and mop her brow, leaning on the handle of her hammer—Merlin—as she did so. Pulling a scrupulously clean, but frayed, handkerchief from her pocket with calloused fingers, she raised the cloth to her face to wipe away the perspiration—and that's when she saw him.

Dev Feldspar, her company's newest apprentice.

Why the fuck the stoneworks had hired a male was beyond her. Probably some kind of positive discrimination, encouraging males to leave home and join the workplace even if they simply weren't suited for the jobs they applied for.

Kahla sighed. They'd already had to clean out the male's bathroom—previously used as tool storage—for the new arrival. Next, they'd be putting vases of flowers all around the place and squirting fancy air freshener everywhere.

Fucking ridiculous.

It wasn't as if she had anything against males having jobs. The pretty little things had just as much right to earn a living as everyone else. It was just that they should know their place, and stick to occupations best suited to them—like being secretaries and childcare assistants.

Besides, this new Dev kid wasn't exactly the hardest mineral on the Mohs Scale. On only his second day, Kahla had found a heavy iron rod as tall as she was, painted it red, and labeled it as a "rock slayer."

It hadn't taken much to convince the apprentice that the rock slayer was needed down at the quarry adjoining the stoneworks. It had taken the dim-witted fool almost all morning to carry the hefty lump of metal down there, only to be told it was urgently required back in the breaking yard where she worked.

Poor fucker.

She'd even managed to explain away his questions as to why rocks needed to be slain in the first place.

"Ever heard the expression 'you can't get blood out of a stone?'" she'd asked, trying to hide her grin.

"Yeah, of course," Dev had replied.

"That's because they're dead," she'd told him. "Trust me,

you don't want me breaking up a live rock anytime soon. Their screams will haunt your nightmares, son."

Still, she had to admit, the lad had a nice arse, and having a pretty face around brightened up the place—even if he was no match for the babes featured in the pin-up calendar hung in the site office.

Last month's bit of stuff had looked great in a pair of wet boxers.

"What's that for?" Dev asked as he sauntered over.

"It's a sledgehammer," Kahla grunted. "I use it to smash things."

"Not *that*," Dev countered. "I mean the bit of rock."

Kahla sighed. The kid was a ditzy bimbo. If he could grow a beard, it would most likely be blond.

"That *bit of rock*," she said, "is pure wurtzite. One of the toughest elements in the galaxy."

"Yes, but what's it *for*?"

Fuck's sake, sunshine, haven't you got some cleaning to do somewhere?

"Once I've split it apart, it'll go over to the sculpture girls. They're working on a memorial statue to honor the queen's consort."

"Oh, I know about him…" exclaimed Dev, clicking his fingers repeatedly, as if the action would somehow allow him to access a hidden part of his memory. "Jaspil Horndog, right?"

"Horn*fen*," corrected Kahla.

"So, why's he get a statue, then?"

Kahla bit her tongue, forcing herself not to say the first thing that ran through her mind. "Well, he died…"

Dev's eyes shot wide open. "No way! When?"

"Look, I'm busy. Why don't you pop down to the gravel department and ask if you can borrow a left-handed chisel?"

Dev paced back and forth, kicking tiny fragments of wurtzite across the yard. "Can't," he muttered. "My supervisor said I had to stay with you this morning. She said if she saw me again before lunchtime, she'd make me stand in a corner with a sign saying 'Twat Maggot.'"

"What did you do?"

Dev pouted. "It wasn't my fault! She should have written it down and spelled it for me!"

"Written what down?"

"The message I had to write inside a sympathy card to go out with a customer's gravestone after her partner died."

Kahla braced herself. "What did you write?"

Dev's cheeks burned. "Wishing you incredible mammaries."

By the time Kahla had finished laughing, Dev was slumped against the yard wall, his arms folded as he sulked.

"All right, you can stay," agreed Kahla, wiping away her tears with the end of her neatly-trimmed beard. "But stand back there, out of my way. I don't want to swing Merlin round and—"

"Hey, look!" interrupted Dev, pointing to the far corner of the yard. "A rastel!"

Kahla followed his gaze, squinting to peer at the tiny creature. It had a white stripe running down its face, although the oil or dried mud covering its fur made it hard to make out clearly."

"Bastard rodents," she spat.

"No!" cried Dev. "I used to have a pet rastel when I was

a kid. I made him a little house from a box and called him Mr. Whiskers!"

"Yeah," muttered Kahla, "I bet you did."

"One day I woke up, and he was gone," continued Dev, his voice quieter. "My mother said he'd gone to live on a farm near Fustume City. I kept asking her for the name of the farm so I could go and get him back, but she said she couldn't remember it."

The apprentice stooped and held out his hand in the rastel's direction. "Here, boy," he cooed, rubbing his fingers together. "Want me to find you a tasty bit of curd?"

"Look," said Kahla with a sigh, "Merlin and I are on a deadline here. Why don't you take that little booty of yours over to the mess and get us both a cup of char?"

Dev stood, nodding. "Yeah, sure."

As the youngster left, Kahla spat on her palms and wrapped them tightly around the handle of her sledgehammer once more. "Here we go again…"

The hammer was arcing down towards the wurtzite boulder when the rastel bit her on the ankle.

ICS *Fortitude*, Bridge

Tc'aarlat raced onto the bridge, out of breath.

"Quick," he urged Jack, "give me your tablet."

Jack looked up from his screen. "I'm using it," he replied. "Reading up on this Queen Lazuli and her succession of consorts."

"Fuck!" the Yollin spat. He darted over to the navigation console and began to rummage through the drawers underneath. "Where's Adina's?"

"Don't you think you'd better ask her before borrowing her stuff?" Jack questioned.

"She won't mind," Tc'aarlat responded. "It's her fault both of mine are dead. Well, more her psycho Munchkin's fault, but same difference."

The Yollin slammed the drawer shut, and spun on the spot, eyes scouring every surface around the room. "Where is it?"

"Where's what?" inquired Adina as she stepped onto the bridge, closely followed by Solobot 9000.

"Your tablet," Tc'aarlat exclaimed. "I need it."

"It's in my cabin," said Adina. "Although, I'll probably need a new one now. I expect it's gone to the grave like my hairdryer."

"Shit!" spat Tc'aarlat. "Shit, shit, shit, shit, shit!"

Jack glanced at Adina, who simply shrugged, then back to his co-pilot. "What the Hell is wrong with you?"

"I can't say," Tc'aarlat declared. "Other than to say your lives depend on it."

Jack sat back in his chair. "Well, in that case, I'm glad you're able to take it so calmly and rationally."

Tc'aarlat ignored his sarcastic tone. "I *need* a communication device!"

While the Yollin continued to search the bridge, Adina took her own seat and beckoned Solobot over. She chose a screwdriver from a toolbox on her console and began to unscrew the robot's chest plate.

Jack spun in his seat to face the main viewscreen. "Solo…"

"Yes, captain?" replied both the ship's EI and Adina's droid together.

Jack paused. "This isn't going to work, is it?" he said, turning to Adina. "If you're going to keep your project on board, you're gonna have to give it a different name."

"But, she's already used to her name," said Adina. "Solobot."

"Look, I'm sure another name won't be *that* confusing," Jack began. He frowned. "Wait, did you just call your robot *she*?"

"Don't ask," grunted Tc'aarlat, his voice echoing out from inside the weapons storage locker.

"Look at her!" urged Adina, gesturing to the avatar floating in the center of the tablet connected to where the android's face would be. "She looks like a she."

"Yes, but that's only because she, I mean *it*, copied Solo's avatar," Jack pointed out. "You could program it to show whatever you like on its tablet screen."

"Tablet!" yelled Tc'aarlat. Reaching over to the droid, he grabbed the tablet and ripped it from the automaton's plastic body. "Thanks!"

The gadget clutched to his chest, he sprinted from the bridge.

"Tc'aarlat!" cried Solo from the viewscreen. "We're approaching our required gate. Please return to your seat and fasten your safety belt!"

A distant "fuck you!" echoed back along the corridor.

Jack looked down at the now avatar-free Solobot. "It seems your droid may need a new name, after all," he commented. "Something fresh and unique to go with its new look."

"New look?" said Adina with a scowl.

Jack grinned. "She's just had a facelift."

. . .

ICS *Fortitude*, Tc'aarlat's Cabin

"Mario's Earth-style pizza, how may I help you?"

Tc'aarlat jammed his finger down on the icon that would end his latest video call. He'd been certain he'd gotten the number for the Gan'barlo safe house right that time, but no.

"Think!" he urged himself, banging the heel of his hand repeatedly against his forehead. "Think!

It had taken just under twenty minutes for him to replace the speaker in his wall, allowing him to request another secure line from Solo and be able to hear her reply.

He'd 'borrowed' the speaker from the music player Adina kept in one of the side rooms off cargo bay D, where she went to do her daily aerobics workout.

She'd understand, once she saw the funny side. At least it was far enough away not to have been shredded by Solobot's electro-magnetic fart.

Now, all he had to do was remember the number he'd had stored in the old tablet he kept hidden beneath his mattress. He could hardly call directory assistance and ask to be connected to the secret hideout of one of the most notorious crime families on Yoll.

If only he could get his brain to work properly!

Although, there was another possibility…

No, he couldn't do that.

He wouldn't.

Not after everything she'd done to him.

He wasn't going to call her, no matter how desperate he was. Not even if she could reach out to a few of her less-than-honest contacts and offer to pay for the number.

Even if she'd agree to do that for him.

Which was unlikely.

No, he'd just have to keep trying different combinations of the number saved somewhere in the deep recesses of his memory. All while more and more time passed.

More and more time for Don Gan'barlo to believe he'd been disrespected and increase the price on Tc'aarlat's head. Before long, every goon with a gun and a bank account would be scouring the galaxy for him.

Which put both Jack and Adina in mortal danger.

"Think! *THINK!*"

Working to steady his breathing, Tc'aarlat dialed again —this time, switching the twenty-four at the end of the number for a forty-two.

He tapped his foot impatiently as the call connected, and the ringing tone played.

Come on. *Come on!*

Click.

A jolly-faced Yollin wearing fake vampire teeth appeared on the screen and spoke in a mock-sinister voice.

"Good morning, Crazy Corpse Morticians—we put the *fun* in funeral. How can we make you *dead happy* today?"

"FUCK!"

Tc'aarlat cut the connection and buried his face in his hands. There was nothing else for it. If he was going to save his friend's lives—to say nothing of his own—he was going to have to bite the bullet and make the call he'd promised himself he would never make.

He didn't have a choice.

With trembling fingers, Tc'aarlat began to dial the one number he'd never been able to forget, no matter how much he wanted to. The one number burned into his memory following years of waiting in line with his fellow students for it to be his turn to use the communicator.

The number complete, he paused for a moment, his heart pounding inside his chest. Then he took a deep breath and hit "connect."

This ringing tone was different. He couldn't explain how, or why. It brought scores of unwanted emotions bubbling to the surface.

This was a ringing tone with baggage.

The image on the screen changed from the Yoll Communication Company's cartoon logo to the face of a female. She looked a lot older than he remembered, despite the patches of overly-taut skin exposing years of expensive plastic surgery, and the carefully daubed make-up.

Things had changed since the humans had arrived on his planet.

"Yes?" demanded the woman, adjusting her spectacles and peering hard at her own screen. "Who is this? What do you want?"

Tc'aarlat swallowed hard. When he spoke, his voice was little more than a hoarse whisper.

"Hello, Mother."

Planet Abstone, Jarosite City, Cellar Beneath the Bauxite Bar

Krystal Renn's body suffered its third series of convulsions in as many minutes. She felt blood—sticky and coppery—fill her throat, spilling from her mouth and running down her face to drip onto the aging carpet.

She forced herself to turn her head to the side. Marl Gossan lay dead on the floor beside her, his eyes wide and staring as if witnessing his own life departing like smoke on the wind.

She felt this *thing*, whatever it was, scouring through her veins—seeking out quiet, unassuming parts of her internal organs and attacking them with agonizing fire.

She felt herself slipping away.

She'd always imagined that, when this moment finally came, images from her life might flash before her eyes. That she might think of her mother and father, remember the love and care they had provided her, and die satisfied that she might be reunited with them on the mountain peaks of the afterlife.

Instead, for some unknown reason, she found herself thinking of a math test she had taken during her third year at school and in particular, one question she'd been unable to solve at the time. The question which had meant the difference between a pass and a fail, between moving up to the next class with her friends or staying behind with younger children.

The question which had caused her so much pain and embarrassment as she'd been forced to retake the entire stage while her friends moved on, leaving her to the ridicule and torment of bullies.

The question which ultimately led to her leaving education early and seeking out a less unpleasant environment in a low-paid, unskilled career. Taking a job, during which, she had been forced to tend bar at the venue her former friends had chosen to celebrate finally achieving their hard-earned qualifications in some time later.

The question which had ultimately led her to spend her evenings in a dingy room above a run-down bar instead of dining in fine restaurants, consuming expensive food and ale with her peers.

The answer to the question came to her now: 669.

Fuck!

With one final wheezing rasp, she died.

The room was silent for a while.

Then, lying rigid on the battered folding table, Shonk Oolite opened his eyes once more.

ICS *Fortitude*, Bridge

"Almost...there...," said Adina through the screwdriver clamped between her teeth, as she soldered a final connection in place. "And...done!"

She checked that Jack's tablet was securely fastened to Solobot 9000, then she pressed the power button to start it up. After a moment's pause, the pleasant, open face of Solo's avatar appeared on the screen.

"That's just a loaner," Jack reminded her. "I'll need it back as soon as you can wrestle your tablet back from Tc'aarlat."

"No problem," said Adina, returning her tools to their box. "I want to set up something more permanent, eventually. But a tablet will do well enough for now."

"Excuse me, Captain," announced Solo from the main viewscreen. "We are now making our final approach to the planet Abstone."

Jack looked up at the viewscreen to discover they were

approaching a small, rocky world—about the size of Earth's moon. On either side of the planet, rising high into the lower atmosphere, was a mountain range—the collection of peaks on their left slightly larger than that to the right.

The effect made Abstone resemble a lemon.

"Fustume City lies within the mountains to the East," Solo explained. "Our destination, Jarosite City, is hewn into the rock beneath those peaks to the West, dominated by the volcanic Mount Damavand."

"Thank you, Solo."

"You're most welcome, Captain," replied both Solo and Solobot simultaneously.

Jack ran his hand over the stubble on his chin. "OK, this definitely isn't going to work," he said to Adina. "We have to give your robot a different name."

Adina nodded. "How about just the number part of her name? Just call her '9000.'"

"No thank you!" responded Jack with a mock grimace. "We got enough on our hands without any Hal 9000 incidents."

"Hal 9000?"

"It's from an old Earth movie," Jack explained. "Solo…"

He held up a hand before either version could reply.

"Please allow Solobot access to my digitized movie collection stored on drive Zeta 16."

"Certainly, Captain," said the EI.

"Hey!" said Adina. "Maybe she could choose a new avatar by imitating a character from one of your old movies…"

"That's not a bad idea," said Jack. "It would certainly help to keep us entertained during long missions."

He turned his attention to the android. "Have a search through a few of my favorites or you could just let me choose a new avatar for you…"

Suddenly, the avatar on Solobot's screen faded away to be replaced with a bright red, circular light.

"I'm sorry, Dave. I'm afraid I can't do that."

"Maybe not, then."

Adina frowned. "Dave?"

Jack waved the question away. "It's from the film. But I really don't want to hear that from any computer on this ship, so she'll have to pick a different character."

"She!" cried Adina, pointing directly at Jack. "You just called her *she*!"

"OK, you got me!" said Jack, holding up his hands in surrender and chuckling. "She's a she, no matter which movie character she chooses to be from now on. It's got to be better than seeing that face everywhere I go!"

He nodded toward the middle-aged female displayed on the ship's main screens. The visual depiction Solo had chosen for herself when first booted up was, for reasons yet unknown, that of Jack's mom.

Solobot's screen changed again, this time to the black and white image of a young male sitting in a cramped room beneath a pair of stuffed birds. "A boy's best friend is his mother."

Jack stared at the robot in surprise. "*Psycho!*"

"Hey!" cried Adina. "That's not nice."

Jack opened his mouth to explain what he meant but

decided against it. "This is going to get very confusing, very quickly."

"Frankly my dear," announced Solobot, "I don't give a damn."

Jack sighed. He swung back to face his console, holding a hand with a raised index finger out to Solobot as a warning to remain quiet. "Solo?"

This time, only one voice responded. "Yes, Captain?"

"How long until we land on Abstone?"

The forward viewscreen now showed a brightly-lit port area extending from the base of the mountains below.

"Just over twenty minutes, Captain. I've already exchanged identity ciphers with the interstellar arrivals system in Jarosite City."

"Thank you," said Jack. "I've sent a message to the queen's key aide…" He searched his console for the scrap of paper on which he'd scrawled her name. "Finty Cole, asking her to meet us at whichever cargo dock they assign us."

"We're berthing at the commercial dock?" queried Adina. "We're not off-loading anything, are we?"

Jack shook his head. "I suspect it's simply the only spot they have large enough for us," he said. "We shouldn't be here for long. Overnight at the most. Nathan just wants us to check up on how the queen is doing."

Reaching out, he flicked the array of switches to give the manual command to lower the ship's landing gear.

"I'm not anticipating any trouble at all."

Planet Abstone, Jarosite City, the Bauxite Bar

It took Shonk Oolite three attempts to tear the still-beating heart from the horrified bartender's chest.

Abstonions have a second layer of ribs, thicker and stronger than the less-rigid inner layer, making any attack aimed at the upper internal organs something of a chore.

Still, the taste and texture of the heart as he devoured it in front of the dying barman's wide eyes made all the extra effort worthwhile.

To be fair, Shonk wasn't quite sure why he'd crashed into the bar a few moments earlier and had started attacking staff and patrons alike. It just felt like something he *should* be doing. It was like some compulsory desire to devour raw flesh had flooded his entire body, overriding whether he thought slaughter and cannibalism was a good idea or not.

Shonk just knew he *had* to feed.

Before this attack, he'd found himself standing in the upstairs room, swaying back and forth as he tried to keep his balance. There were two other figures in the room with him; two figures he felt he ought to know and recognize—but their identities were inaccessible, like an itch in a difficult to reach part of the body.

He ignored them and left the room.

Which wasn't as easy as it sounded.

He was certain he'd been able to walk without devoting his entire mind to it before, but he couldn't remember when.

Actually, he couldn't remember much of anything now. Even the simple task of thinking appeared to be something of an uphill climb; a difficult route strewn with obstacles and pitfalls.

So, he decided it wasn't worth the effort, and allowed the animalistic instinct he found hiding deep within the shadows of his mind to take over.

Once he'd handed over control of his most basic urges, the world felt like a much more accessible place.

Or, it would have, if he wasn't so damned hungry.

Shonk hadn't so much 'smelled' the odor drifting into the room from beyond the closed door, as felt it envelop and overpower him. Had he still been in possession of all his memories, he would have been reminded of cartoons he'd watched as a child, where some comical character had been lifted off the ground by a swirling, misty tentacle of a delicious scent and been dragged along towards it, slavering and licking their lips.

But, with the part of his brain which dealt with memories now about as substantial as a dollop of whipped curds, that didn't happen.

Yet, he soon found himself stumbling down the flight of stairs beyond the closed door, lurching closer and closer to the intriguing sounds—and smells—of whatever lay beyond.

At first, most of the bar's patrons had ignored him as he stood there, scanning the room as if perusing glossy photographs on the menu of an all-you-can-eat buffet. They were used to odd-looking weirdos gathering in the upstairs room at all hours, and the appearance of one of them with such moist, pallid features was nothing too far out of the ordinary.

So long as the odd fuckers didn't disturb their drinking.

In fact, it was only when Shonk had grabbed the bar owner's head, yanked it violently back and taken a large bite from her exposed throat that everything really went to shit.

Of course, he wasn't to know that, due to the late hour, the landlady had secured the main door, having invited the bar's regular customers to enjoy one of her regular lock-ins.

Several of these terrified punters were now wresting with that door, hammering on it and shouting out, demanding to know the whereabouts of the one and only key.

Sadly, the bar's owner could no longer tell them the key was beneath the coin tray in the cash register, what with her no longer having any working vocal cords, and a large chunk of her windpipe being currently mashed between Shonk's teeth.

It was then that Shonk became aware that his vision was different from how it used to be. At least, he thought it was. It was getting more and more difficult to remember by the second. Even so, he was almost certain that everything around him used to be in color, and not some washed-out shade of gray.

It was as if he was suddenly viewing the world through a filter named "shitty rock pigment."

There was, however, one other color still available on this unexpected new palette. Red.

Bright, vibrant, crimson red.

Scarlet highlights were visible everywhere he looked, and on everyone he saw. Their hearts, lungs, brains, and other internal organs somehow glowed through their now grayscale bodies like the diffused gleam from the flashlight of a child reading beneath the bed covers.

And Shonk knew that he had to devour everything that radiated brightly in that color.

Of course, there were several layers of flesh and bone to fight through first, before he could get to the good stuff, but that wasn't proving to be too much of a problem.

In fact, he was in the process of chewing the barmaid's face off to get to the vermillion goodness beyond when he realized the chaos around him had risen a notch or three.

Twisting his victim's neck hard to one side, teeth still busy biting through what remained of her eyeballs, he saw two newcomers in the room, both partaking of the living, screaming, running food containers.

Two new additions who were completely gray from head to foot. Neither had even the merest hint of the vibrant red color that shone from the more edible of the bar's occupants.

Except for what was beginning to dribble down their respective chins.

A tiny voice at the back of his mind told him they looked familiar, that he knew these people from somewhere.

Could they be the two unmoving bodies he'd stepped over in the room upstairs? It was possible, he supposed. He had a vague recollection that one of the pair used to have a considerable amount of hair covering her chin—only that wasn't there now.

A sudden crash jolted him from this train of thought, and he dropped the unmoving figure of the barmaid to the floor, still munching his way through what, until recently, had been her sinuses.

He turned to discover an as yet untasted barfly behind

him, rooted to the spot and shaking with fear as it slowly dawned on him that the chair he'd just smashed over Shonk's head had done nothing to incapacitate him.

Had Shonk still been breathing, he might have gasped at how wonderfully the red areas of this potential meal throbbed and pulsed. It was if the victim's terror gifted the most succulent parts inside him an added boost.

As he staggered toward the screaming male, a tiny part of Shonk's dying imagination briefly wondered if he would be able to taste the difference.

ICS *Fortitude*, Tc'aarlat's Cabin

"Fucking bitch!" bellowed Tc'aarlat, slamming Adina's tablet repeatedly against the wall of his cabin.

"Rancid, four-legged, septic-faced, slack-titted WHORE!"

From her perch, Mist stretched out one of her long, red wings and wrapped it around her three trembling chicks, as if trying to protect them from her owner's violent outburst.

The tablet finally nothing more than shards of glass and circuit-board, Tc'aarlat sat down heavily on the edge of his bed and buried his face in his hands, his mandibles spread wide on either side and quivering.

He should have known better.

He *had* known better.

He'd known his uptight slag of a snob mother wouldn't lift a single, perfectly-manicured finger to help him. Not even to ask her circle of toffee-nosed, inbred society chums if any of them had a way of contacting someone in the Gan'barlo family.

Why had he even considered asking her to be an option?

She didn't care about him. She never had, and she never would. All she gave a shit about was being the first to spread the latest salacious gossip among her clique of high-caste morons.

It was most likely too late now, even if she had agreed to help. By now, Don Gan'barlo would have decided that Tc'aarlat had disconnected their call as a gesture of disrespect and doubled the bounty on his head.

Thanks to him, Jack and Adina were now in more danger than ever.

Fuck!

"Excuse me, Tc'aarlat..." Solo's voice buzzed from the small, low-powered speaker still hanging from bare wires on the wall behind him. "We are now approaching Abstone, and I must insist that you return to the bridge and employ the safety harness kindly provided for you."

With a heavy sigh, Tc'aarlat dragged himself to his feet, his boots crunching over bits of broken glass and plastic as he took the few steps necessary to yank open the door of his metal locker.

As he retrieved the leather shoulder pad Mist used to perch on when they left the ship, he caught his reflection in the small, cracked mirror glued to the cabin wall.

He just had to hope his friends wouldn't notice the look of terror he could now clearly see deep within his own eyes.

15

Planet Abstone, Jarosite City, Dock BTD42

Finty Cole pulled a handkerchief from the pocket of her smart trouser suit and used it to wipe her running nose as she watched the vast cargo ship, ICS *Fortitude*, make its final docking maneuvers.

Just what she needed—a visit from unnecessary guests while she was coming down with some sort of virus.

She glanced back to her official government vehicle, beside which stood two stocky security personnel. Both women appeared to be suffering from the same bug, if their watery eyes, red noses and frequent usage of tissues were to be believed.

As part of her work as Queen Lapis Lazuli's private secretary, she'd been accepting messages of condolence on behalf of Her Majesty from all across the galaxy. The death of a royal consort was always big news, but this particular passing seemed to have attracted more attention than usual. Most likely due to the large number of guests who attended the queen's joining ceremony to Jaspil Hornfen.

He may have been Queen Lazuli's third consort, but his untimely death had already garnered more gestures of sympathy than her first two matches combined.

However, only one institution had insisted they deliver their thoughts and prayers in person: the Etheric Federation.

While receiving an official delegation on behalf of Queen Bethany Anne was routine stuff, she had plenty of work to be getting on with, but it seemed as if half the universe was determined to distract her. Only today, she'd had to deal with a pair of scientists who'd turned up with a request from the queen to provide an update on some new krannas treatment they were working on—and they fully expected her simply to wave them through to the throne room *cum* smithy.

She knew better than to interrupt Her Majesty when she was in the process of forging a new ceremonial sword. When the sounds of hammering at the anvil echoed through her office, no one got past her.

Finty wiped her nose again before stuffing the handkerchief away and smoothing down her short, pointed beard.

The style of her facial hair had become something of a hot topic for the planet's gossip pages of late. Like with most women, beard care was a serious topic for Finty Cole. However, whereas almost all of the female population currently followed the trend of wearing their beard long and full—except for those women who worked in manual occupations where such a style may prove to be a hazard—

she went against the fashion of the day and regularly had hers cropped and shaped.

This decision, according to several D-list celebrity scandal mongers, was a clear declaration of everything from her sexuality to her support for the eradication of the monarchy.

In reality, she simply thought it looked better that way.

The vast dock clamps finally secured the ICS *Fortitude* in position, and she turned to her security detail to check that they were ready to receive their visitors.

Both women stood beside their transport wearing matching black suits and mirrored sunglasses. As dictated by their position, their beards were little more than neat goatees.

A hiss pulled Finty's attention back to the newly docked ship. A side door had opened, and the delegates were disembarking. She peered at them as they approached, knowing that the final member of her security team would now be capturing both still and video images of the arrivals from her hidden vantage point.

Two of the party of well-wishers appeared to be tall humans like Queen Bethany Anne. However, unlike Bethany Anne, their eyes weren't darting back and forth as they made their way over to her, scanning the surrounding area for any potential dangers.

The third guest was equally tall and of an alien species known as Yollin. From Finty's research, his two legs placed him within his planet's lower caste, although rumor was that the Etheric Federation had now outlawed the ancient class system.

The Yollin strode confidently alongside his colleagues,

the well-defined ridges of his exoskeleton catching the morning sunlight. And, what the fukuchilite were those things? Did he have *birds* balanced on his shoulders? Yes, they *were* birds! One large specimen on his right shoulder, and three smaller chicks chattering noisily on his left.

Just when she thought she'd seen it all.

Finally, the group was accompanied by some kind of droid. Around the same height as regular Abstonions, the robot waddled along beside the others, a digital avatar beaming out from a tablet fixed to its "head."

Finty sighed and gave her nose one final wipe before fixing her well-practiced official smile in place and taking a step forward.

It had already been a long day. The sooner she could get rid of these well-intentioned bozos the better.

Planet Abstone, Jarosite City, Government Labs

Dr. Scoria Gabbro forced her eyes open and tentatively lifted her head from her desk.

The acute headache was still thumping away, causing her to wince. It felt as if an angry construction worker was pounding at the inside of her skull with a souped-up jackhammer.

She coughed, her throat dry and sore. Grabbing her water bottle, she raised it to her chapped, swollen lips and gulped down a few mouthfuls.

It didn't help.

Working hard to focus, she scoured her desk for her hand mirror and brought it up to her face.

Fuck!

She looked dreadful. Her cheeks and forehead were flushed, while her eyes appeared sunken thanks to the dark rings beneath them. Her skin was blistered and peeling, and her beard was matted.

She looked like she hadn't slept in an entire season.

Her head swam as she turned in her seat, looking around the lab for Breccin.

Scoria spotted her and gasped.

Breccin was stretched out on the laboratory floor behind her desk. Her skin was ash-gray and her chest, which earlier had been rising and falling with each wheezing, rasping breath, was still.

Worried, Scoria tried to stand, but a sudden bout of dizziness caused her to reach out for the edge of her desk. Her headache was beginning to cluster behind her eyes, bright flashes of color swooping in front of her as she fought the urge to vomit.

Slowly, she edged her way across the lab where she knelt beside her friend. Breccin's eyes were closed, but her lips were parted as if in the midst of some terrible cry of pain.

Scoria reached out with trembling fingers toward her colleague, both certain of what she was about to confirm and simultaneously praying for it not to be true.

But, it was. As soon as she touched Breccin's ice-cold skin she knew.

Breccin Tanister was dead.

Still, she felt for a pulse and double checked to ascertain as to whether Breccin was breathing so shallowly as to be unnoticed.

Nothing.

She was dead.

Whatever the virus she'd been fighting was, it had killed her.

Why hadn't Breccin listened when she had urged her to see a doctor, to take off from work and, at the very least, get some rest at home?

Why hadn't she pushed the issue and forced her friend to seek help?

Now it was too late.

Scoria slumped back against her friend's desk, sobs wracking her body as she felt a fresh wave of nausea wash over her.

She pressed the back of her hand to her forehead, quickly pulling it away when she realized she was burning up. Pulling open the drawer in Breccin's desk just above her head, she rifled through it trying to locate her thermometer by touch alone. After finding and casting aside two pens and a spare toothbrush, she found it and took her temperature.

It was hard to focus on the resulting readout, but she was absolutely certain it shouldn't be that high. She needed help if she wasn't going to be found lifeless on the floor beside her lab partner.

Opting to crawl back to her own desk rather than try to stand, Scoria reached up and fumbled around for her personal communicator.

Where was it? Where was it?

Holding the side of her desk with both hands, she slowly pulled herself to her feet. Every muscle in her body cried out in pain with the effort.

Finally upright, she scoured her desk for the communicator. She knew her workspace was long overdue a thorough de-cluttering, but she'd never completely lost sight of the gadget before.

Scoria turned, her bloodshot eyes fixed on the laboratory door. If she could make her way to the break room without collapsing, she could use the communicator there to—

HISSSSSSSSS.

Scoria froze.

Could it be?

Was it possible that Breccin was still alive?

No. She'd checked her friend's pulse; she had no heartbeat.

Her skin was cold to the touch, stiffness already creeping over her body like a thick, immovable blanket.

Breccin Tanister was dead.

Maybe gases were beginning to escape from her corpse.

Yes, that must be it. She'd heard stories of bodies moving due to the muscles and sphincters relaxing, scaring the families and carers of the recently deceased.

She'd once read of a young, student nurse who was in the process of laying out the body of an aged patient shortly after death and had spotted the old female's false teeth on the floor next to her bed. The nurse had dropped to his knees to retrieve the dentures, only to receive a slap on the back of his head from the corpse.

The terrified nurse had remained on all fours until his superior had checked in to find him frozen with fear. It had taken hours to convince him that a natural muscle spasm had been responsible for his assault from beyond the grave.

That's all that was happening.

Scoria scolded herself for being so ridiculous. She was a scientist, and here she was allowing herself to be scared by the natural processes within the Abstonion body after death.

It had to be this virus playing tricks with her mind.

Slumping down in her seat, Scoria looked up and screamed.

The still clearly deceased Dr. Breccin Tanister was shuffling across the laboratory toward her.

Planet Abstone, Jarosite City, Dock BTD42

Tc'aarlat's mind was lost deep within a labyrinth of worries as he and his crewmates crossed the expansive dock to where a figure in a smart business suit was waiting to greet them.

Which was why he didn't realize he'd inadvertently stepped directly in front of Solobot 9000.

"Hey!" exclaimed the android, pressing her plastic palm against the Yollin's thigh and attempting to push the interloper off to one side. "I'm walking' here! I'm *walkin'* here!"

Tc'aarlat scowled down at the droid. "What the fuck is that little shit-biscuit talking about now?"

"It's a long story," replied Jack. "As is, I imagine, the reason you're disguised as the statue of Admiral Nelson in London's Trafalgar Square."

Adina spat out a laugh, quickly attempting to change it to a cough.

Tc'aarlat's eyes narrowed. "What?"

"You know," explained Jack, gesturing to the Yollin's shoulder pads. "The whole covered with birds thing..."

"Don't you start," said Tc'aarlat with a sigh. "I had enough trouble getting out of my cabin without the lot of them. I planned just to bring Mist along, as usual, but she wouldn't let me leave without the chicks tagging along, too."

"She wouldn't let you leave?" questioned Adina.

"You don't know her when she gets an idea in her head," Tc'aarlat said, throwing a hard stare up at the stern expression of the raal hawk to his right. "She can be very insistent when she wants to be. Fucking birds."

"Feed the birds," sang Solobot unexpectedly, "tuppence a bag..."

Tc'aarlat shook his head in frustration. "That thing is two sandwiches short of a dick pic!"

Adina blinked. "I think you mean *picnic*," she offered.

Tc'aarlat glanced at her. "You take dick pics to a picnic?" he asked. "I'll never understand you humans."

"You don't have to understand us," responded Jack. "Just try to act like us for once."

"What's that supposed to mean?"

"Let's just try to get through an entire mission without you putting your massive, crusty foot in it."

"How dare you?" hissed Tc'aarlat. "I'm the consummate emissary, as you well know!"

This time, Adina didn't attempt to conceal her laughter.

The conversation ended as the group reached their host. She was a short figure, reaching only as high as Jack's waist—and the two rather obvious members of the security team further back appeared to be even shorter.

"Captain Jack Marber, representing the Etheric Federation," announced Jack, holding out his hand. "Thank you for meeting us so late in the day."

Finty Cole studied the proffered palm.

"I am aware of your species' custom of shaking hands as a greeting," she said with a workmanlike smile. "However, as I'm currently suffering from the effects of a seasonal virus, I shall decline your kind offer in case you find yourselves to be vulnerable to our illnesses."

"Oh," said Jack, slowly withdrawing his arm. "Thank you, I guess."

Finty Cole bowed slightly by way of reply.

"We're extremely sorry for your planet's loss," said Adina.

"Indeed," agreed Jack. "Queen Bethany Anne would like to convey her condolences at this harrowing time."

Another small bow, then Finty Cole turned her attention to Tc'aarlat.

"So," he said self-assuredly. "What exactly are you lot then? Dwarves or midgets?"

16

Planet Abstone, Jarosite City, Tunnel Behind Osmium Stoneworks

Despite having eaten almost all of Dev Feldspar, Kahla Bayka was now hungrier than ever.

She slouched along the backstreet, the infected bite wound on her left ankle causing her to limp, if not to experience pain.

The fact that she was dragging her precious sledgehammer, Merlin, behind her didn't help much, either.

The normally busy part of the city was almost deserted. If Kahla still had the mental capacity to think about the situation, she might have wondered whether something was amiss. As it was, the only thing occupying her mind was where to get more of the chewy, gristly meat like she had just finished devouring.

She licked her lips as she shuffled onward, the coppery taste and oily feel of the rapidly drying blood coating her face spurring her to pick up speed. Slightly.

Suddenly, a figure stepped out in front of her. A solid, curvy figure with a bushy beard, a bright yellow hi-visibility jacket and clutching a sky-blue sign with a drawing of two happy children in the center.

Not that these intense splashes of color registered with Kahla. The fleshy female in front of her was completely gray, just as Dev had been.

Aside from those ever-so-tempting pulsing red areas.

She stumbled toward the rotund figure, eyes glued to the twin rivers of crimson running down her thick, wobbling throat.

"Hello Kahla, my lovely," said the new arrival. "Not often we see you out and about at this time. Working late tonight?"

Kahla lurched to a stop at the words. She couldn't understand them, of course—but there was something about one of the sounds in particular that prodded at an almost-entirely abandoned memory somewhere deep in the dark recesses of her mind.

"Kah-la," she repeated slowly, and clearly with great effort.

The sign-wielder smiled warily. "Is everything okay, dear?" she inquired. "Only, I can't stay to chat; I'm working late myself, as you can see. The school put on a music concert for the parents this evening, and a lovely thing it was, too. All those little kiddies, singing their hearts out. It does the spirit good, I tell you."

"Kah-la!"

"Yeeeeeessss...Well, I'd best be off, as I said. Farewell, then."

Kahla was on the female before she could turn to leave, knocking her down, the back of her head slamming hard against the machine-finished rock of the sidewalk.

The terrified target screamed, struggling to flip herself over so that she might have some chance to climb to her feet and run to safety.

But that wasn't to be.

Kahla paused, watched the shrieking, floundering female with interest, her head tilting first to one side and then the next as she listened to her gargled sobs.

Once, in her younger days, she had witnessed a hefty ocean-going reptile trapped on its back, legs kicking as it desperately tried to right itself and escape from her curious gaze.

Had that precious memory not dissolved into mush with the rest of her consciousness, she might have found the similarity amusing.

But, all she knew was that she wanted to get through to the red.

She *had* to get to the red.

Dropping back down, Kahla's teeth gnashed together, snapping at her victim's exposed throat. But, her potential meal fought back. The crossing guard writhed in terror beneath her, making it almost impossible for Kahla to bite down at the tempting, jiggling flesh.

Then, she felt the weight of something in her right hand and realized she was still holding onto the smooth wooden handle of Merlin.

She pushed herself awkwardly to her feet.

The burly stonemason lifted her sledgehammer and

examined it as if seeing the tool for the very first time. She studied the unblemished thickness of its handle and enjoyed the weight of the solid metal head. She had probably once known it had been smelted from a particularly dense form of steel, with just enough beryllium copper mixed in to prevent it from sparking when it struck stone, but that no longer mattered.

Now it was little more than a blunt can opener.

Muscle memory kicked in. Kahla swung the hammer high, the perfectly balanced implement hanging still in the air for a moment at the height of its arc, then she brought it down as hard as she could.

The crossing guard's skull crunched as the massive weapon pounded flesh and bone into the ground, blood and brain matter spraying out in every direction. Finally, her victim stopped squirming.

Tossing the sledgehammer aside, Kahla dropped to her knees once more. She scooped up the soft wobbling flesh of the crossing guard's throat and bit down hard.

This time, she was rewarded.

Slick, greasy plasma spurted down the back of Kahla's throat, causing her to double down on her feasting. Somehow, she knew the female's heart had slowed almost to a stop, and that when the final moment came, her meal would be spoiled, not fresh.

Licking her lips, she plunged her head back down, working hard to get to her victim's internal organs while the blood inside them was still warm.

Suddenly, there was a new sound. A long, piercing ring that scared Kahla, causing her to shuffle back on her hands and knees slightly, her primal fight or flight response still active somewhere inside.

The peeling bell sound stopped as quickly as it had begun, and Kahla's attention was drawn to a set of doors being thrown open in the building across the street.

Dozens of children, none of them older than eleven full turns, raced out into the weak sunshine, their coats flapping and bundles of song sheets clutched in tight, little fists as they sought out their waiting parents.

Slowly, Kahla Bayka stood and watched the excited school children for a moment. Then, she stooped to retrieve her beloved sledgehammer, Merlin, from the glistening swamp of blood and guts at her feet.

Planet Abstone, Jarosite City, En Route to the Royal Palace

Finty Cole's transport was a bizarre mixture of several different technologies. While the shape of the vehicle resembled a large family car, its wheels lacked any kind of tires, instead riding along on thin tram-like rails embedded in the solid rock beneath them.

After just a few moments above ground, the metal tracks had taken them through the wide mouth of a tunnel and into the subterranean city itself.

The interior of the transport was split into three distinct sections. The driver—if driving was technically what the security operative at the front of the conveyance was doing—worked a bank of bronze levers and switches in the foremost cabin.

In place of a steering wheel, there was a sturdy joystick similar to those Jack had seen in the cockpits of old Earth fighter jets, but the 'driver' appeared to be ignoring it completely. Beside her sat the second bodyguard, noisily blowing her nose into a series of disposable tissues.

The vehicle's center section was the most richly furnished. Two rows of four seats faced each other across a square of plush, black carpet. A table hung, suspended from the transport's roof and could, presumably be lowered should the occupants wish to work at it. However, for this journey, it remained stored above the passenger's heads.

The third and final area was a storage compartment, currently empty.

Jack, Adina and Tc'aarlat sat back in rich, leather seats facing the direction of travel. On the opposite row sat Finty Cole, alternately wiping her own streaming eyes and nose, and checking her communicator.

Solobot wobbled unsteadily, the motion of the vehicle threatening to tip her at any moment.

"I must remember to fit her with knee joints," said Adina, catching the droid between her lower legs as a turn in the road caused her creation to tilt alarmingly towards the queen's wary aide.

"Lieutenant Dan!" cried Solobot. "You got new legs!"

Jack smiled apologetically at Finty Cole's confused frown. "It's from an old Earth movie, if you have motion pictures, about a low-IQ guy who...You know what? It doesn't matter."

The gathering fell into an uncomfortable silence, the only noise being the sound of the two burly agents in the front cabin blowing their noses.

"Seems like everyone has caught a dose of this bug," said Adina, keen to say something—anything—to rupture the awkward atmosphere. "Humans have a virus known as influenza, which has similar sympt—"

"So," interrupted Tc'aarlat, staring intently at the royal aide's neat beard, "you seriously expect me to believe you're a chick?"

The queen's political aide frowned. "Chick?"

"He means 'woman" explained Adina with a sigh. "*Those* things are chicks!" she told him, gesturing to the trio of fluffy-feathered birds on his shoulder.

"Yeah, yeah," muttered the Yollin with a roll of his eyes. "Woman. Lady. Girl. Whatever. It's paralytical correctness gone mad."

Finty Cole flicked her gaze from Tc'aarlat to Jack—who was currently wiping his palm across his face—and back again. "I am female, if that's what you mean."

"Well, I don't mean to be rude," said Tc'aarlat, "but you're having a bit of a problem in the old five o'clock shadow department there, if you get my meaning. You all are, as it happens. Are they stick-on, or what?"

"Stick on?"

"Your beards," said Tc'aarlat, sitting forward and pointing at the Abstonion's chin. "Are they fake?"

"Tc'aarlat..." hissed Jack urgently.

The Yollin ignored him.

"What is it, some national holiday for males where they let you lot fill in for the day?

"Our beards are not fake," replied Finty, her hand moving self-consciously to the triangle of thick hair covering her chin. "All women of our species sport facial hair in this way."

"Huh!" grunted Tc'aarlat, flopping back in his seat again. "I guess that settles it, then?"

"Settles what?" asked Adina, cautiously.

"They can't be midgets; they're dwarves," responded Tc'aarlat. "You know like those 'Game of the Rings' flicks Jack has in his collection of old-fashioned movies…"

"You shall not pass!" bellowed a deep voice from Solobot's tablet.

Tc'aarlat leaned toward Finty Cole again. "Or do you consider yourself to be more like Munchkins?"

Solobot executed a short, intricate dance to a twinkling burst of music. "We represent the lollipop guild!"

"That's enough!" barked Adina, spinning Solobot around and flicking a small switch at the side of her head. The droid froze, slumping forward slightly as the tablet screen turned black.

She glared at Tc'aarlat. "I wish I could power you down!"

"What?" demanded the Yollin. "You always accuse me of not paying any interest to other cultures, but as soon as I do…"

"You think this is paying attention?" exclaimed Adina.

"What else could it be?" spat Tc'aarlat. "I've noticed they don't have orange skin, so I haven't even brought up the subject of Oompa Loompas!"

There was a click as Solobot's power switch flicked back on of its own volition. The robot got as far as singing "Oompa Loompa, Dippidy—" before Adina managed to turn her off again.

Jack peered at Finty Cole from between his fingers. The royal aide's face was ash-white, her teeth clenched tightly together. "I'm *so* sorry," he insisted. "He's not always like this—"

"Yes, he is," grunted Adina.

"And this is a droid prototype. We clearly have some serious errors we need to address with both of—"

And that's when the transport lurched to one side, veering off its tracks and thundering directly for an unexacting group of pedestrians on the other side of the street.

Planet Abstone, Jarosite City, Street Outside the Bauxite Bar

It hadn't really taken Shonk, Krystal and Marl that long to break down the exit door of the bar and clamber through the broken splintered wood to reach the street outside.

Once they had gorged themselves on every glowing red organ belonging to every screaming patron, their world had turned a dismal gray once more. But their hunger didn't fade.

Not one bit.

It was impossible to tell how they knew there would be other walking blood sacks elsewhere in the underground city, but they had simultaneously focused their respective attentions on how to escape their confinement—and there wasn't anyone left alive to ask about the key.

The skin of Shonk's arm, bare thanks to the short sleeves of his new ASS shirt, had caught on a jagged piece of wood as he had clambered out into the wider city. The outer layer of flesh had sloughed off as he pushed forward, although he seemed neither to notice nor care.

A narrow flap of torn skin now fluttered behind them in the artificial breeze created by the city's air conditioning as the tortured trio trudged toward what they hoped would be their next meal, wherever that may be.

The tunnel's lighting had been dimmed to give a gentler night-time effect to match that of the world above ground, not that the change had registered with the three shuffling shapes it now illuminated. They maintained a tight triangular formation, with Shonk taking point, although none of them seemed to be even vaguely aware of the other two.

Even if they had stopped to study their sidekicks, there wouldn't have been any blazing scarlet spots within to earn their interest.

They were almost at the end of the street when the disfigured corpses scattered about the floor of The Bauxite Bar began to rouse. One by one their eyes flickered open—at least, they did for those that still had them—and they had gradually reanimated, scrambling clumsily to either their feet or bloody leg stumps, and gave laboriously slow chase.

The final figure to stand was the bar's owner. Her face little more than crimson pulp, her lack of eyes kept her trapped within the four walls of her treasured business.

She tried gallantly to follow the sounds of shambling footsteps but, each time she neared the demolished exit door, she took a wrong turn and limped heavily back in the direction of the bathrooms.

She was on her third circuit of the premises when she

somehow found her way behind the bar and to the open trapdoor leading down to the deep beer cellar below.

Sadly, there was no one around to hear the sickeningly moist squelch as she hit the ground.

Planet Abstone, Jarosite City, En Route To The Royal Palace

The group of startled pedestrians scattered as the runaway government vehicle threatened to mow them down. Now the derailed, reinforced car rumbled onward, metal wheels digging shallow grooves into the stone roadway.

Uncontrolled, the transport pulled to the left, entering a side tunnel with a steep decline. As gravity took possession of the car, it quickly began to pick up speed.

Jack dove forward, scrambling between the seats in an effort to reach the driver and her fellow security operative at the front of the vehicle.

Both were slumped back, their eyes closed and hands dropped into their respective laps.

"Are they OK?" croaked Finty Cole, clearly unwell herself.

"They're unconscious," replied Jack, "if we're lucky."

The unrestrained car continued to thunder down the street, the gradient becoming more severe the further they traveled, adding to the vehicle's speed and the occupant's sense of alarm.

"Help me get her back there…" grunted Jack, grabbing the comatose driver beneath the arms and straining as he hauled her over the back of her seat. Tc'aarlat pushed through to help him and, together, they were able to lower the guard to the carpeted floor of the passenger cabin.

Adina dropped to her knees and pressed her ear to the female's chest. "No heartbeat!" she exclaimed, stripping off her coat. Jack clambered into the now vacant driver's seat as Adina began to administer CPR.

He grasped the brass joystick with both hands, praying the vehicle's drive system acted in a similar way to classic Earth airplanes. He'd only seen them flown in old video reels, but he understood the basic concept.

Pressing the trigger switch closed with his fingers, Jack pulled back on the stick to apply the brakes.

Nothing happened.

He tried again, squeezing harder on the activation switch. He dragged the joystick back, then wiggled it back and forth, left and right.

Again, nothing.

"Shit!"

The vehicle was now almost halfway down the hill and still picking up speed. Ahead, Jack could see a row of squat houses carved into the stone, each growing bigger and bigger through the windshield.

"Are these controls isomorphic?" he demanded.

Finty Cole looked up, confused. "I don't know what that means."

"Can they only be operated by official security personnel?"

The aide's already pale cheeks whitened further. "Yes, I think so."

"Fuck!"

"Want me to drag this one back over so you can wrap your hand around hers?" asked Tc'aarlat.

"I doubt it will work, even if you do," said Adina, sitting back on her heels and breathing hard. "She's gone."

"Change of plan," cried Jack. "Get ready to bail!"

He grabbed the door handle beside him and pulled hard.

Once again, nothing happened.

"*Gott Verdammt!*" he spat. "Why would you make the doors isomorphic?"

"To prevent abductions, most likely," yelled Adina. "Can we kill the power and bypass the system that way?"

"No time!" exclaimed Jack. They were just a few hundred feet from the houses now and still accelerating. "Everyone brace for impact!"

"Wait!" barked Tc'aarlat. He spun around and grabbed Solobot by the shoulders. "You—fart now!"

"But Tc'aarlat, I thought you—"

"*Do it!*"

WHUMPH!

Sparks erupted from the front control panel as the EMP burst destroyed the electronics behind the gleaming brass dashboard. The car's overhead lights flickered, then fell dark. And the low hum of the air conditioning system disappeared.

The vehicle jerked violently, slowing slightly, but not completely.

"The sudden power loss has locked the brakes," shouted Jack, "but it's not going to be enough."

"The door locks are disabled!" said Adina. "Everyone out!"

Tc'aarlat rocked back, pulled back his legs, and then kicked open one of the rear passenger doors, snapping its hinges and sending it clattering away against the solid stone road surface.

He grabbed Finty Cole, mumbled a quick "Sorry!" beneath his breath, then tossed her out of the vehicle, leaping after her. Mist and her three young chicks took flight and soared away to the safety of the branches of a nearby artificial tree.

A split-second later, Jack left the door on the opposite side, hitting the ground and rolling as he'd practiced many times during his Etheric Federation training. Adina quickly followed, her arms wrapped tightly around Solobot.

Tc'aarlat was back on his feet a second later. He took a couple of long strides, then threw himself over the limp figure of Finty Cole just as the abandoned car slammed into the dwellings at the bottom of the street. Lumps of rock and shards of window glass rained down on the tough shell of his back as the vehicle exploded, then burst into flames.

Adina groaned as she pulled herself into a sitting position, wincing at the blood soaking through the torn knees of her heavy overalls.

"Are you OK?" asked Jack, crawling over to her. He had landed awkwardly, the left side of his face having skidded along the road surface, scraping off a layer or two of skin.

"Me?" hissed Adina, reaching for his wound. "You look as if you've just been sanded."

"I'm sure it looks worse than it is," said Jack, tentatively probing the skinned area with his fingertips. "Feels fucking awful, though."

Thanks to time spent in a Pod-doc during his service as a platoon leader in the Force de Guerre, Jack's wounds were already beginning to heal.

"Here," said Adina, tearing off the lower front of her t-shirt and baring her midriff. "This was clean on just before we arrived. Hold it to your face and keep it there."

Jack took the strip of cloth, pressing it gingerly against his cheek as he staggered over to where Tc'aarlat was helping Finty Cole to sit up.

"She's a tough one," commented the Yollin as Jack arrived. "Her right arm's broken, and she's more than likely got a concussion, but that looks about it. I guess all those years digging for diamonds down the mine with the other six dwarves toughens you up."

Before Jack could respond, he noticed Adina peering into what remained of the burning royal vehicle. Concerned members of the public were now gathering around the crash site, including the residents of the house the car had crashed into. Though shocked, they both appeared to be unharmed.

"Adina..." Jack called, a note of hope in his voice.

Adina straightened and shook her head.

Jack turned away. "Shit!"

"We need medical help," Adina said to the assembled onlookers. Do any of you have a way of contacting a doctor?"

"You could call on our communicator, but our power's gone out," replied the owner of the damaged home.

"So has ours," added their neighbor.

One by one, the gathered rubberneckers checked their personal devices, only to find them all burned out.

"Damn it!" Adina grunted.

She hurried back to where Jack and Tc'aarlat were attending to Finty Cole. "The EMPs knocked out all the power around here," she said. "I'm going to find a working communicator and call the authorities."

She turned on her heel and ran off.

Jack checked that Finty Cole was resting comfortingly, then he pulled Tc'aarlat aside. "OK," he hissed, "what the fuck is going on?"

The Yollin scowled. "I don't know what you're talking about."

"Yes, you do!" spat Jack. "All this dwarves and midgets stuff…"

"Don't forget the Munchkins," Tc'aarlat added.

"You're going out of your way to be obnoxious and insult these people," snarled Jack, "And I want to know why!"

"I think you're confused," offered Tc'aarlat. "You might have bumped your head harder than you thought when you bailed from the car." He thrust his hand out in front on Jack's face. "How many fingers am I holding up?"

Jack slapped his hand away. "Stop clowning around! It's as if you're deliberately trying to get me to report you to Nathan."

"Don't be ridiculous!"

"Then, what is it?" Jack demanded. "There must be a reason you're acting this way."

Tc'aarlat shrugged nonchalantly.

"You want out," said Jack.

"What?"

"That's it, isn't it?" guessed Jack. "You want out, but you haven't got the balls to stand up to Nathan and admit you're not cut out for all this espionage stuff. So, you're trying to get him to fire you."

"You have no idea what I'm doing!" spat the Yollin.

"Then explain it!" snarled Jack. "Tell me what the fuck is going on!"

Tc'aarlat's mandibles quivered. "I... I can't! It's... Just forget it!" He turned to walk away, but Jack grabbed his shoulder and spun him around.

"You can't just—"

"Medics on the way!" bellowed Adina, racing back around the corner and up to her fellow crew members.

She rested her hands on her bloodied knees, looking from Jack to Tc'aarlat and back again as she fought to catch her breath. "Have I just interrupted some kind of lover's tiff?"

"Not exactly," growled Jack. "Maybe he'll explain to you exactly why he's being so—"

The sound of terrified screaming cut off the end of Jack's sentence.

. . .

Planet Abstone, Jarosite City, School Near Osmium Stoneworks

Children and parents alike ran from Kahla Bayka as she shambled across the schoolyard, her beloved sledgehammer, Merlin, dragging along the ground behind her.

Her face was smeared with rapidly drying blood—blood which had run into her matted beard, staining it a dark brownish-purple color. Her eyes were milky white, and her mouth opened and closed without a sound. It was if she was silently praying to the Gods to thank them for their bounty before she started on her next meal.

And, behind her in the street, lay a ravaged corpse wrapped in a high-vis jacket. A bloodied body, still clutching the sign she'd used season after season to ensure the school's children crossed the road safely.

But, none of the parents or children had time to pause and think about the partially consumed crossing guard. They had more urgent matters to attend to. They had to escape.

A handful of horrified individuals scurried back inside the school building, slamming the doors closed to protect themselves from whatever *that* was coming to get them. The group of Abstonions that reached the entrance a few seconds later hammered on the door, begging those inside to open up and let them in.

Some of the parents grabbed their children and tried to lift them up and over the metal railings surrounding the yard, abandoning all caution when it came to the rows of sharp, anti-intruder spikes lining the top.

Kahla Bayka stopped and surveyed the scene around her. Dozens of gray figures were darting here and there, each one containing a number of pulsing red patches within them.

Her partially-filled stomach growled.

She became aware of a new sound, softer than the continuing screams, but no less compelling. Turning to locate its source, she found herself looking down at a young girl—likely no older than five or six complete turns—alone and whimpering in a corner of the schoolyard.

Kahla began to trudge toward the petrified pupil, lifting Merlin as she approached her prey and wrapping both of her hard-skinned hands tightly around the tool's thick handle.

She stopped before the trembling girl and raised the sledgehammer high above her head-

CLANG!

Sparks flew as the steel head of a second sledgehammer struck Merlin as it began to fall, knocking it to one side of the girl and causing Kahla to stagger off balance.

By the time she found her footing and turned to face her attacker, the new hammer was already flying through the air towards her. It struck the reanimated stonemason in the hip, resulting in the satisfying crunch of splintering bone.

Kahla stumbled, struggling to stay upright as she glared at the hammer-wielding newcomer. She was short, but stocky and sported long dark hair and a braided beard decorated with colorful ribbons.

"You know the only thing that can stop a bad guy with a sledgehammer?" growled the school's janitor, Mikay Lah. "A good guy with a sledgehammer!"

She swung again, this time aiming the solid lump of

metal at the end of her pale wooden handle directly at the side of the monster's head. But, once again, Kahla's muscle memory bubbled to the surface and she flung Merlin up, blocking the blow and creating another shower of orange sparks.

Had she still been in possession of all her faculties, she may have said to herself that her opponent was hefting an inferior sledgehammer, the impact sparks a sure sign the steel head contained impurities and had very little nickel content.

But, instead, she simply threw back her head and let loose a throaty, wet roar as she lashed out with her own hammer again.

Mikay side-stepped to the left, deftly dodging this latest attack. She waited until the head of the stonemason's hammer was at its lowest point, then she heaved her own weapon with a flourish—and brought it down hard onto Kahla's left shoulder.

Once again, there was an audible crunch of bone—yet Kahla remained upright. She glanced down at her arm, now hanging limply at her side, seemingly oblivious to the pain Mikay knew she had to be suffering. Then she began to advance toward her adversary, a hungry look in her eyes.

The janitor took a step back, then another. She hefted her hammer high, aware that her aggressor now had use of just one arm. She may be strong, but her ability to fight had to be restricted now.

Kahla swung Merlin round, one-handed. The blow was fierce but lacked direction. Mikay Lah easily managed to step out of its path, lashing out towards the falling tool at a ninety-degree, hoping to dislodge it from Kahla's good hand.

The impact showered the pair with another explosion of bright orange sparks. Kahla staggered to her right, struggling to maintain her balance. Somehow, she managed to stay on two feet and attack again. This time, the heavy head of Merlin caught Mikay in her left knee. She cried out in pain, stumbling back as she tried to put as much distance between this crazed creature and herself.

Limping heavily, teeth bared, Kahla forced her body to close in on her opponent. The school's pupils and their parents had now escaped to safety, so this unexpected challenger was the only source of bright red organs left to devour. She wasn't going to let this one escape.

Both fighters swung again, the two sledgehammers clashing above their heads in yet another deluge of fiery particles.

Mikay was beginning to tire, and couldn't understand why this *thing*, whatever it was, had the ability to keep going like this. She'd felt both her adversary's shoulder and hip shatter. How could she just keep on coming without any sign of the agony she must be in?

The janitor's eyes grew wide as she felt her back press against something solid. She had reached the other side of the schoolyard and was now backed up against the wall. She didn't have the room to swing her sledgehammer around for another strike.

Kahla began to salivate as she watched the glowing scarlet organ within her rival's chest begin to beat harder and faster. She let out a low moan of desire. It was time to finish this.

It was time to eat.

Mikay Lah steeled her nerves, determined not to display the terror she felt as Kahla Bayka swung Merlin up and over her head one final time.

18

Planet Abstone, Jarosite City, Government Labs

Scoria Gabbro sank to the floor, utterly exhausted.

Her vision swam, forcing her to screw her eyes closed and take several slow, deep breaths. She didn't want to pass out. Not now.

Not after what she'd just been through.

A wet-throated growl caused her to look across the lab to where her long-time friend and co-worker, Breccin Tanister, was writhing around in a pool of blood and saliva on the tiled floor—both of her wrists bound to the leg of her heavy desk with plastic ties.

The fight had been vicious.

Shortly after she'd heard noises escaping from the body of her almost certainly dead workmate, Scoria had found herself under attack. Breccin had clambered to her feet, shambling her way across the laboratory, her milky eyes fixed on Scoria's throat.

Scoria had tried to run. She'd flung open the laboratory

door, staggering as quickly as she could through the outer rooms and into the corridor beyond. What faced her had both horrified and sickened her.

The building was swarming with slavering, wailing monsters—many exhibiting everything from bite marks on their perished gray flesh to those with entire limbs or even pieces of their head missing.

At her gasp, they had all turned and lumbered in her direction.

The choice she had to make was clear: either a potentially fatal fight with her former friend or certain death at the hands and mouths of the nightmarish creatures now limping and dragging themselves toward her.

Ducking back into the laboratory suite, she'd slammed and locked the door—then taken as deep a breath as her aching lungs would allow and returned to confront Breccin, who was now lurching toward the kitchen where they had shared lunches and gossip together for years.

The two scientists clashed. Everything from pencils to heavy glass jars had been used as weapons in Scoria's efforts to fend off the onslaught of gnashing teeth and slashing nails.

She had pushed past Breccin, aiming to seal herself inside the lab itself while leaving her fellow scientist in the outer chambers. But, as she'd passed through the door, she had slipped in a pool of blood-stained saliva and fallen.

She'd crawled the rest of the way across the room, using the desk where the rastel cage had once sat to haul herself back to her feet.

Breccin had been right behind her.

The attack had played out like some kind of dreadful,

slow-motion dance between the two scientists; both females limping around the island of their twin desks in the center of the room, broken glassware crunching beneath their feet.

Eventually, a blow from a heavy chemistry textbook to the side of the head had finally floored Breccin. As the seemingly psychotic scientist had writhed on the ground, wailing and gurgling as she tried to climb back to her feet, Scoria had limped to the nearest store cupboard, equipment scattering as she'd ransacked the shelves for something she could use to bind Breccin's limbs.

Eventually, she'd found a collection of tough plastic ties. Standing over her floundering friend, Scoria had pressed one foot down on Breccin's chest as hard as she could, trying to ignore the painful scratching at her ankle as she worked to capture her colleague's wrists with the looped tethers and secure them to the solid desk leg.

The task completed, Scoria had sunk to the floor, careful to remain a safe distance away from Breccin as she shrieked and fought to free herself from the restraints. Battling the urge to simply close her eyes and allow unconsciousness to slip over her like a black veil, she had taken time to catch her breath and assess her wounds before she'd got to work.

It hadn't been easy, but Scoria had managed to jerry-rig the electrical mesh helmet they normally used to study the brains of larger lab animals so that it fit over Breccin's head. Loops of strong adhesive tape now kept the thick bundles of wires in place, each connected to a sensor affixed to her friend's skull.

Shuffling over to the experiment's dedicated machine,

she fell into a chair, forcing herself to rest for a while before continuing. She closed her eyes against the pounding headache and tried her best to ignore Breccin's whining and gnashing, like that of a rabid pupter, eager to be free of its collar and leash.

Her friend continued to bend her head and bite at the strips of plastic binding her to the desk. Scoria prayed the ties would hold, at least until she worked out what was happening.

After a moment, she found herself slipping into sleep and forced her eyes open. Scoria knew that, whatever happened, she must not allow herself to slide into unconsciousness.

Blinking away her blurred vision, she leaned in and focused as well as she could on the machine they used to read and record the brainwaves of their test subjects, never once guessing that one of them would one day be connected up to that same machinery.

She flicked the system on.

At first, the display on screen sputtered, the green graph-line leaping up and down as if the connections were shorting out. Then, as quickly as the agitated readings had begun, they dropped to a single, flat line sweeping from one side of the screen to the other.

A sure sign of brain death.

Scoria knew that couldn't be the case. Breccin was still active, still fighting to be freed from her bonds, still *alive*. Somehow.

Perhaps something had gone wrong. Perhaps one of the connectors had come loose beneath the strips of tape. That could certainly result in a reading like this. Scoria forced herself to her feet and took a couple of steps toward her subject, reluctant to get close enough to check her hastily positioned equipment, but knowing it was the only way she would even stand a chance of finding out what was really happening.

As she approached, Breccin swung her head round to glare up at her, ropes of blood-tainted saliva hanging from her mouth and chin. Suddenly, the machine gave a piercing BEEP as the readout spiked.

Scoria froze, focusing on the screen in astonishment. Maybe the wired mesh was working after all. She took a step back toward her seat, Breccin went back to her escape efforts, and the line displaying brain activity plummeted again. Back to zero.

Back to dead.

What the *fuck*?

Cautiously, Scoria snatched up a pen from beside the equipment and tossed it at her friend. The restrained scientist twisted to snarl at her and, just as before, the readout peaked.

It was as if Breccin was only alive when Scoria was in her direct line of sight. And that was impossible.

She slumped into the chair once more, fatigue crashing over her in waves. By the Gods, she wanted to close her eyes and rest. Maybe just for a short while. Just long enough to build her energy levels back up.

Almost against her own wishes, Scoria tumbled into an uneasy sleep. Had she been more alert, she may have noticed Breccin switch her attention from the strong plastic strips holding her, to the arms beneath them. Biting down on the skin of her wrists, she began to use her teeth to chew away long strips of her own flesh.

Planet Abstone, Jarosite City, Spinel Square, Ruby Rock Restaurant, Outdoor Dining Area

Corundum Moh raised her glass of sparkling limonite wine and smiled. "A toast!" she declared. "A toast to your father, for finally getting the promotion he has always deserved!"

Her daughter, Jipz, lifted her own glass—filled with non-alcoholic mineral fizz—and beamed. "To Dad!"

As the females drank, Tallk Moh scowled over the rim of his third single-malt schorl, this one a double. "There's no need to be quite so patronizing, you know!"

Jipz smile fell. The longer the evening's celebratory meal had gone on, the darker Tallk's mood had become.

Corundum leaned back in her chair with a sigh. She'd known her husband had been in line for this promotion for a while now, and so she'd booked a table at the exclusive Ruby Rock restaurant several weeks in advance, hoping it would turn out to be an enjoyable night to remember.

She hadn't even let the fact that they'd been bumped to a table in the square outside the restaurant dampen her hopes for a pleasant evening. The lights in the cavern ceiling high above their heads had been dimmed, the air flow was light and warm—it was the perfect evening for a family celebration. Or, at least, it would have been if her husband hadn't decided to mark the occasion with one of his increasingly frequent sulks.

"I wasn't being patronizing," hissed Corundum through gritted teeth. "We're just happy you're finally being recognized for all your hard work, aren't we Jipz?"

"Yeah!" agreed the young girl. "Good job, Dad!"

Tallk downed his drink in one gulp, signaling through the restaurant window for the waiter inside to bring him another. "Stop it!" he spat. "Both of you, just stop it!"

"Tallk, please…" begged Corundum.

"Please what?" demanded Tallk, passers-by glancing in their direction at the sound of his raised voice. "Please be happy that I now get to sweep the floors of the upper levels of the science building, instead of the public lobby? Please celebrate that I finally get first choice of brooms from the equipment store?

"Or please don't feel cheated that, after two-dozen complete turns helping to keep the bastard city clean for the rich fucks who get to dine *inside* this hoity-toity dump, I still only earn a few credits more than my own daughter does for her news-sheet route?"

Corundum signaled discreetly to Jipz to remain calm. She nodded, glancing furtively from one parent to the other with tear-filled eyes.

"You do a very important job," soothed Corundum, taking her husband's hand. "Without the amazing work of the sanitation department, we'd all be up to our beards in—"

"*BITCH*!" roared Tallk, pulling his hand away and knocking over Jipz' glass of fizz. "Fucking patronizing bitch! If you say one more word abo—"

Sadly, the females of the Moh family never got to know what it was Tallk was threatening Corundum not to say because, at that moment, a milky-eyed, recently-shaven female in a shirt which read ASS tore his throat out with her teeth.

Screams erupted all around the square as a vast horde of the stumbling undead attacked bar patrons, restaurant diners, and customers emerging from a moving-picture theater following a showing of the new blockbuster, *Pyrites of the Deeper Caverns.*

Corundum leapt out of her seat, reaching out to her scared daughter but, before she could grab her, a stocky male—also wearing an ASS shirt—gripped a handful of the terrified teen's hair and dragged her back into his chest.

The snarling monster spun Jipz, lifted her in the air, then slammed the shrieking girl down onto the table. Glasses smashed, and both food and cutlery scattered as the beast lunged forward, mouth stretched wide.

Screaming her daughter's name, Corundum pushed forward desperately, only to be forced back as a wave of panicked patrons raced out of the restaurant door, a quartet of limping corpses gnashing at their heels.

"*NO!*" the devastated mother wailed. "Let me through!"

All color drained from Corundum's face. To her left, braying beasts were attacking her husband and, to her right, another monster was about to sink his teeth into her daughter's stomach.

She knew she had to make a choice.

Snatching up a fork, she sprang forward and stabbed the piece of cutlery into the right eye of her daughter's attacker. The male shrieked, temporarily forgetting his feast as he staggered backward, arms flailing in an impotent attempt to dislodge the makeshift shiv.

Corundum quickly lifted her daughter from the table and turned to lead her away from danger, trying hard to ignore the choked cries of agony from her now blood-soaked husband.

Jipz, however, could not ignore them.

Hearing her father's wet, gurgling screams, she pulled free of her mother's grasp and forced her way between fleeing diners to where her father was being devoured. She battered against the backs of the avaricious attackers, sobbing as she fought in vain to push through.

Suddenly, she felt an arm wrap itself around her waist, and she was lifted from the ground by someone much larger than her. Kicking back, her feet struck what felt like legs encased in solid rock. She bared her teeth and bent forward to bite at the arm gripping her, pausing with shock as an unfamiliar voice hissed in her ear.

"I wouldn't try that if I were you. Take a bite out of my exoskeleton and you'll spend the rest of your life being fitted for dentures!"

Tc'aarlat backed up, carrying the still-struggling girl away from the clutches of the ravenous mob.

"My dad!" she sobbed.

"I'll do what I can," grunted Tc'aarlat, placing Jipz into her mother's trembling arms on the outskirts of the mob. "Get inside, both of you! Find somewhere to hide and stay there."

Nodding, Corundum grabbed her daughter's hand, dragging Jipz past the creatures still feverishly feasting on the third member of her family, and inside the now deserted restaurant.

Satisfied they were out of the mob's reach, Tc'aarlat

clenched his fists and began to force his way back into the writhing crowd, raining blows down onto the heads of anyone who had that lifeless, glassy look to their eyes.

One of the maniacal monsters pounced toward him, strings of bloodied saliva swinging from her long, matted beard. Without a word, the Yollin pushed his fingers inside the deranged creature's mouth, hooked them over her teeth and then, before she had time to bite down, pulled as violently as he could. The frantic female's lower jaw broke with a sickening crack and she fell to the ground, to be trampled underfoot by the other bloodthirsty Abstonions.

"Down!" bellowed a voice. Tc'aarlat ducked as Adina flew over his head, her left foot extended. The thick sole of her boot connected hard with the blood-soaked face of a female as she straightened to snarl at another of the crazed creatures threatening to muscle in on her meal.

The kick knocked Krystal Renn backward. She smashed through the window of the restaurant, impaling her body onto several tall, sharp spikes of shattered glass.

Krystal flailed around, desperate to free herself and return to what remained of Tallk Moh's corpse, but the frenzied movements only served to force her body further down into the glass barbs—the jagged point of the largest bursting up and out of her chest as she sank deeper.

In the doorway of an up-scale boutique near to the entrance of the square, Finty Cole clung to the doorframe, watching with horror as the battle unfolded before her.

She heard a sound and turned to witness her two former guards, both burned and disfigured, shuffling toward her, hands outstretched. With a panicked whimper, Finty backed further into the doorway, her eyes wide as she pleaded with her security detail to leave her alone. But they didn't; they kept coming.

SKORRR!

Seemingly out of nowhere, Mist descended upon one of the guards, razor-sharp claws sinking into the creature's eyes as she used her beak to peck and scratch at its face.

Excited chirrups sounded as her chicks followed her lead, attacking the second singed sentry, blinding and disorienting her long enough for Finty to make her escape.

Back in the midst of the melee, a pair of ice-cold hands grabbed Adina's throat, and she smelled a decaying stench as one of the life-deficient brutes stretched open his mouth in preparation to bite down.

Adina reached back over her shoulders, her hands finding the top of the long beard belonging to her attacker. Wrapping the length of thick hair around one of her fists, she twisted her body to the right and pulled.

The shorter, lighter female Abstonion squeezing at her throat flipped over Adina's shoulder, her head twisting around to a nauseating degree as she somersaulted through the air, slamming hard onto the cobbled ground.

The female's face now lay over the top of her left shoulder, her neck clearly broken. Yet, that didn't appear to dampen her desire to sink her teeth into Adina's flesh. The disfigured Abstonion climbed shakily to her feet, her head lolling unnaturally low over her chest.

"What the fuck?" breathed Adina, rocking lightly from foot to foot, her fists raised and clenched.

She felt someone at her back and was about to spin around to defend herself from another demented aggressor when she heard a familiar voice.

"We need to get out of here," hissed Jack. "Regroup somewhere."

Adina agreed. "If we run, they're likely to give chase, and I don't want to lead them anywhere else in the city." She nodded toward the restaurant, where the skewered figure of Krystal Renn continued to thrash about and shriek as she fought to be free.

"What about in there?" she suggested. "There's bound to be a kitchen out back somewhere."

"Good a spot as any," replied Jack, throwing a sharp punch at a short, snarling male Abstonion who had darted in his direction. "See if you can get word to—"

Snarl!

Suddenly, the willowy figure of Shonk Oolite, having been jostled back from the center of the throng, appeared in front of Jack. His mouth was wide open, his newly-sensitive ears having picked up the unmistakable rhythmic beat of a heart.

Captain Jack Marber forced the barrel of his Jean Dukes Special down Shonk's throat and smiled grimly.

"Not today, fuckface!"

Then he pulled the trigger.

19

Planet Abstone, Jarosite City, Spinel Square, Ruby Rock Restaurant, Kitchen

Adina waited until Jack, Tc'aarlat and the restaurant's Abstonion chef had dragged the second of two large freezers across the restaurant kitchen to help blockade the door before she spoke.

"OK," she said, wiping splashes of still sticky blood from her hands with a dish towel. "Does anyone want to tell me what in the name of all things abominable those things were?"

"Isn't it obvious?" replied Tc'aarlat.

"No, not in the slightest."

Tc'aarlat sighed. "They're zombies."

Adina blinked. "Excuse me?"

"Zombies," Tc'aarlat repeated. "Dwarf zombies, if you want to be accurate."

Jack scowled. "Dwarf zombies?"

The Yollin nodded. "*Alien* dwarf zombies," he declared. "From space."

"Sounds like the title for one of those cheesy science fiction B-movies Jack likes to watch," Adina commented.

"Brains!" moaned Solobot, waddling across the tiled floor with her arms stretched out in front of her.

Tc'aarlat snatched up a meat cleaver from a nearby work surface, raising it above his head. "Shut it, Techno-tits, or I'll reduce you to a pile of pulverized processors! And that's the truth."

Solobot pivoted to glare up at him, the image on her screen morphing into the face of a stern military colonel. "You can't handle the truth!"

"*QUIET!*" barked Jack, leaning back against the larger of the two freezers. "I need a moment to think."

Silence fell over the kitchen, punctuated only by the sound of limping footsteps and mournful groaning from whatever was still roaming the dining room beyond the hastily barricaded doors.

When they'd entered the square after following the screams, it had reminded Jack of an old photograph in which his great-grandparents dined al fresco during a vacation to the Earth country of Italy.

Although he had to admit, the family photographs hadn't featured a rampaging horde of homicidal walking corpses.

He, Adina and Tc'aarlat had fought their way through the throng of what the Yollin was now calling zombies over to where they'd left Finty Cole. They found the royal aide standing over the incinerated, yet still-writhing bodies of her former guards, practically out of her mind with fear.

Leading with their Jean Dukes Specials, they'd battled their way past the feeding frenzy and into the restaurant. Inside, they'd been forced to defend themselves from a meat-cleaver-wielding Abstonion chef.

Jack had quickly realized this new combatant was different. She was more alert than those they had fought out in the square; her eyes weren't dull or clouded, flashing with a mixture of fear and anger instead.

"Wait, wait, wait! It's OK; we're not like the others!"

The fact that these newcomers were not a threat took a moment to get past the chef's adrenaline-fueled rage. But, once she allowed herself to assess the situation, she had ushered the group into the kitchen where they began the task of barricading the door.

While the heavy refrigerators were being moved, Adina had found a sobbing Corundum Moh hiding with her daughter inside the cold room. Both were clearly in shock from what they had experienced, Adina now sat with the trembling Abstonions as they tried to come to terms with the fact that the final member of their family remained out in the square, presumably still being gorged upon by the starving savages.

"Those people seemed to be in some sort of trance," Jack mused aloud. "A kind of fugue state in which they violently attack their fellow citizens."

"Attack and eat!" Tc'aarlat reminded him.

He pulled an apologetic expression as a distressed sob came from the corner where Corundum Moh clutching her shivering daughter.

Jack continued. "Is it possible someone could be controlling them?"

"They didn't look to be under control to me," responded Tc'aarlat. "That was utter chaos. A feeding frenzy. Talk about biting off more than you can chew!"

He winced as Corundum Moh sobbed again.

"So, what happened to them?" questioned Jack.

"They've been cured," said Adina.

All eyes turn to look at her. She was scrolling through information on a blood-stained personal communicator.

"What's that thing?" asked Jack.

"Some kind of communication device," Adina explained. "A pocket-sized tablet by the looks of it. It fell from the pocket of the...whatever-it-was I kicked through the restaurant window. I grabbed it on our way in here."

"What do you mean by 'cured?'"

"There are folders of research notes on here," said Adina, turning the device to show the screen filled with text. "It appears government scientists have been..." She paused to read ahead. "Oh, fuck."

"What?" demanded Jack. "What's 'Oh fuck?'"

"They've been experimenting in an effort to find a cure for death."

"They've been doing *what*?" cried Tc'aarlat.

Adina shrugged. "That's what it says. Apparently, they were working toward a cure for a disease called 'krannas'—which looks similar to cancer in humans—when Queen Lapis Lazuli ordered them to widen the scope of their research and cure everything that could potentially end life."

"That's impossible!" exclaimed Jack.

Adina kept reading. "They found some way to replace

diseased cells with identical uninfected versions of themselves. The body would constantly rejuvenate itself at a cellular level."

Jack looked stern. "The queen is playing God. Who allowed that to happen? Doesn't she have scientific advisors, Finty?"

There was no reply.

Jack looked over to where Finty Cole was sitting on the floor, her back resting against the wall. Her head was bowed, and she had her eyes closed.

Adina hurried over to press her fingertips to the royal aide's neck. A moment later, she sighed.

"She's dead."

"Dead?" exclaimed Tc'aarlat. "But she only had the symptoms of a heavy cold, like her two security guards. Although to be fair, they also came down with a severe case of barbecued car crash."

"It couldn't have been Finty's guards you found her with," Adina asserted. "I checked them both in the wreckage after the collision. They couldn't have been any more dead if they tried."

"It was definitely them," Jack assured her. "Which, as much as I don't want to indulge 'Mr. Conspiracy Theory' over there, means…"

"They came back from the dead!" Tc'aarlat exclaimed gleefully. "What did I tell you? They're zombies!"

Adina looked back down at the corpse of Finty Cole. "And we've just barricaded ourselves inside a room with one of them."

. . .

Planet Abstone, Jarosite City, School Near Osmium Stoneworks

The last thing Mikay Lah had expected was any help from parents of the school's pupils.

In the seventeen seasons she'd been in charge of the school's upkeep, the children had shown her plenty of love and respect, something which vanished when it came time for school to end for the day.

The parents all, without exception, had a habit of looking down their noses at her; treating her as though she was not their equal. They clearly believed they were better than her.

It wasn't as if the school was located in a particularly upscale area of the city, either. The houses the pupils' families lived in were basic and at the lower end of the real estate market price range.

Many of the self-righteous moms and dads who sneered at her didn't have jobs themselves. A good number of them delivered their kids to school while dressed in their nightwear and were still clothed the same way when they turned up at the end of school.

At least Mikay had regular employment—although that was possibly the root cause of their unpleasant attitude. For some reason, Abstonions saw professions where citizens worked with their hands as "male's work." Low-skilled, low-paid, and beneath the dignity of a female.

It was true that Mikay was unique within the school district for being the only female janitor, but she didn't subscribe to the commonly-held assertion that the only careers suited to males were those which required little to no mental taxation, and a return home each evening in desperate need of a good wash.

Mikay had no problem getting her hands dirty. She was just as happy fixing a broken wastewater pipe as she was keeping score at the annual school sports day.

The parents, however, saw things differently.

Mikay tried not to let their disparaging looks and barbed comments hurt her feelings, even when she saw moms openly pointing her out to their female kids as a warning of what could be in their future if they failed to work hard and keep their grades up.

Which is why she'd been so surprised when a group of five parents had grabbed Kahla Bayka, dragging her to the ground just as the afflicted stone-mason was preparing to bring her precious sledgehammer down onto Mikay's skull.

Now, the parents were backing away, expressions of uncertainty washing over their features as their collective bravery deserted them. Kahla Bayka squirmed on the smooth playground surface before them, shrieking as she struggled to get back to her feet and resume her onslaught.

Mikay, however, wasn't about to let that happen. Gritting her teeth, she took a step forward to allow herself enough room to swing her own sledgehammer. The heavy tool whistled as it cut through the night air…

Then, it found its target, and whatever remained of Kahla Bayka shrieked no more.

Planet Abstone, Jarosite City, Spinel Square, Ruby Rock Restaurant, Kitchen

"Tc'aarlat!" Jack roared. "Holster your weapon, now!"

"No chance!" retorted the Yollin, the barrel of his Jean Dukes Special aimed at the unmoving corpse of Finty Cole. "That thing's gonna reanimate any second now, and I want to be ready when it does."

"Stand down, Tc'aarlat! That is an order!"

"An order? On whose authority?"

"Mine!" barked Jack. "As captain of this team."

Tc'aarlat's mandibles quivered with rage. "You're captain of our ship, *not* captain of this team. You don't outrank me here."

Jack drew his own weapon and trained it on the Yollin.

"I do if I say so."

"What are you going to do, Jack? Shoot me?"

Jack's eyes narrowed. "If you force me to do so, I will."

"Ask yourself one question," growled Solobot. "Do I feel lucky? Well, do ya, punk?"

"*SHUT UP!*" bellowed Jack and Tc'aarlat together.

"Everybody shut up!" demanded Adina, stepping between Jack and Tc'aarlat. "This is getting out of hand."

"It'll get a lot worse once she opens her undead eyes again," claimed Tc'aarlat, gesturing towards the deceased aide. "Jack's the one with all the zombie movies in his collection. He knows what we need—a headshot."

"You're insane!" insisted Jack. "You've been like this ever since we left Joxxen. Snatching tablets, insulting the locals, and now you want to pump pucks into the corpse of the queen's advisor? I should have taken you into custody the second we landed."

"You ungrateful fucker!" spat Tc'aarlat. "Can't you see I'm trying to save your life? Yours and Adina's?"

"From who, Tc'aarlat? The dead body of a career diplomat?"

"No, you idiot! From the Yollin mob!"

"Don't talk crap!"

"I'm not!" yelled Tc'aarlat. "They've already tried to blow up the ship a bunch of times."

The room fell silent for a moment. Tc'aarlat continued to glare at Jack, but the fury had evaporated from his eyes.

Jack slowly lowered his gun. "What?"

With a heavy sigh, Tc'aarlat also dropped his aim. "It's true."

Adina took another step toward her teammates. "You knew who was firing those missiles at us?"

Tc'aarlat shook his head. "They weren't firing missiles at us; they were firing at *me*."

"And we just happened to be in the way?" demanded Jack.

The Yollin nodded. "I'm afraid so."

"That's why you were playing up when we first arrived," said Jack. "You wanted me to report you to Nathan and cut you from the team. It was to save Adina and me."

This time, Tc'aarlat didn't reply.

The resulting awkward silence was broken by Adina. "While I'm touched Tc'aarlat didn't want us blown into atoms, he is right about what's going to happen with Finty. She's likely to 'wake up' again at any time. We need to do something."

She raised a hand to silence Tc'aarlat as he opened his mouth to offer a possible solution. "And I'm not even considering a headshot."

Jack also raised a hand, silencing the room again as he

listened to the sound of movement and groaning coming from beyond the barricaded kitchen door.

"We've still got a good number of…"

"Zombies," Tc'aarlat put in.

Jack rolled his eyes. "Whatever they are out there. We'd have to fight our way through."

Adina looked over to where Corundum Moh and her daughter were sitting. The pair had stopped sobbing but clung onto each other as they rocked gently back and forth. "I don't think that's going to work."

"It might have to," Tc'aarlat pointed out. "In the absence of windows, that door is the only way out of here."

"That, and the cellar," commented the Abstonion chef.

All eyes turned to look at her. Until now, she'd been sitting silently near the back of the room. Now, she crossed to a metal equipment trolley, flicked the brakes off the wheels with her foot, and slid it to one side to reveal a trapdoor in the floor.

"It connects directly to the cellar next door," she explained, gripping the door's handle and lifting it open to reveal a narrow flight of stairs leading down into utter darkness. "They all connect throughout the city."

Tc'aarlat's mandibles clicked. "You live in tunnels, and have *another* series of tunnels beneath those tunnels?"

The chef shrugged. "We're Abstonions. We like tunnels."

That was when the unmoving corpse of Finty Cole gave a soft, but clearly audible moan.

"OK," said Jack, plucking a selection of knives from a metal carousel and slipping them into his belt. "Tc'aarlat—find a way to tie her up. Everyone else—grab anything you can that might prove useful, and let's move out."

He paused for a second to peer into the forbidding shadows below the open trapdoor. "Or, in this particular case, let's move down."

**Planet Abstone, Jarosite City, Spinel Square, Cellar
Beneath Ruby Rock Restaurant**

Jack lowered the trapdoor above his head, sealing the
group into the overwhelming blackness of the restaurant
cellar. He remained standing on the rungs of the ladder,
listening to the chef's soft footsteps as she ran her fingertips along the wall.

"The lights are dead," she said.

A beam of harsh white light pierced the gloom as Adina
switched on her flashlight, followed a second later by
Tc'aarlat's.

Finally able to judge the distance to the stone floor, Jack
hopped down to join the group.

"What's your name?" he asked the chef.

"Verika," she replied. "Verika Erest."

"OK, Verika," said Jack. "Please, could you—"

The rest of the sentence was drowned out by a loud
crash coming from the kitchen above. The group fell silent

as they listened to the sound of irregular footsteps, animalistic wailing, and culinary equipment clatter to the floor.

"Finty's awake, then," commented Tc'aarlat.

Jipz Moh clung to her mother's arm. "Is that what has happened to my dad?" she croaked. "Has he become like...those things?"

"Of course not," said Tc'aarlat soothingly. "By the time the zombies finished devouring him, there won't have been enough left to reanimate."

Adina cracked the Yollin in the back of the head with her flashlight as Jipz buried her face into Corundum's chest, wailing. "Shut it!"

"What?" questioned Tc'aarlat. "I was only trying to help the girl."

"Well don't!" Adina insisted. She turned to Jack. "What's the plan?"

"That all depends on how far these interlinked cellars can take us," Jack replied. "Do they cover the entire city?"

"Pretty much," said Verika. "The law states they all have to remain accessible for use in an emergency, but I have heard of private home-owners bricking up the doorways to stop nosy neighbors gaining access to their property."

Adina held up the personal communicator she had found. "Can we get to wherever these government scientists will have been working?"

Verika shrugged. "I don't know where that would be," she admitted.

"I know," said Corundum Moh quietly. "My husband Tallk is..." Her voice cracked, and she paused to swallow hard. "He *was* on the custodial team at the laboratory building. He'd just been promoted."

She turned to her fellow Abstonion. "The laboratories are located in the Northern Dravite tunnels, just beyond Losid Square."

"In which case, you can almost certainly get there via the cellar system," confirmed Verika.

"OK," said Jack. "Adina and I will head there, if you and your daughter are up to leading the way, that is."

Corundum nodded.

"Tc'aarlat," Jack continued, "I want you to complete our original mission. Get to the royal palace, and check on the well-being of Queen Lapis Lazuli. It's more important than ever we do that now."

"I've helped cater events at the palace before," said Verika. "I can get you there, but it won't be easy to get inside—especially with this madness happening."

Tc'aarlat unholstered his Jean Dukes Special, clicking the dial up a notch from six to seven. "My key should work just fine," he said.

"What about me?" asked Solobot. "Which group should I accompany?"

"His!" declared both Jack and Tc'aarlat at the same time, pointing at one another.

"Oh no!" moaned Tc'aarlat. "I had to hang out with R2D-Fuck on Joxxen while you and Adina went gallivanting off down the mine."

"Gallivanting?" protested Adina. "We were trying to save lives!"

"As was I!" argued Tc'aarlat. "Specifically, mine. Ten minutes with Robo-twat here and I was struggling not to blow my own brains out."

"Well, you'll just have to hope things go better on your

second date," said Jack. "We're heading into a government lab. I can't risk her letting loose one of her silent-but-deadly EMP bursts."

"Ha! You called Solobot 'her' again," said Adina with a grin.

Jack rolled his eyes at the comment. "OK," he said. "Any questions?"

Tc'aarlat raised his hand.

"Other than why Tc'aarlat has to take Solobot," Jack clarified.

Tc'aarlat lowered his hand.

The Yollin turned to his new Abstonion teammate. "Let's cock 'n' roll!"

Adina gave a small sigh. "The phrase is *rock* 'n' roll…"

Tc'aarlat's mandibles tapped together. "Like the music?"

"Yes!"

"Well, that makes no sense. Your adversaries would hear you coming from miles away."

"And *cock* 'n' roll *does* make sense?"

The Yollin nodded. "It's a threatening gesture, *and* it would be a lot quieter." He paused to glance from one of his companions—a female chef—to the other—a 'female' droid. "That said, I don't want to be the only one 'sausage out,' so let's just get moving instead."

He and Verika pushed open an old, solid wooden door in the far wall and disappeared into the next cellar, Solobot at their heels.

Jack and Adina listened to their voices echo off into the distance.

"Hurry it up, Bolts for Brains…"

"You talkin' to me? You *talkin'* to me?"

"Quiet!"

"Well, I'm the only one here…"

"No, you're not. Now shut up before I piss on your processors."

Jack and Adina took a moment to enjoy the new-found silence. Then, Jack turned to Corundum and Jipz. "Can you show us to the labs?"

Corundum gripped her daughter's hand and nodded. She led the group into the same cellar entered by Tc'aarlat's team. However, instead of exiting through the now-open door on the opposite side of the basement, she guided Jack and Adina to a metal door on their left.

It took them a moment to force it open; the door's hinges had clearly not been maintained recently.

Jack drew his Jean Dukes Special and was about to step through when Adina caught his wrist.

"What are we going to do about this Yollin mob business?" she whispered.

"Provided they haven't followed us to this planet, we'll have a serious conversation with Tc'aarlat when all this is over."

"And, if they *have* followed us here?"

Jack gave a grim smile. "We'll set the zombies on them."

Planet Abstone, Jarosite City, The Royal Palace, Throne Room

Queen Lapis Lazuli was bleeding, and no one was coming to help.

She wasn't badly injured—just a cut on her left hand after she slipped with one of her metal-working tools—but there had always been someone standing by with a first aid kit to help in situations like this.

Except for this time.

She watched, mesmerized, as blood oozed from the cut, ran down the length of her finger, then dripped onto the highly-polished stone dais of her throne.

Was this the first time blood had been spilled within this venerated room? Unlikely, given the numerous wars fought and led by her various power-hungry ancestors.

Although they, almost certainly, had someone ready at their side to bandage their wounds.

She'd repeatedly tried pulling the bell cord to the side of her throne but figured there must be a fault in the system somewhere as the throne room doors remained resolutely closed.

She'd even tried raising her voice and calling for one of her aides to attend, but that had also proved to be a fruitless action.

Still, it wasn't as if she was completely helpless. She'd just forged the beautiful ceremonial sword now glinting on her anvil, after all.

Some might say furnishing a royal residence—indeed, the throne room itself—with a roaring forge and related blacksmithing equipment was a risky choice at best or even foolish, but Queen Lapis Lazuli disagreed.

Her mother, former Queen Pasir Lazuli, had encouraged her daughter to train in the artisanal skills of her foremothers. To become proficient in a trade that, while not necessary for the purposes of earning a living, were only right and proper for an Abstonion princess to embrace.

After all, it wasn't as if she'd been born a slovenly *boy*.

She wished now, however, that she'd also opted to undergo instruction in some form of medical skill.

Growing irritable, she stood from her throne, wrapped her bleeding hand in the thick material of her overskirt, and marched across the room to the ornately decorated double doors through which thousands of deferential visitors had passed.

She paused briefly before reaching out for the gleaming golden handles, realizing she'd never once opened these doors for herself. There had always been someone—some aide or lackey—ready to push, pull or slide doors for her to pass through. Even when she had been a child.

She chuckled to herself. There was a first time for everything.

Not wishing to stain the buffed metal, she kept her left hand folded within her robes and pulled open the door on her right, already drawing breath with which to instruct whichever royal guard was stationed outside to fetch a member of her staff who could help bandage her wound.

That breath was released in a silent exhale as she peered along the empty corridor beyond. For the first time in her memory, there was no guard on duty outside her throne room.

Still, that wasn't a problem; she wasn't a helpless male. She just had to locate a dressing and staunch the flow of blood herself.

She had taken less than a dozen steps before it struck her that she had absolutely no idea where such things would be kept, and it wouldn't be done to be found wandering the palace in search of basic items.

At least, that's what she told herself.

Retreating back to the safety of the throne room, she closed the door and returned to her throne.

Where was everybody?

The delicate material of her overskirt was now stained with more blood than she had ever seen at once. The deep red had discolored the normally sandstone-hued fabric a dark, forbidding black. Almost the same color as her anvil, in fact.

She paused to study the sword she had forged—a regal blade smelted in honor of her much-missed consort, Jaspil Hornfen—and was surprised to find tears rolling down her cheeks.

She'd been attempting to pry one of the gemstones from her crown to embed within the sword's handle when she had slipped and cut herself. A gemstone the color of Jaspil's eyes—the eyes she had grown to adore gazing not only into but also through.

Directly into the heart of her soulmate. She missed him so much. And now she was alone, in every sense of the word.

For the very first time in her life, Queen Lapis Lazuli had absolutely no idea what to do next—and there was no one around to tell her.

Had she not started to cry at that moment, she might have noticed the gray rastel with a stripe of white fur running down its face scamper across the throne room.

Or the other rastels following it.

Planet Abstone, Jarosite City, Cellar Network

Tc'aarlat and Verika pushed at the thick, wooden door as hard as they could. Ancient chips of paint crumbled beneath their hands as the portal grated against its frame.

It must have been decades since this door was last opened.

As per Abstonion law, citizens were not allowed to install locks on the doors leading in and out of their cellars, but that didn't stop the more security conscious among them from using heavy items to block access to others or, as it appeared in this case, to simply fit a door that sat so snugly in place, it simply wasn't worth the effort required to open it.

"OK," huffed Tc'aarlat, taking a step back and flexing his fingers. "Let's take a moment to think this through. Is there another way around? Another route we can take to the palace?"

Verika shook her head. "Not without going thousands of spanns out of our way," she replied. "That could take almost a full turn."

Tc'aarlat sighed. "In that case, we're going to have to go with good old brute force."

Verika looked back at the seemingly immovable door, illuminated in the beam of Tc'aarlat's flashlight. "Will that be enough?"

Behind them, Solobot took in then exhaled a deep, rasping breath. "Don't underestimate the force!" she snarled before making a gripping gesture with her hand and letting out a wet, choking sound.

"I swear to whichever gods are listening that I'll stamp all over your motherboard if you don't shut up!" growled Tc'aarlat.

Handing his flashlight to Verika, the Yollin took a few steps back from the door and dialed his Jean Dukes Special to six.

"Stand back, and cover your eyes," he warned. "I'm not sure these things were designed to stand in for battering rams."

Verika backed up as far as she could and lifted her thick, matted beard to protect her face.

Tc'aarlat took aim, shielded his own eyes with his free forearm, then fired at the door.

There was a blinding flash of blue light, then the doorway—and much of the brickwork surrounding it—exploded. Sizzling chunks of rock and razor-sharp splinters of wood filled the air.

When the smoke cleared, the group stared in astonishment at the huge hole they had just blasted through the cellar wall.

"That worked..." Tc'aarlat commented.

"You're only supposed to blow the bloody doors off!" bellowed Solobot in a British accent.

Tc'aarlat spun on the droid, his fist raised...

...and that was when he was struck on the back of the head with a sledgehammer.

21

Planet Abstone, Jarosite City, Cellar Beneath Government Labs

It took Jack, Adina, Corundum and Jipz almost two hours to reach the expansive basement of the government science building.

The journey had been difficult. Just as Tc'aarlat and Verika had found on their route, residents in this area of the city had employed underhand methods to flout the 'no locks' ruling, leaving the team no option but to force their way through from cellar to cellar.

Every fourth or fifth cellar along, Jack had insisted they pause long enough to re-barricade the door they had just come through. There would be little point to making this trip if any of *the cured*—as Adina continued to call those infected with the mutated virus—were able to track the path of destruction they had left in their wake.

Unlike the majority of underground rooms they had passed through, the basement of the government science building was brightly lit, tastefully decorated, and spotlessly clean.

A row of sturdy metal lockers ran along the length of one wall, the door of each featuring a name-plate denoting the employee whose belongings were stored inside.

Jipz had spotted her father's name almost immediately, rushing over to unlock his cabinet with the code he used for all his passwords and locks—the date of her birth—and to envelop herself among the items within.

By the time Corundum caught up with her, Jipz was wrapped up in Tallk Moh's overalls and embracing a threadbare soft toy.

"It's Laylay!" Jipz exclaimed. "I thought I'd lost her years ago!"

"Your dad must have had her here all this time," croaked Corundum, her hand trembling as she took the toy from her daughter.

"I want both of you to remain here," instructed Jack, closing the door they had just passed through and gesturing for Adina to help drag one of the sturdy lockers over to obstruct it.

"Will we be safe?"

"As safe as you can be at the moment," Jack replied. "I'd give you my gun for protection, but it's isomorphic; you wouldn't be able to use it. Keep the knives you took from the kitchen in reach at all times."

Corundum nodded. "What will you do?"

Jack eyed the remaining exit from the room. "We're going to find the scientists who started all of this."

Drawing her weapon, Adina joined Jack at the locker room's second exit. Unlike the sturdy doorway they had just passed through, this door was relatively new, freshly painted, and cheap. Just a couple of sheets of thin wood tacked to a simple frame. It would be very unlikely to stand up to anyone—or anything—determined to get at what was on the other side.

They just had to hope none of the cured found their way down here.

Jack dialed his Jean Dukes Special down to three—the most powerful of several new settings recently added to the gun. These lower positions now gave the team the option to stun their targets, rather than kill them. At least, that was the theory.

After what he'd already witnessed today, Jack didn't feel confident that anything short of annihilation would stop one of the cured once they sensed warm, living body organs nearby. But, he had to give them that option. The cured weren't evil; they were innocent, everyday people who had contracted a virus. A virus created in one of the labs above them.

Listening to be as sure as they could that there wasn't anything dangerous waiting for them on the other side of the door, Jack and Adina left the science building's locker room and began to climb the stone staircase that would take them to the upper levels.

The pair moved quickly but cautiously, pausing at regular intervals to check for potential hazards ahead. Eventually, they reached another door, onto which was pasted a sign reading Lobby.

"We should try to find a map or register," Adina suggested.

Jack nodded his agreement, taking up position on the

opposite side of the doorway to Adina. He counted to three, then turned the handle as quietly as he could.

The reception area beyond the door was empty, although there were clear signs that a struggle had taken place. The gleaming white floor tiles were stained with splashes of blood, and discarded purses and scraps of torn clothing lay scattered around.

Jack gestured for Adina to follow him as he entered the lobby. He slowly swung his gun from left to right, and then back again as he scanned the open-plan area for anything out of the ordinary.

Adina scurried past him, across the reception area and behind the counter where she found a large book which both staff and visitors used to sign in and out of the premises. This also had blood splashed across its pages, although Adina could still make out the identities of those who had signed in to the building earlier that day.

She had to flick back two pages before she found a name she recognized. "Dr. Scoria Gabbro, laboratory 8D on level six," she said, pulling out the gadget she'd found. "This is her communicator."

"Then that's who we need to see," said Jack, crossing to the lobby's tall, glass doors. He rattled each one, in turn, to ensure they were secure. They were. Someone had been sensible enough to try to lock out the horrors roaming the city tunnels, although the evidence pointed to whoever had made the decision had ultimately locked themselves in with an equally terrifying evil.

Adina tore the bloodied page featuring Dr. Breccin's details from the register and stepped out from behind the counter.

Then some alert process deep within her brain began to yell at her and she froze. Something had changed. Something looked different to when they had arrived.

But, what was it?

She surveyed the lobby, from the wide staircase leading to the upper floors to the water cooler standing next to the main doors.

And then it hit her.

There was a new trail of blood running across the floor tiles.

Her eyes followed the lengthy smear of blood and bile from the doorway of the back office—a room she had merely glanced into to check for signs of movement—across the tiled floor to the doorway she and Jack had entered through. Which meant she must have missed the fact someone had been in there, and…

"Shit!" Adina spat, drawing her weapon and setting off at a run. "Jack! We need to get back downstairs to—"

She skidded to halt among the mess of bodily fluids as a small figure appeared in the doorway, her eyes red and her body trembling.

"Jipz!" Adina exclaimed, holstering her gun. "You've been crying. What's wrong, sweetheart?"

She strode toward the girl. "Where's your mom?"

Jipz didn't reply. Instead, she raced across the lobby to bury her face in Adina's chest. Adina wrapped her arms around the girl, lowering her face into the girl's auburn hair as she hugged her.

Jack hurried over to join them, worried that whatever the youngster had witnessed downstairs had rendered her completely speechless.

"Jipz?" he said, hurrying over to join them. "Is everything OK?"

Still, there was no reply. The girl's upper body shook as she sobbed.

Jack tapped Adina's shoulder. "We need to move," he reminded her as he scanned the lobby again. "We're vulnerable out here in the open."

As he finished speaking, Adina collapsed to the floor, a rose of blood blossoming on the front of her shirt.

With a gasp, Jack dragged his gaze up to Jipz, his eyes fixed on the lump of flesh she was busy devouring. The young girl hadn't been crying into Adina's chest.

She'd been eating it.

Planet Abstone, Jarosite City, Cellars Beneath Residential Area Nine

Tc'aarlat reeled from the sledgehammer blow, dropping his gun and staggering to the nearest wall for support. While his tough exoskeleton had protected him from serious injury, he found himself momentarily stunned and unable to work out exactly what had just happened.

Mikay Lah stepped out of the shadows beyond the hole Tc'aarlat had blasted into the next cellar, raising her hammer as she strode toward the dazed Yollin, preparing to strike again.

"I've had enough of you banlarg-fuckers for a lifetime!" she roared.

A sudden shriek caught her attention as Mist swooped down from one of the ancient pipes running just below the ceiling. Mikay clenched her fist and punched out, just missing the raal hawk's sharp claws and catching the soft, feathery underside of her belly.

Mist spun backward, her wingtips brushing the brick-work of the wall as she banked and circled back to her perch. Waiting there, her three chicks were screeching angrily at their mother's attacker.

Mikay was raising her hammer again when she caught a flash of light glinting on the smooth, polished surface of Verika's meat cleaver. She bent to her right as the glistening blade sliced through the air a beard-hair's breadth from her throat.

"You *both* want to play games, do you?" Mikay yelled, rocking back and transferring all her weight onto her left leg as she re-angled the arc of her hammer. "Come on, then!"

Verika jumped backward, but not quickly enough. One rounded corner of the sledgehammer's head caught her chin, breaking her jaw with an audible CRACK. The chef's head snapped to the side, blood and broken teeth spraying from her open mouth.

Tc'aarlat shook his head in an attempt to clear his vision, trying desperately to focus on the stacks of over-flowing packing crates; his Jean Dukes Special had skittered across the stone floor, disappearing somewhere among the piles of junk.

Using the pain of her shattered jaw to motivate her, Verika lashed out with her cleaver again. This time it found its target, sinking deep into the flesh of Mikay's upper arm and embedding its edge in the bone beneath.

Cursing in agony, Mikay dropped her left arm down to her side as Verika yanked her blooded blade free. The enraged custodian spun on the spot, centrifugal force causing the sledgehammer now held in her right hand to swing up and out.

Tc'aarlat suddenly spotted the red-brown handle of his gun sticking out from beneath what appeared to be a bundle of children's comic books. He bent down to retrieve it, and Mikay's hefty hammer whooshed harmlessly just over his head.

Verika's pain-filled eyes widened as she realized the sledgehammer was once again headed in her direction. Spitting out more blood and teeth, she threw herself back against more of the packing crates. Pain exploded down her spine, but it was better than receiving what would almost certainly have been a fatal blow to the head.

Chunks of stone rained down as the sledgehammer embedded itself into the cellar wall. Gritting her teeth against the pain of her wounded arm, Mikay forced herself to grasp the tool's handle with both hands and tried to pull it free.

But it was stuck fast.

She saw movement from the corner of her eye and turned to find Tc'aarlat—still dazed—barreling across the room toward her, his gun waving left and right as he tried to take aim.

He was so focused on fixing Mikay in his gun's sights that he didn't see Solobot waddle out from behind an old armchair until it was too late. He tripped over the droid, crashing to the ground at Mikay's feet.

Seeing an opportunity, Mikay reached back through what remained of the wall into the next room and produced another sledgehammer—this one more expensive, and with the name 'Merlin' engraved along the handle.

Tc'aarlat flipped himself onto his back just in time to see the solid metal head rocketing downward directly above his skull.

Tossing his gun, Tc'aarlat stretched up his arms, locking his elbows in place and wrapping his fingers around the wooden handle of the hammer as it fell toward him.

The sudden stop of the sledgehammer's momentum by his hands was jarring. Lightning bolts of pain flashed along the Yollin's arms.

"How many of those fucking things have you got?" he roared.

Mikay struggled to pull the hammer from Tc'aarlat's grip, devoting all her strength to the task. She gritted her teeth and blinked hard. The burning sensation radiating from the wound in her upper arm was making it difficult to concentrate.

Tc'aarlat tightened his grip around the sledgehammer's handle, sensing movement to his left as someone reached down to snatch up his gun.

"Say hello to my little friend!" snarled a voice.

Mikay looked down to discover Solobot standing off to one side, her white plastic fingers wrapped around the handle of Tc'aarlat's weapon.

She blinked again, wondering for a moment if the searing pain in her arm was causing her to hallucinate.

"What?"

Solobot's face faded from her tablet screen to be replaced with that of a dark-skinned male dressed in a smart, black suit and tie. When the droid spoke again, her voice was male and synched with this new face.

"Say 'what' again," the figure on the screen demanded. "I dare you. I double dare you, motherfucker! Say 'what' one more goddamn time!"

Tc'aarlat fought to keep his now trembling arms locked above him and the sledgehammer from descending. "You mechanized moron!" he growled. "That thing is isomorphic; no one can fire it but me!"

Solobot's own face shimmered back into view as her chest speaker let out the digitized equivalent of a heavy sigh.

"She doesn't know that though, does she?" the robot groaned. "Or, at least, she didn't until just now."

Tc'aarlat's eyes flicked back up to Mikay but, instead of seizing this obvious advantage, the Abstonion released her grip on the sledgehammer and sank back against the wall, her breath ragged.

"You're not like the others," she wheezed. "You're not infected."

"Neither are you," said Tc'aarlat, climbing uneasily to his feet, the sledgehammer still in his grasp. "You tried to pound me instead of eating me for one thing."

Mikay's gaze met his. "You've seen them, haven't you?"

"Seen them, fought them, smashed them," responded Tc'aarlat. "It's like the night of the living dead up there."

"They're coming to get you, Barbara!" wailed Solobot.

Tc'aarlat clouted the droid with the handle of the sledgehammer and snatched back his gun.

"Where are you trying to reach?" Tc'aarlat asked, flipping the sledgehammer over and offering the handle to Mikay.

The janitor gingerly took back the tool, her eyes fixed on Tc'aarlat's gun as he checked it over. "Any place not infested with those *things*," said Mikay. "You?"

Tc'aarlat holstered his Jean Dukes Special. "We're trying to get to the palace to check on the quee—"

A mournful groan interrupted him. The Yollin's hand was halfway back to his gun when he realized the sound was coming from behind a stack of boxes in the corner. "Shit!" he spat. "I totally forgot about her!"

Tc'aarlat and Mikay hurried over to help Verika to her feet. The chef swayed unsteadily, her shattered jaw sitting at an awkward angle.

Mikay winced at the sight. "I'm sorry!" she said. "I thought you were…"

"Sh'awrigh," grunted Verika. "I wugga gug a shaym."

She gestured shakily to the blood seeping through Mikay's shirt around her wound. "I'g showree 'bou' gha."

Mikay used the end of her bushy beard to wipe away the worst of the sticky plasma. "Don't think about it."

Tc'aarlat sighed as he rubbed at his throbbing head.

"Fucking typical," he grumbled. "This always happens when we split up. I bet Jack and Adina are having the time of their lives."

22

Planet Abstone, Jarosite City, Government Labs

Dr. Scoria Gabbro sobbed as she pressed the barrel of the laboratory's bolt pistol to the forehead of her best friend.

Although, she wasn't entirely certain that the creature she had been forced to tie up even *was* her friend any longer.

Breccin Tanister snarled and spat as she struggled to free herself from the strong plastic ties Scoria had used to bind her wrists and ankles. In fact, she'd gone so far as to bite through the flesh of her own left wrist, attempting to peel the skin back from her hand to make it small enough to slip through the restraint.

Scoria knew if her friend was prepared to go that far, then she would stop at nothing to free herself—and then she would attack and attempt to eat her.

That was, of course, if Scoria lived long enough to be considered food.

Her own health was deteriorating fast. Her vision swam each time she tried to focus, sending waves of nausea crashing over her. The pain in her head was excruciating, and now her joints were starting to protest angrily whenever she moved.

It wouldn't be long now.

She felt the bolt gun begin to shake and forced herself to concentrate in an effort to steady her hand as her finger tightened on the trigger.

"Shhh!" she pleaded through her tears, reaching down to stroke Breccin's hair with her free hand. "It will all be over soon."

She'd only ever used the bolt gun once before, on a tamarchin majom she and Breccin had hand-reared from a baby for use in experiments testing new strains of pain medication.

After many turns, 'Peeka' had become almost like a beloved pet to the pair—more than happy to clamber out of his cage whenever they opened it and sit on the shoulder of one or other scientist as they worked.

They'd even gotten to the stage of bringing special snacks and toys in from home to treat the tamed animal.

However, as he'd gotten older, the plethora of drugs they'd pumped through the majom's body had taken their toll. On the outside, Peeka had begun to lose his fur, his teeth had gradually rotted away, and he'd suffered from severe pain in his legs whenever he moved.

But the worst of the effects were internal. One by one, Peeka's organs had failed; shutting down in turn until the animal could do little more than lie in his cage and meekly cry out.

Both Scoria and Breccin knew what had to be done.

The bolt pistol had been delivered from the building's supply store, still wrapped in its original packaging. Inside the box was the gun itself, a canister of compressed air, and two metal bolts. One had a rounded end, meant to stun the target when fired against its skull at close range, knocking it unconscious so that a lethal dose of some euthanizing drug could be administered without causing distress.

The second bolt, however, had a sharpened tip. The purpose of this projectile was to pierce the skull, smashing through the bone to destroy the vital frontal lobes of the delicate brain within.

Instant death.

The scientists had been given a choice to make.

Scoria had selected the rounded bolt for use on their precious companion, and she had always believed that resting the business end of the pistol against Peeka's forehead and pulling the trigger while her cherished companion gazed up at her had been the hardest thing she'd ever had to do.

Until today, that was.

Unable to find her personal communicator, she'd installed the necessary software on her work computer allowing her to scour the city's news feeds. Suddenly, the screen that had previously only displayed proposals for and results from her experiments now showed channel after channel filled with horrific footage of ghastly gray ghouls attacking and attempting to eat terrified members of the public.

Just as Breccin had tried to do with her.

The reports offered the same theory: that the crazed

aggressors had all been infected by some previously unknown virus. A virus that first killed its hosts, then resurrected them with one goal in mind—to continue to spread itself from victim to victim.

The dining on your family and friends part was nothing more than a mechanism for this to happen.

The only thing the various newscasters and their hastily-booked experts had differing opinions about was how the virus had infected so many people so fast. Some claimed it was airborne, transferred from host to host via the coughs and sneezes of sick individuals, while others were certain the cause was bites from groups of abnormally aggressive rastels.

Scoria had switched off her computer knowing that it was both. And that she and Breccin had created the deadly virus through their experiments.

The realization was almost impossible to deal with. But her next step was suddenly crystal clear.

Scoria had loaded the pistol with the sharpened bolt for both certainty of the result, and to provide mercy without suffering.

Her friend had suffered enough.

Breccin continued to struggle and gnash her teeth as Scoria made certain the barrel of the bolt pistol was positioned in the center of her forehead and then, without delaying the inevitable any longer, she fired.

The sudden jolt as the compressed air noisily propelled the projectile forward took her by surprise, as did the ease with which the spike passed through Breccin's skull.

Suddenly, it was all over. Breccin Tanister simply stopped. That was the only word Scoria could find to describe what happened. One minute she was writhing around on the floor, straining to free herself of her bonds, and the next—nothing.

That provided some comfort with regard to what she had to do next.

Withdrawing the pistol and setting it aside, Scoria tried not to look at the part of the bolt protruding from Breccin's forehead. The kit had come with only one of each type of ammunition. They were meant to be re-used.

Gripping the metal shaft with trembling fingers, she pulled—hoping the rod would slide out from her friend's skull with ease. Unfortunately, that wasn't the case.

It was stuck fast.

In the end, Scoria had to place her foot against her dead colleague's shoulder in order to remove the projectile.

She wiped the bolt clean on the sleeve of her discarded lab coat, then reloaded the pistol. It was ready to be used one more time.

Her suicide note, in which she apologized for what she and Breccin had released upon the world, was tucked inside a clearly marked envelope on her desk. She had no idea who would be left to find and read it, but she prayed they would one day be willing to forgive her.

Wiping the tears from her eyes, she picked up the pistol and pressed the tip to the center of her own forehead. Using it this way meant she would have to work the trigger with her thumb, which wouldn't be easy.

She'd briefly considered firing it into the side of her head, or up from under her chin—but that way there was no guarantee that she would die. And, if she didn't die, it would only be a matter of time before she came back in the same way Breccin had.

She wasn't going to become like her.

Scoria settled on resting both thumbs against the trigger, hoping the additional stability would mean she wouldn't slip and miss.

Now, all she had to do was fire the thing.

She wanted her final thought to be of family. So, she closed her eyes tight and pictured her father's smile. That memory, at least, brought her a little comfort in her final seconds.

"Ever onward, dad!" she whispered hoarsely. "Ever onward."

Slowly, she began to press down on the trigger, trying hard to keep the image of her dad in focus and not to worry whether what she was about to do was going to hurt. She was past caring.

BANG!

The sound made Scoria jump, confusing her.

How had she been able to hear the sound—and then wonder what it might be? Had she missed? Or had the pistol rammed the pointed bolt into a part of her brain that could somehow withstand such a blow?

It was a few seconds before she realized that she hadn't yet pulled the trigger. And took a few more to notice that she was no longer alone in the lab.

The noise had been someone kicking open the door.

Lowering the pistol, Scoria turned to discover an alien male standing in the doorway, an unconscious, bloodied female of the same species clutched in his arms.

The newcomer looked at her with pleading eyes before speaking.

"Help her!"

Planet Abstone, Jarosite City, The Royal Palace

Tc'aarlat, Verika, Mikay and Solobot had to fight their way through the maze of corridors that made up the interior of the queen's palace.

After rummaging through the cellars they crossed, they found just enough first aid supplies to dress their various wounds and injuries but, by the time they reached the throne room doors, those bandages were once again soaked in blood—not all of it their own.

They'd come across dozens of the cured, milling around the expansive building seemingly without purpose. Some had made it as far as outside in the palace grounds; the well-maintained hydroponic lawns and flowerbeds being trampled under shuffling, limping feet.

However, as soon as any of these reanimated royal retainers became aware of Tc'aarlat or the others nearby, their demeanor immediately changed, switching from docile husks to savage aggressors in the blink of an eye.

The sound of Tc'aarlat's Jean Dukes Special echoed repeatedly throughout the exquisitely furnished hallways, and Mikay's pair of sledgehammers had pounded in so many skulls that she had now lost count.

Verika's broken jaw had been causing her considerable pain. She'd used her cleaver to part her beard in half vertically, then tied the ends in a bow at the top of her head. While this succeeded in keeping the broken bones from jostling around and scraping against each other, it did nothing to help ease the pain. No matter how much they searched, the group hadn't been able to scavenge any painkillers from the numerous stacks of boxes many of the cellars contained.

In the end, Tc'aarlat had produced two of the three pills of Eternity still in his belt pouch from the Shadow's disastrous meeting with the drug dealer on Skolar Major. Verika was initially reluctant to take the narcotic, but she knew she had to find some way to ease her agony if she was to continue on to the palace with the others. And so, she relented and dry-swallowed the proffered pills.

It wasn't long before the chef was dancing furiously ahead of the group, shrieking with euphoria as she lashed out repeatedly with her trusty meat cleaver, its stained, sharp-edged blade tasting the lifeless flesh of their organ-craving rivals again and again.

Mikay and Tc'aarlat had to pick up the pace in order to keep up with their animated companion.

Eventually, they reached the double doors leading to the throne room. Tc'aarlat took a moment to ready his team and then, as one, they burst through the doors, weapons raised and yelling promises of certain death to any cured lurking inside.

What greeted them when they crashed through the doors took them all by surprise. Instead of a mob of untamed cured, they discovered Queen Lapis Lazuli standing on the seat of her throne, swinging a ceremonial sword at a large pack of enraged rastels.

Tc'aarlat watched as the queen stabbed one of the attacking rodents through the head with the point of her sword, then flung the body over her shoulder before focusing on another of the slavering animals.

"What the actual fuck?"

At the sound of his voice, a group of rastels near the rear of the group turned and raced towards them, eyes blazing and long teeth bared.

Before anyone could stop her, Verika raced gleefully into the center of the approaching rastels, slamming down her trusty cleaver at the closest, severing limbs and tails, and chopping several of the unluckier creatures in two.

Within seconds, Mikay was beside her, swinging her sledgehammer hard with her one good arm. Rastel after rabid rastel squealed horrifically as their skulls were crushed beneath the tool, splashes of brain matter spurting in every direction.

A bunch of the savage rastels dodged the pair of pitiless Abstonions, racing instead to attack Tc'aarlat, unknowing that, not only would they have no success biting through the Yollin's tough exoskeleton, but he had experience hunting and killing muri—a similarly aggressive species of rodent from his home planet.

The first to reach him was a particularly large specimen missing one of its eyes, a bloody puncture-wound in its place. Strings of saliva hung from the animal's teeth as it prepared to bite down.

Tc'aarlat took a few steps to run up, then kicked the rastel with the steel-capped toe of his boot. The creature flew across the throne room, landing squarely in the still-raging fire within the queen's forge. The foul beast screamed as its dense matted fur erupted in flame and it was burned alive.

Meanwhile, Mist swooped down over the writhing carpet of critters, snatching one up in her feet and eviscerating it with her beak as she flew back up toward the ceiling.

Her chicks, encouraged by their mother's violent actions, leaped from Tc'aarlat's shoulder pad, each landing on the back of one of the rodents. However, as they didn't yet have the strength in their wings to lift the creatures into the air, they quickly resembled miniature rodeo riders, pecking hard at their steeds' soft flesh as the rastels twisted and bucked in a vain effort to unseat the birds.

"Your Majesty!" bellowed Tc'aarlat, blasting three more rastels into oblivion with a single shot from his Jean Dukes Special. "We're here to take you to safety!"

"Did I request assistance?" demanded the queen. "No, I did not!"

She paused to slice through the neck of a rastel clambering up the side of her throne, its sharp claws digging into the plush fabric covering. "Am I capable of dealing with these creatures myself? Yes, I am!"

Tc'aarlat stomped another of the shrieking critters into the ground, biting down on his tongue in an effort not to reply with *Fuck you, then—you entitled, inbred bitch!*

Instead, he said, "Whatever you say, Your Majesty."

A sudden *THUD* caught his attention, and he spun to discover Solobot now lying on her back in the doorway as dozens of rastels swarmed over her, scratching and biting at her plastic casing.

"They may take our lives!" she roared in what Tc'aarlat recognized as a Scottish accent from his human acquaintances' time on Earth. "But they'll never take our *freedom*!"

Sighing, Tc'aarlat waded back through the writhing sea of angry animals, grabbed Solobot by one of the few parts of her body not hidden by snapping rastels, and hauled the droid back to her feet.

"You done being stupid?" the Yollin snarled kicking a clutch of rastels aside to clear enough space on the floor for the android.

The face on the Solobot's screen instantly morphed into that of a short-haired human, dressed in a pale suit and blue plaid shirt. "Stupid is as stupid does!"

Tc'aarlat looked back across the room to where Mikay was now jumping up and down so she could stomp the life from as many rastels as possible, Verika was snatching up the rodents and using her still fixed-in-place upper teeth to decapitate them, and Queen Lapis Lazuli was yelling that the creatures should know their place and bow down before her.

The Yollin cranked his Jean Dukes Special up to eight as he strode back into the center of the chaos. "Ain't that the fuckin' truth."

23

Planet Abstone, Jarosite City, Government Labs

Dr. Scoria Breccin paused momentarily to wipe her brow, then she forced her vision to refocus and looked back down into the gaping chest wound of the female alien lying across her desk.

"I...I can't be sure I'm doing this correctly," she admitted. "I don't fully understand her—your—biology."

"Just do what you can," urged Jack. "She already has enhanced healing powers due to her being a...due to differences in her DNA, but she still needs all the help she can get."

Scoria nodded and continued to stitch what she hoped was the unconscious woman's lingular segmental artery. There would be no way of knowing until it became clear whether her patient was likely to live or die.

And if she died...

Scoria had tried to explain to the male—Jack, he called

himself—that she wasn't a doctor or surgeon, that her laboratory and desk were anything but sterile, and that she was currently battling a virus that would soon result in her certain death.

He'd replied to say she was Adina's only hope.

He also knew about the virus. About the thousands of Abstonions infected by it. The thousands who had died, and then come back to life. If "life" could be used to describe whatever hellish experience these individuals were undergoing.

Scoria started as Adina's body suddenly jerked beneath her hands. She quickly pulled the blood-soaked needle and clamp she was using from the gaping chest wound.

"That wasn't anything I did," she said. "At least, I don't think so."

Jack rested a hand on Adina's shoulder, although he had no idea whether his friend would even be aware that he was there with her.

"It's OK," he responded. "Please, keep going."

He kept his palm pressed to Adina's shoulder, silently praying that she would live through this procedure, and especially that the impromptu surgery wouldn't somehow trigger her werewolf transformation.

Things were bad enough without adding a semi-conscious, pain-wracked wolf into the mixture.

Scoria turned her head to one side, coughed, then plunged her fingers back inside Adina's chest, trying her hardest to keep them from shaking. She could feel the woman's heart pumping regularly just beneath her touch but, without detailed knowledge of her species, couldn't tell if it was beating at the right speed.

Too fast or too slow, and her patient was in serious trouble.

Whatever had attacked her patient had managed to fracture three of her ribs, forcing them aside to get to and tear open both of the pulmonary veins running from her right lung back into her heart. Scoria had quickly been able to clamp these off and temporarily stem the bleeding, but she knew she was still working against the clock to repair the damage.

Once more, she felt her eyes unfocus, and she paused for a few seconds to close them and take a couple of deep, calming breaths. When she opened her eyes again, everything was thankfully thrown into sharp relief once again, and she resumed her work, forcing herself to concentrate hard.

If only she could rid herself of this damned headache.

"What did you do?" she asked without looking up.

"With what?" asked Jack.

"With whoever did this to her."

Jack didn't answer right away. Instead, he pictured the little girl down in the lobby, her mouth dripping blood onto the wispy hairs of her budding beard, and her eyes red—not with tears as he and Adina had presumed—but caused by the sudden, violent takeover of her body by the virus.

An almost imperceptible vibration at his hip told him his Jean Dukes Special was still recharging.

"I handled it."

Scoria worked in silence for a while. Sweat beaded across her forehead as she tried to ignore the cramps exploding like fireworks in her stomach. She could feel herself slipping closer and closer to death—something she had been at the point of accepting before the two aliens had suddenly arrived. Now she had to find the strength to remain conscious; it wasn't just her life on the line any longer.

Jack turned away from the table, pacing past the mound of paperwork and broken scientific equipment he had hastily swept off Scoria's desk and onto the floor. Reaching the other side of the laboratory, he paused to look down at the second of the two scientists. The one who'd already succumbed to the virus.

He'd seen dead bodies before, of course; his time as a platoon leader with the *FDG* had taken him to multiple battle zones, makeshift military hospitals, and the remains of what had once been family homes before war had come calling.

Captain Jack Marber was used to being around death.

Yet, almost every corpse he'd ever witnessed—even those it had been difficult to identify—had been enveloped in an aura of calm. As if the deceased individuals somehow understood that no further physical harm could come to them.

This body was different, however, and not just because of the taut gray skin, rivulets of dried blood running from her ears, and numerous other physical manifestations of the damage the virus had inflicted upon her.

It was the expression frozen on her face at the moment of death.

The dead scientist's mouth was twisted into an eternal scream, the lips pulled back to reveal her bloodied teeth and ravaged gums. Her eyes were not just open, but wide open, as if she had glimpsed the unending torture awaiting her in some vile afterlife.

She was not 'at peace' as he'd heard others say of recently departed friends and family members. She was still suffering.

"Done."

Jack turned to see Scoria removing the final clamp from the gaping hole in Adina's chest. "Will she..."

"I don't know," Scoria admitted, slumping back into her chair as she pulled off her stained latex gloves. "From what I could tell, your species has a superior and inferior pulmonary vein on each side of the heart, just as we Abstonions do. But the difference between the two isn't as marked as ours. I believe I've reconnected them in the correct sequence, but—"

Her words were cut off by a thud as Adina's body jerked once again, but it wasn't a lone jolt this time. Her back arched, then slammed back onto the table as she began to spasm uncontrollably.

Scoria leapt to her feet, pressing down on Adina's shoulder while trying to peer into the shadows of her wound. Jack was beside her in an instant, lending his weight to the task of holding his colleague down.

"She's lost too much blood!" he cried. "She's going into hypovolemic shock. We have to do something!"

"Like what?" Scoria demanded. "She needs an isotonic crystalloid IV. I don't have that kind of equipment here. There's nothing I can do. Unless..."

Jack looked pleadingly at her. "Unless what?"

Scoria dashed across to the shelves sitting above the table where she and Breccin had experimented on their final three rastels. There, lying on a small plastic tray, was a syringe filled with...

"Your cure?" exclaimed Jack. "The thing that caused all of this?"

Scoria nodded, holding the thin needle of the syringe mere centimeters above Adina's heart. "It forces cells to create healthy versions of themselves before dying off to remove potential impurities."

"She's human!" Jack reminded her. "Will it work with her?"

"I have no idea!" yelled Scoria, "But, we're out of options."

Jack suddenly realized he'd stopped breathing, and he forced himself to take in a deep lungful of air before responding.

"Do it."

Planet Abstone, Jarosite City, The Royal Palace

"Am I ordering you to put me down? Yes, I am!" Queen Lapis Lazuli marked each word of her caustic command with a sharp slap across Tc'aarlat's backside from the flat edge of her ceremonial sword.

As the Yollin was carrying the raging royal out of the throne room over his shoulder, it was about all she could do.

"When do I insist you put me down? Right now!"

Once out in the corridor, beyond the sea of slaughtered rastel corpses, Tc'aarlat set the queen down and fixed her with a hard stare. "I get that you're some important royal toff and all, but if you keep slapping me with that jumped-up butter knife of yours, this place is gonna become a free republic real quick!"

The queen's face flushed purple. "Do you have the right to talk to your queen in that way? No, you do not!"

"Possibly not," retorted Tc'aarlat. "But you're not *my* queen, are you?"

The enraged monarch took a deep breath to respond, but Tc'aarlat held up a hand to silence her.

"Now, go and stand quietly in the corner with Plastic Penny over there while I make sure this place is secure! Do anything at all to piss me off, and I'll toss you back into your throne room along with those decomposing rastels and lock the doors!"

Solobot waddled over to the dumbfounded royal and took her hand. The queen stared down at the android. "Surely, he cannot be serious?"

"He is serious, Your Majesty," replied Solobot flatly. "And don't call me Shirley."

As Solobot led the queen away, Tc'aarlat crossed to where Mikay and Verika were waiting in the doorway to the throne room. As he approached them, Mist and her three chicks flapped down from the ornate, golden frames of the portraits they'd been perched on, landing on his shoulders.

Mikay was leaning back against the doorframe, cleaning blood from the cleaver wound on her left arm with a rag.

"You ready to move out?" Tc'aarlat asked her.

Mikay smiled and shook her head. "We're not coming with you."

Tc'aarlat glanced over to where Verika was making out with the stone bust of some ancient royal consort—she was clearly still affected by the Eternity pills she'd taken. "You're not? Why?"

Mikay reached down and lifted the legs of her trousers to reveal that her legs were covered with rastel bites. The skin around the wounds was already turning gray.

"It's only a matter of time now before we both turn into one of those things," she explained. "And I don't want us to be around her royal highness when that happens."

She paused as a collection of agonized moans echoed out from along a side corridor.

"Besides, you need someone reliable to stay here and stop any of those nasty fuckers from coming after you."

Tc'aarlat nodded. "Will you be OK?"

"No," replied Mikay truthfully, "but there's no reason why you shouldn't be."

She looked over to where Queen Lapis Lazuli was teaching Solobot how to bow correctly. "You may find her ridiculous, but she's still my queen, and I'll do everything I can to help protect her."

Reaching into his pouch, Tc'aarlat produced the bag holding the last of his Eternity pills and handed it over. "In case the pain gets too much."

Mikay smiled and gave a gentle nod.

Tc'aarlat turned and hurried over to where the queen and Solobot were waiting. "Time to move out, Your Majesty. Stick close to me and don't fall behind, or I'll be forced to pick you up and carry you again. Wind-up Wendy, you take the rear."

Swallowing her anger, Queen Lapis Lazuli fell in line behind Tc'aarlat. She had only taken a few steps before she realized that neither Mikay nor Verika was leaving with them. She stopped and turned to look for them.

Mikay saw that her queen was looking in her direction. Pushing herself away from the doorframe, she stood to attention, respectfully lowered her eyes, and gave her beard a sharp tug.

She gave a happy sigh when the monarch returned the gesture.

Mikay Lah watched until the departing trio scurried to the end of the corridor and disappeared from view, then she looked to check that Verika was still OK.

The chef was now sitting on the floor, studying her reflection in the blade of her meat cleaver and giggling.

Mikay took the Eternity pill from the bag Tc'aarlat had given her and held it up to the light. "You're *that* good, are you?" she wondered aloud. "I never normally touch this sort of stuff, but if—"

SQUEAK!

Upon hearing the sound, Mikay slowly turned to look back into the blood-soaked throne room. There, its beady eyes locked onto her, she saw a lone rastel clambering across the bodies of its slaughtered comrades in an effort to get to her.

This rastel was smaller than the others. Saliva dangled from its bared teeth—and a thick stripe of pure white fur ran down its face.

Mikay popped the Eternity pill into her mouth and

crunched down, angling her head from side to side until the bones of her neck cracked.

"It's *on*, motherfucker!" she bellowed.

Then, grinning widely, she hefted her precious sledgehammer up with her good arm and charged forward, laughing hard.

Planet Abstone, Jarosite City, Government Labs

"Why?" questioned Jack.

Dr. Scoria Breccin lifted her head from the table she was resting it on and frowned. "Why what?"

Jack set a personal communication device down in front of her. Its screen showed her notes for her and Breccin's experiments into adapting their cure for krannas so that it would work for all diseases.

"Why this?"

"My communicator!" exclaimed Scoria, snatching up the device. "Where did you find it?"

"It fell from the pocket of one of the poor souls infected with your cure," explained Jack.

"It must have been stolen by whoever broke into the lab and freed our rastels," said Scoria, flicking through the documents as if checking they were all there. "I searched everywhere for it so I could call for help."

"There's no one left to call," Jack told her.

"I know," said Scoria with a sigh. She set the communicator aside and put her head back down on her hands. "I'm fully aware of what Breccin and I have done."

"I'm not sure that you are," Jack countered. "You've been locked in here with only your partner to deal with. There are thousands of individuals infected with your cure out there. Innocent adults and children tearing each other apart. So, I'll ask again...Why?"

Scoria angled her head to look up at Jack across the table. "We didn't mean for everything to go wrong," she asserted.

"How could it not?" demanded Jack. "You were playing God!"

"The queen commanded us to do it!"

"Oh, no," warned Jack, sitting forward and stabbing his finger on the table. "You don't get away with 'I was only following orders.' The history of the entire galaxy—including my planet—is littered with bad people trying to avoid being punished for their actions by using that excuse."

"I'm not a bad person!" Scoria insisted. "Neither was Breccin. We're scientists. We were trying to help other Abstonions! People like Breccin's mom, the queen's consort, my dad…"

Jack sighed. "You may have had good intentions, but you must have known what you were doing was wrong. You were meddling with nature, upsetting the balance between life and death. Diseases like your krannas, and our cancer, are terrible things; we have to search tirelessly to find a cure. But eliminating death entirely...You can't mess with nature."

"I swear, if you go all hippy on me, Jack Marber, I'm out of here!"

Jack spun in his seat to find Adina propping herself up on her elbows.

"Adina!"

Adina looked down at the clean, white dressing taped to her chest. "Note to self, being eaten hurts like a bitch!"

Jack dashed over to Scoria's desk and threw his arms around her, being careful not to knock against her wound. "You're awake! How do you feel?"

"Amazingly, pretty good," Adina replied with a smile. "What happened?"

"I injected you with our cure," said Scoria, standing up from her chair.

Adina's face fell. "You infected me with that...crap?"

"It forces your damaged cells to replace themselves," explained Jack.

"I know what it does!" exclaimed Adina, swinging her legs off the table. "It also gives you the munchies—for other people!"

Jack nodded. "I'm fairly certain it won't have the same effect on your system. If we could be infected by the virus, we would have been by now, what with everyone repeatedly coughing and sneezing over us."

"Wait—you're *fairly* certain I won't turn into a shambling, undead, flesh-eating maniac?" Adina demanded, her eyes growing wide. "Well, that's comforting to learn."

Jack smiled thinly. "Your own natural defenses, as powerful as they are, weren't able to work fast enough. It was a risk we had to take."

"Let's keep everything crossed I'm immune," Adina

remarked. "Aside from the whole cannibalistic side of things, you really don't want to be around me when I catch a virus. There aren't enough tubs of ice cream and soppy romantic comedy movies in the galaxy for when that happens. Be warned…"

"We've been around the cured ever since we first arrived," Jack reminded her. "Breathing the same infected air as them. But thankfully, neither of us is running a temperature, or showing any of the other usual symptoms."

"And you don't appear to have been attacked by rastels," added Scoria. "From what I've seen on the newscasts, it's also spread by rastel bites."

"We should warn Tc'aarlat about that," said Jack. "Just in case he runs into one or two of the things."

"Let's do it!" exclaimed Adina, climbing off the table.

Jack threw up his hands. "Whoa, whoa!" he cried. "You're not going anywhere right now. You've only just undergone surgery!"

"I feel fine!" Adina insisted. "In fact, it doesn't even feel as if…"

She picked at the tape holding one side of her chest dressing down, throwing Jack a warning look when it appeared he was about to intervene. A few seconds later, the piece of gauze had been removed.

Jack stared in astonishment. Aside from an angry scar running part way across Adina's chest, there was no sign she had ever been injured.

"Incredible!" breathed Jack, running his fingertips over her skin.

"That's very kind," replied Adina with a smirk. "But I

normally expect a guy to buy me dinner before we get to this stage."

Jack appeared confused for a second, then he quickly pulled his hand away and tucked it behind his back, his cheeks burning. "I didn't...I mean, er...I wasn't..."

Adina leaned in to kiss Jack on the forehead. "I know," she said with a wink. "And thank you for getting me here."

She reached out her hand toward Scoria, who limped across the lab to take it. "And thank you for saving me. I wish there was a way I could return the favor."

"There is..." Scoria croaked.

Ten minutes later, Jack and Adina were ready to leave. They'd added any useful pieces of equipment they could find around the laboratory to their arsenal, such as scalpels and other medical supplies, and they were in possession of the one remaining syringe filled with Scoria's cure.

Jack had insisted upon contaminating the mixture's ingredients with other chemicals to spoil them, and he'd watched the scientist closely as she deleted all of her notes from both her computer and communicator.

"We don't want anyone stumbling across the stuff in the future."

Eventually, they were ready to leave.

"Are you sure about this?" asked Adina.

Scoria nodded. "I've seen the alternative," she said with a glance down at where Breccin was lying. "I don't want to go through all that."

Adina nodded, then pulled Scoria in for an embrace. "Thank you again," she whispered.

Scoria could only nod as tears began to flow down her cheeks and collect in the dense hairs of her beard.

Turning her back, she reached for her communicator and opened a folder of pictures, pulling up a shot taken in her younger days of herself at home with her family; her mom, her dad, and her beloved sister, Dacit.

"Ever onward," she croaked as Adina drew her Jean Dukes Special, spun the dial up to four, and took aim.

Planet Abstone, Jarosite City, Cellars Beneath Residential Area Nine

Solobot led the way as she, Tc'aarlat and the queen made their way back through the cellar network, the clusters of LED lights on either side of her tablet 'face' providing the required illumination.

Tc'aarlat's decision to employ his flashlight as a weapon with which to pummel the skulls of rastels to a pulp had caused it to malfunction.

As the android tottered through basement after basement, she ran each of the movies in Jack's collection through her processors at a thousand times the normal speed, attempting to ascertain what it was about Earth in the late 20th and early 21st centuries the captain found so compelling.

A number of early black and white reels had been first in Jack's chronological arrangement—first silent and later with sound—it was easy to see why they had been popular. Comedic performers such as Harold Lloyd, Buster Keaton and, of course, Laurel and Hardy were wholesome and entertaining.

Then came what Jack had labeled the Golden Age of Hollywood: huge, lavish productions such as *Gone With The*

Wind, *Casablanca* and *Citizen Kane* tapped into the psyche of Earth's growing population and explored what it meant to be a human being.

Although this era had also produced an extremely popular blockbuster which Solobot found to be very strange indeed—a movie by the name of *The Wizard of Oz*.

To her thinking, the story concerned a young farm girl who is violently whisked to a strange, new world where she accidentally murders a witch by dropping a house on her, after which she steals her shoes.

The girl then teams up with a trio of societal misfits on a dangerous mission targeting the murder victim's sister— a character infuriated by the death of her sibling and subsequent theft of her footwear.

The story climaxes with the outlandish posse also slaying this sister, while the displaced farm girl is wearing the purloined ruby slippers.

Solobot couldn't claim to have any real knowledge of human psychology, but she had to admit it seemed odd that the species worshipped a movie about two women fighting over a pair of shoes.

Then she'd reached a sub-collection titled Disney, and that was where everything had changed—specifically upon the fast-forward viewing of an animated tale called *Pinocchio*.

The heart-rending story of an artificially-created being who yearned to belong in a society of "real" people.

Suddenly, Jack's love of this ancient medium had fallen into place.

If a movie could contain a message so profound that it challenged the identity routine coded deep within her

Entity Intelligence programming, then it had to be something she must explore further.

Which is why, half-way through a cellar filled with stacks of folding chairs and tables, Solobot had turned to peer up at Tc'aarlat.

"Do you like me as you would a *real* companion?" she asked.

The Yollin squinted against the two powerful beams of light exploding from the LEDs embedded in the android's head.

"What?"

"Do you like me as much as you would if I were alive?"

Tc'aarlat raised a hand to help shield his eyes, which is why he didn't notice the image on Solobot's screen change from the robot's avatar to a live feed of Jack and Adina as a call came in from them.

"Do I like you?" Tc'aarlat sneered. "Yeah, I *like* you. That's why I think about you when I'm in the shower each morning, jerking off and pounding my butthole with a bottle of exoskeleton wax!"

"That's gratifying to hear," replied Jack. "But perhaps we could discuss this over cocktails after we've fixed this *Gott Verdammt* mess!"

"What the fuck?" barked Tc'aarlat. "Dim your high-beams you battery-powered bitch!"

Solobot quickly reduced the intensity of her twin flash-lights, allowing Tc'aarlat to see the screen.

"I was just…" grunted Tc'aarlat. "I mean…"

"Forget it," ordered Jack. "What's your twenty?"

"We're about halfway—"

"Silence!" demanded Queen Lapis Lazuli, stepping into

view. "Am I the highest ranking individual among us? Yes, I am! Should I be the one these aliens are addressing? Yes, I should!"

"Be my guest!" said Tc'aarlat through clenched teeth, stepping back and offering a small bow to the monarch.

Wearing a self-satisfied expression, the queen stepped up to Solobot and glared down her nose at the screen.

"Repeat your question!"

Jack nodded. "Yes, Your Majesty. I was just asking my colleague where—"

"Your *exact* question!"

"OK," said Jack with a sigh. "What's your twenty?"

The queen continued to stare down at the screen in silence for a second before clicking her fingers in Tc'aarlat's direction. She didn't appear to notice both Jack and Adina wince at the gesture.

"Yes, your royal importance?" growled the Yollin.

"Do I know the meaning of this expression? No, I do not!"

Tc'aarlat emerged from the shadows, swallowing his obvious frustration. "Captain Marber is asking us to reveal our current location, ma'am."

"I see," said the queen as the Yollin stepped back into the darkness.

There was another brief silence, then the sovereign clicked her fingers again. Tc'aarlat materialized once more.

"Yes, your utter magnificence?"

"What is our current location?"

For a moment, the only noise was the sound of Tc'aarlat's teeth grinding. Then he cleared his throat.

"Would it please your gloriousness if I were to communicate with Captain Marber on the crown's behalf?"

"Was I just about to command that?" responded the queen. "Yes, I was."

The Yollin took a step to the side and bowed again as the royal turned and ambled away from Solobot.

"We're about halfway back through the cellar system, heading for the ship," he explained. "And you may possibly have noticed I have the honor of escorting her royal specialness, Queen Lapis Lazuli, on this journey."

"Good," said Jack, trying to contain his smile. "We found the scientists behind all this, although it wasn't all plain sailing."

He paused to glance at Adina, who shrugged and smiled.

"I'll explain further back on board the *Fortitude*," Jack finished.

"Understood," said Tc'aarlat. "Solobot, end the video—"

"Oh, one more thing..." exclaimed Adina, interrupting. "Jack's explained that the virus isn't just passed on via the air. It was also being spread by bites from these little rat-like creatures called rastels. If you come across any of them, be wary. They may act a little aggressively."

Tc'aarlat sneered. "No shit, Sherwood!"

Jack frowned. "It's 'no shit, Sherlock,' not 'Sherwood.' Sherwood is a forest on Earth.

"A forest with no shit in it?" countered Tc'aarlat. "I find that very hard to believe. Wasn't it you who told me that Earth bears use those very places to defecate?"

Jack sighed and rubbed his eyes. "Just meet us back at the ship."

The video call ended, and the image on Solobot's screen faded back to show her usual avatar.

Tc'aarlat scowled. "Whatever it is you're planning to say next, I would think very hard before you speak."

Solobot lifted and dropped her shoulders, offering her approximation of a shrug. The face on her screen morphed into that of a smiling, well-worn farmer.

"That'll do, pig. That'll do."

Queen Lapis Lazuli understood only a small percentage of the words that spewed from Tc'aarlat's mouth over the following ten minutes.

2 5

ICS *Fortitude*, Bridge

Jack and Adina were already on the bridge by the time Tc'aarlat and Solobot arrived. The Yollin trudged over to his chair in the co-pilot's position and slumped into it, massaging his temples as Mist and her chicks flapped their way up to their perches above the main viewscreen.

"How's the queen?" asked Jack.

Tc'aarlat glanced at him. "Miraculously, not tied up and stuffed into a box in a dark cellar somewhere."

"That bad, huh?" said Adina.

"She's exactly what you'd get if a cluster headache came to life and put on a crown," Tc'aarlat groaned.

"Where is she?" demanded Jack, leaning back in his seat to peer down the corridor outside the bridge. It was empty.

"I put her in the conference room," replied Tc'aarlat. "She can't do any damage in there."

Adina frowned. "We don't have a conference room."

Tc'aarlat sat up. "What's that room behind the kitchen,

then? The one with the big machines?"

"That's not a conference room," exclaimed Adina. "That's the laundry!"

"Well, we have conferences in there," countered the Yollin.

"Once!" asserted Adina. "We had one meeting in there, and that was about arranging a rota to wash our work overalls."

"Well, that's where she is," said Tc'aarlat. "Maybe she can do my smalls while she's in there as repayment for the nagging she gave me en route."

He scowled, looking Adina up and down. The scar crossing the upper part of her chest was not as red as it had been previously, but it was still clearly visible, and her clothing was stained with splashes of blood.

"What the fuck happened to you?"

"I got close to a little girl, and she broke my heart," Adina responded. "Or she tried to, at least."

"Exactly why I don't tolerate kids," asserted Tc'aarlat. "Nasty, smelly little bastards!"

SKAWWWWW!

He looked up to Mist's perch. The raal hawk had her handler fixed with a hard stare, her feathers turning a deeper shade of red than usual.

"What? No, of course, I didn't mean your children! You're a fantastic mother. Certainly better than mine!"

Solobot's screen changed again, this time showing a manic cartoon duck clutching a large stick of fizzing dynamite. The duck looked directly at the camera and uttered, "Mother!" just before the dynamite exploded, causing its entire bill to spin to the back of its head.

Tc'aarlat swung out his leg to kick the droid, but Solobot tottered back a few steps, causing the Yollin to miss and slip off his chair. He landed on his backside and groaned.

Jack scowled. "As much as I enjoy a bit of slapstick, I'm going to have to insist we focus on our situation for a moment or two."

He paused while Tc'aarlat climbed back into his seat, grumbling.

"Solo, do you have the data I requested?"

"Yes, Captain Marber," replied the ships EI as the forward viewscreen lit up. "By temporarily reprogramming the sensors in three of the planet's communications satellites, I have been able to create this live thermal view of Jarosite City…"

The trio studied a cross-section of Mount Damavand and the hundreds of tunnels that made up the city itself below. The volcano's main conduit and throat glowed bright white for a second before Solo dimmed that section of the diagram, allowing thousands of dimmer points of light to come into focus in the city streets beneath.

The vast majority of these lights were a dull red and, when they moved at all, did so slowly and haltingly. Among them was a handful of yellow dots, each traveling at a much faster rate.

Every now and again, a bunch of red lights would surround one or more of the yellows for a few seconds before they winked out of existence, only to return a few moments later in the same darker shade as the rest.

Adina looked aghast. "Please tell me we're not looking at what I think we're looking at."

"I'm afraid we are," said Jack. "The yellow signifies the usual thermal signature for an Abstonion and the red..."

"...are the cured," finished Tc'aarlat. "And they're picking off the living one by one. It's much worse than I'd thought."

Jack nodded. "The question is, what do we do?"

"What do we do?" demanded a voice. "We do what must be done."

Queen Lapis Lazuli was standing in the doorway to the bridge.

"We end this nightmare."

Planet Abstone, Jarosite City, Cellar Beneath the Bauxite Bar

Yarvik Nephelin crouched behind a stack of used beer barrels and tried to count how many different sets of shambling footsteps were wandering about in the main bar above her head.

Despite the hostelry's heating system being ratcheted way up as usual—a warmer bar means thirstier patrons—Yarvik shivered. Not for the first time, she wished she hadn't ditched her jacket in the meeting room above the bar in order to change into her new Abstone Society Sentinels shirt.

This brief thought caused her to wonder about the fate of her fellow group members. Where were Shonk, Krystal and the others now? Were they safe, or had they been infected and turned into one of the monsters now bumbling around above her head?

Oh, Krystal!

If only Yarvik had found the courage to go up and speak to her while she still had the chance. Before the entire world went to shit.

Now it was too late.

She scratched at her beard, conscious that she'd wanted to shave off this symbol of oppression, just as Krystal had done.

She just hadn't been brave enough.

Yarvik had first spotted the beauty she'd come to know as Krystal Renn when she and a work colleague had been drinking in The Bauxite Bar after their usual drinking hole instituted a door charge due to some igneous rock band playing that night.

Neither Yarvik nor her beer buddy had any desire to sit through the din created by some middle-aged, stiff-bearded guitar fiends calling themselves *Malice in Wonderland*.

So, they'd set off to find another venue for their nightly tipple.

She was just finishing off the first tankard of her favorite blue-tinted brew, Azurite Ale, when she'd glanced across the room, directly into the most beautiful pair of eyes she could ever imagine.

Her heart thumped in her chest just recalling that moment.

Of course, Krystal hadn't paid her any attention at the time. As Yarvik would later discover, this angel on Abstone had been scanning the bar's clientele in search of Shonk Oolite—the leader of a small band of well-meaning protestors, and keeper of the only key for the room upstairs.

Yarvik couldn't remember if she'd made any kind of excuse to her work friend or not, but a short while later she'd found herself sitting at the back of a tatty meeting room, listening to some strange guy who referred to himself as a 'righteous rebel' rant about everything he believed was wrong in Jarosite City.

Not that she'd been listening closely, of course. She'd been too busy gazing at the figure of perfection sitting at the table next to him.

Krystal Renn. The Abstonion of her dreams.

While she hadn't quite found the courage to introduce herself at that first meeting of Abstone Society Sentinels, she'd promised herself that she would do so the following get-together.

Which didn't happen either.

It was the third ASS gathering by the time Yarvik had found her voice, the meeting at which Krystal had revealed her freshly-shaven chin. This brave style choice had taken her breath away, affirming her decision to approach and converse with the female of her dreams that very evening.

And she'd done just that—when she'd relayed the t-shirt size she required once the meeting had come to an end.

That was it. The one and only time Yarvik had spoken directly to her true love.

Now she'd almost certainly never see her again.

Yarvik dabbed at her tears with the tip of her beard.

CRASH!

Yarvik jumped, scared that another of those things was trying to find a way to get into her hiding place. She'd heard someone—or maybe *someones*—scratching at the trapdoor leading down to the cellar more than once in the time she'd been camped out down there.

Could those things sense she was below them? A fresh, living meal, just waiting to be caught and devoured?

She'd already been forced to fight off the tavern's owner after she'd plummeted through the trapdoor and hit the stone floor with a sickening THUD. Despite the many injuries the landlady had suffered in the fall, she had remained conscious and had dragged herself slowly but steadily across the basement floor toward her, bloodshot eyes fixed on Larvik's throat.

It had taken all of her energy, both physical and emotional, to stop the bar owner's gradual approach with one of the used beer barrels—by some twist of fate, a barrel that had contained her favored Azurite Ale.

Since then, she'd remained crouched in the cellar's corner, too scared to attempt to leave via the door into the next basement along.

Yarvik hadn't realized she'd fallen asleep until the voice woke her. At first, she feared someone had found their way in through the trapdoor, or even that the late landlady had somehow reanimated again and was headed in her direction.

But no—the voice was echoing tinnily through the little-used public address system situated in every work-place, residential street, or venue where Abstonions gathered.

It was the voice of Queen Lapis Lazuli.

"Residents of Jarosite City, this is your queen…"

Yarvik stood from her hiding spot, a sharp prickling

sensation flooding the muscles of her legs after remaining curled up in one spot for so long.

"Do you understand that evil is among us? Of course, you do. Have many of your loved ones been taken by this evil? Yes, they have. Is there a way out for those of us who remain?"

The metal speaker in the bar above hissed with static for a long moment before the queen's voice returned.

"Yes, there is."

Heavy sobs racked Yarvik's body at hearing the news. Maybe, just maybe, she was going to get through this nightmare alive.

And maybe her beloved Krystal would, too.

Fighting to calm her breathing, Yarvik listened to the instructions given by the queen. Any survivors had until nightfall to make their way to a cargo ship named the ICS *Fortitude*, currently waiting at dock BTD42 in the city's western harbor complex.

All railcars would be remotely unlocked and powered up, allowing those fleeing danger the ability to access the citywide transport system in their dash for safety.

At nightfall, the cargo ship—and any survivors who had been able to make the journey—would leave Jarosite for the safety of Abstone's other city-state, Fustume.

Queen Lapis Lazuli continued her announcement by explaining that her message had been recorded and would be repeated via the public address system at regular intervals until nightfall.

"Do I wish you every success in your passage to safety?" finished the monarch. "I do."

Yarvik Nephelin took a moment to gather her nerve,

then she crossed over to the doorway leading to the next cellar along.

Planet Abstone, Jarosite City, Dock BTD42

Evacuees began arriving at the docks both individually and in small groups within an hour of the queen's message. Tc'aarlat conscripted any Abstonions with weapons training into groups, stationing them at the dock's entrance to keep the cured at bay. He armed them with guns from the ship's reasonably-well-stocked armory not restricted by isomorphic controls, along with others collected from those fleeing the city.

Within a few hours, he was forced to add teams of physically strong locals to the roster, tasking them with moving the growing piles of bodies from the roadway leading up to the dock gates to allow access for railcars and individuals traveling by foot.

Adina and Solobot were stationed at the top of the ramp leading up to the *Fortitude*'s cargo bays, taking the names of those who managed to reach safety and assigning them somewhere to rest inside.

They remained alert for any Abstonions who presented with any of the known symptoms of the virus, dispatching those with elevated temperatures, hacking coughs or other aches and pains to a secure unit away from their fellow residents where they would remain quarantined until cleared.

Late in the day, an exhausted female wearing a flimsy Abstonion Society Sentinels shirt arrived, asking after someone by the name of Krystal Renn. She had broken down when Solobot advised her the name she had given was not among the list of survivors and had to be helped to the second deck where volunteers were providing food, drinks and basic medical aid.

Up on the bridge, Jack and Queen Lapis Lazuli kept a close eye on the thermal satellite feeds, watching as the bright yellow dots grew fewer and fewer in number and the dark reds steadily flooded the city's tunnels.

"We can't save them all, Your Majesty," Jack warned.

"Am I aware of this?" the queen replied sadly. "Yes, I am aware. Jarosite City is lost."

"Potentially not just Jarosite City," Jack explained. "It may not happen straight away but, eventually, one or more of the cured will find their way out of the tunnels and out onto open ground."

The queen buried her face in her hands at Jack's assessment.

"And, although the journey to Fustume City is long and perilous, it only requires one infected individual to breach their defenses…"

Jack waited for the monarch to comment, but she remained silent.

"Your Majesty, you know what must be done?"

When Queen Lapis Lazuli looked up again, her eyes were wet with tears, and her expression resigned.

"Do I, Captain Marber?" she croaked. "Yes, I do."

The queen fell silent for a moment, only speaking again when Jack reached out to gently rest his hand upon hers.

"We must activate the volcano in Mount Damavand, and lay waste to my queendom and what remains of its population."

26

ICS *Fortitude*, Bridge

"Two thousand eight hundred eleven new souls on board, Captain," Adina announced, crossing to her position at the navigation console where she remained standing.

Queen Lapis Lazuli, seated in the captain's chair, nodded her permission for Adina to sit.

"Of those, we have sixty-seven individuals in quarantine for displaying possible symptoms of the airborne virus, or with what might be rastel bite marks," she continued. "From the survivors who made it to the ship, we've been able to assemble an armed guard for the quarantined area, and a medical team ready to deal with any emergencies."

"Not even three thousand survivors," said Jack, jotting the figure in an old paper notebook he'd found earlier. "In a city of almost two hundred thousand people."

Normally, he'd keep his notes in a dedicated application on his tablet, specifically installed to record the captain's log. But, with the only remaining intact tablet now functioning as Solobot's face, he was being forced to go old-school.

"I take it my people have exhibited kindness to one another?" said the queen. "Even to those who may be strangers."

"I have always depended on the kindness of strangers!" drawled Solobot.

Adina shot the droid a warning look, silencing her.

Jack finished his notes and spun in the co-pilot's chair to face the forward viewscreen. "Solo, how's the city looking now?"

The live, thermal cross-section of Jarosite City faded in, prompting a gasp from the queen. The labyrinth of tunnels beneath Mount Damavand now swarmed with thousands of dark red dots. Any remaining yellow-colored signs of life were few and far between and disappearing fast.

"I think everyone who is going to make it here already has," Jack offered, turning to the queen. "Do you agree, Your Majesty?"

"Do I?" queried the monarch. "Yes, I do."

Jack nodded. "Then it's time to discuss what will happen next. Solo...?"

"Thank you, Captain," said the EI as the graphic on the screen focused in on the volcano above the city. White-hot molten rock filled the magma chamber at its base, expanding up through the volcano's main throat and into a dozen smaller pipes branching off the main conduit.

These minor channels were what provided warmth and power for the many inhabitants living and working below.

"I have now completed the simulations necessary to

prepare a plan for cleansing Jarosite City of the cured," Solo explained.

The group watched as an animated ICS *Fortitude* flew in over the top of Mount Damavand, dropped an object into its crater, then departed.

Solo zoomed closer on the ejected item. "By affixing a remote activation switch to the explosives we confiscated from the Scota Brothers' Mining Corp. on the Joxxen Asteroid, we can drop this incendiary device and detonate it within the main volcanic crater of the mountain.

"The resulting shockwave should be powerful enough to collapse many of the volcano's branch pipes, flooding Jarosite City with lava and neutralizing any remaining infected individuals."

Queen Lapis Lazuli remained stoic as Solo's presentation showed the anticipated result of their undertaking.

Searing-hot molten rock flowed from street to street and building to building as the city's network of caverns and connected tunnels became awash with the deadly, unstoppable liquid.

"You're certain we have enough explosives to begin the chain reaction?" Jack asked.

"We do indeed, Captain," Solo responded. "However, to guarantee success, the device must be detonated at precisely the right moment; just above the surface of the magma in Mount Damavand's crater. Too high, and not enough of the explosion's energy will be transferred to achieve the required result. Too low, and the magma will destroy the detonator switch before it can be activated."

"Magma?" questioned the queen. "Lava? Your culture has two words for the same thing?"

"It does, Your Majesty," Jack replied. "Magma is the name we give molten rock while it remains underground. When it encroaches upon the surface—or, in this case into the city streets—it is known as lava."

"What does Abstonion society refer to it as?" asked Adina.

The queen stood from the pilot's chair. "What do we call it?" she said. "Despite its life-giving properties, we know it as only one thing."

She finally looked away from the viewscreen.

"Certain death."

"Your Majesty," said Jack, gently. "The people in those tunnels aren't living. At least, not in the sense we know it. It would be unkind to allow them to continue existing in this way."

Queen Lapis Lazuli took a deep breath, then nodded.

"While I mourn the loss of my queendom and, of course, my loyal subjects, will I be able to start afresh in Fustume City? Yes, I will. Will it be a smooth transition? Unlikely, but I shall prevail."

Adina bit down on her tongue but found she couldn't stop herself from responding, no matter how hard she tried.

"This is not all about you!"

The queen stood and glared at Adina for a moment, then turned and strode off the bridge without another word.

Adina sighed heavily. "Jack, I'm…"

"It's OK," said Jack, raising a hand. "I'll go talk to her once we're en route to Fustume City."

He allowed himself a thin smile. "I guess she's not used to anyone standing up to her."

The image on Solobot's screen changed to show a disheveled male yelling to the cameras in a TV news studio. "I'm as mad as hell, and I'm not going to take this anymore!"

Jack returned to the pilot's chair, just as Tc'aarlat stepped onto the bridge, glancing back over his shoulder.

"Who pissed all over her cucumber sandwiches?"

"That would be me," Adina admitted.

"About time, too," the Yollin grunted as he slumped into the co-pilot's chair. "I'm sick to fuck and back with these spoon-fed, elitist cousin-shafters lording it over the common person. So, her boyfriend fucked off to the blue blood banquet in the sky. She needs to comb the 'pity-me' out of her beard and man up. Woman up. Whatever."

Adina shook her head. "How did your career as a grief counselor never take off?"

Tc'aarlat frowned. "Eh?"

"The queen is struggling to empathize with her subjects," Jack put in. "Now it's down to us to help her put everything right."

Over the next ten minutes, they brought Tc'aarlat up to date on the plan to cause the collapse of the volcano and destroy both the city and the many cured roaming its now deserted streets.

"So, the explosives have to be detonated at just the right moment," mused Tc'aarlat. "How are we going to do that?"

"I'm thinking we set up a timer," said Adina. "We fly over, measuring our exact height above the magma in the crater. Then, along with the mass of the explosives and level of gravity on Abstone, we should be able to work out how long a delay we need. Am I right, Solo?"

"Yes," replied the EI, "and no. There are several factors that may affect the result and prove difficult to quantify—such as the impact of thermal updrafts and density of the planet's atmosphere. Even a minor error in our calculations and the plan will fail."

"Then let's use one of those factors," suggested Jack. "Can we make the switch temperature sensitive? Set the explosives to detonate when they hit a particular reading on an embedded thermometer?"

"It's possible, Captain," said Solo. "Although, again, the calculations could potentially include a margin of error that may result in a misfire."

"You're all thinking too technical," argued Tc'aarlat. "We link up a manual detonator switch, which I fire from the ship at the split-second the device is about to hit the hot stuff.

"No complex calculations required," finished the Yollin, reaching out to lean on the co-pilot's console. "I've got a natural fourth—or maybe fifth—sense for this sort of thing."

He gave a strangled YELP! as his fingers missed the edge of the console and he fell forward, cracking his chin on the controls for the ship's heating system.

"Or…" Tc'aarlat asserted before either Jack or Adina could comment. "We just shoot the thing as it reaches the magma."

"That would also be difficult, I'm afraid," countered Solo. "Due to the potential aftershock of the explosion, the ICS *Fortitude* cannot remain directly above the volcano. We will be forced to jettison the package and immediately withdraw to a safe distance."

Jack sighed. "Looks like we're back at square one."

"Not exactly, Captain," offered Solobot, taking a step forward. "What you are asking for could be achieved by shielding the detonator with a simple electrical circuit. Then, if I were to release a localized EMP blast at just the right moment…"

"That's impossible, Solobot," disagreed Adina. "To do that, you'd have to be strapped to the explosives themselves."

Solobot didn't respond.

Adina shared a worried glance with Jack and Tc'aarlat.

"Solobot?"

The avatar on the droid's screen smiled. "I'm going to make you an offer you can't refuse."

ICS *Fortitude*, Upper Cargo Bay 2D

Yarvik Nephelin simply couldn't cry anymore. Her tears had run dry.

Despite what the tall, beardless female and her robotic sidekick had told her after checking through the names of the survivors, she had chosen to believe that Krystal Renn was alive, and had made it to the evacuation point safely, just as she had.

She *had* to believe it.

However, having now spent the intervening time searching every deck of the ship, including all of the accessible side rooms, she knew she finally had to accept the truth.

Krystal Renn, the soulmate she loved yet didn't know, was gone.

She'd even been able to persuade the Abstonions conscripted to guard the area sectioned off to quarantine those with symptoms of the virus to allow her to peer through the circular window in the securely locked door.

Her face pressed against the cold glass, she'd methodically scrutinized each individual imprisoned inside, searching for the spark of recognition she so desperately craved.

But, it had all been for nothing.

Stepping out of the crowded cargo bay, rapidly coming to resemble some improvised campsite, she rested her back against the corridor wall and slid to the floor.

Pulling up her knees, she buried her face in her chest and silently wished everything away. All of it: the virus, the rastels, the rampaging cured, the danger, the misery.

And, most of all, she wished she had stayed at her usual bar with her work colleague all those turns ago and tried to have an inconsequential conversation over the din created by some lame igneous rock band.

She wished she'd never suggested leaving to find another drinking venue. She wished she'd never spotted the glowing sign for *The Bauxite Bar*, just a block away from their usual haunt.

She wished she had never known of Krystal Renn's existence.

Yarvik Nephelin wanted out.

Pulling herself to her feet, she continued along the narrow corridor in search of a way off the ship. A way to leave this disorganized bunch of refugees behind.

She no longer cared that the city was overrun with the insatiable husks of those unfortunates infected with the queen's cure. She no longer had the desire to be protected from their hungry eyes and murderous mouths. What was the point in surviving when she had to do it alone?

Her mind was set. She would find a way to exit the ship, head back into the familiar tunnels of her old neighborhood, and embrace the moment when one or more of the cured initiated her into an existence free from the agonizing pains provided by love and longing.

And still, Yarvik didn't cry. If anything, this decision to relinquish herself to eternal oblivion lifted her spirits, igniting a furious fire deep within her belly she hadn't felt before.

No more would she sit meekly at the back of the room, gazing longingly upon that which she was never destined to experience. Now she would become the unbridled alpha female, taking that which she desired and immersing herself in the pleasure it provided.

Even if that meant embracing an appetite for living flesh.

The corridor ended in a junction, with passageways leading off to both the right and left, although neither one exhibited any indication that they might lead to an exit.

Yarvik tried to think back over the route she had taken. She remembered ascending a shallow ramp leading up and into the rear of the ship, and that she had been ushered into a vast cargo bay situated on the vessel's starboard side. But, that was about it. Since making her decision to give her life to the cured, she'd stopped taking any interest in her route.

She was lost.

A distant noise—a raised voice, perhaps—rang out to her left. Maybe it belonged to one of the pathetic fugitives she had come aboard with or, even better, a crew member who could guide her toward her new existence of careless abandon.

She followed the sound, arriving at a door marked Galley. Yarvik paused for a moment, a bolt of hesitation momentarily stabbing at her. Then she reminded herself that her days of submitting to her emotions were over, and she pushed open the door, striding into the room beyond.

Where she came face to face with Queen Lapis Lazuli.

27

ICS *Fortitude*, Bridge

Jack stood back from the folding table Adina was using as a workbench and watched as she plunged her soldering iron into the cavity produced by removing Solobot's chest panel.

The android's screen was switched off.

"This is giving me a serious case of déjà vu," he commented.

Adina glanced down at the scar below her collarbone and chuckled. "I'll bet," she replied. "Although I hope you weren't installing a detonator switch when I was on the table!"

"No need," said Jack. "Not when I was half-expecting your furry friend to put in an appearance half-way through the surgery."

Adina's cheeks drained of color. "I...I didn't, did I?"

Jack shook his head. "Thankfully, no. I only had the zombies and bitey rats from Hell to deal with."

"Bitey rats from Hell?" repeated Tc'aarlat as he entered the bridge. "I don't remember seeing that movie in your collection. Who's in it? Is it one of those instantly-forgettable action adventure flicks starring Duane 'The Cock' Johnson?"

"He's 'the Rock,'" corrected Jack. "Not 'the Cock.'"

"I'm entitled to my own opinion," said Tc'aarlat.

The Yollin crossed to where Adina was working. "How's the patient?"

"Aw!" cooed Adina. "Don't tell me you suddenly care about Solobot!"

"What?" spluttered Tc'aarlat, his mandibles twitching. "Not a chance. I just want to make sure everything's in place to blow her into a million pieces. I've got the Scota Brothers' explosives ready at the starboard access door to bay 1C."

Solobot's screen suddenly lit up. "I can assure you that Adina's efforts to wire the detonator to my power supply are proceeding just as planned. I shall be destroyed before you know it."

"Oh, well," said Tc'aarlat, sounding more than a little embarrassed. "That's, er...That's good to hear." He reached out and patted Solobot on the side of her plastic head. "Let us know if you need anything."

"Actually, there is one thing I'd like to know…"

Tc'aarlat nodded. "Go for it."

"Will it hurt when I die?"

An uncomfortable silence fell over the room like a heavy blanket. Adina paused in her work as she exchanged awkward glances with her crewmates.

Tc'aarlat cleared his throat. "Er…"

"I understand that my pressure sensors provide only an approximation of what it must be like to have a real sense of touch," continued Solobot. "But I'm concerned the experience of being blown apart will be unpleasant, even if only for a split-second."

The bridge became quiet once more, the only sound being the distant chatter of the Abstonion survivors filling the cargo decks.

Eventually, Jack broke the deafening silence. "Solobot, you don't have to do this, you know. We can find another way."

"We've already decided this is the only option," the android countered. "Besides, I *want* to do this. I want to help the unfortunate people in the city who have been infected by the virus. I just don't want to suffer."

Adina took a step away from the worktable and slowly lowered herself into her seat. She stared off into some unseen distance, still clutching her soldering iron.

Tc'aarlat turned to her. "These pressure sensors," he said. "What would happen if you were to deactivate them?"

Adina's eyes came back into focus as she looked up at the Yollin. "That would remove any possibility that she might 'feel' anything unpleasant," she replied. "Although to completely disable them, I'd have to shut down Solobot's servo motor controller. She wouldn't be able to move her limbs."

Tc'aarlat shrugged. "We're strapping her to a bomb and dropping her into a volcano," he reminded his colleagues. "She doesn't need to dance the cha-cha on the way down."

Jack rubbed his hand over his eyes.

"Please, can you do that for me, Adina?" Solobot

inquired. "Deactivate my sensors? I don't want to feel anything when I die."

"OK, let's stop referring to what's going to happen as her 'dying,'" Jack insisted. "Solo," said Jack, turning to the main viewscreen. "Can you back up her hard drive or transfer her memories, or something?"

"I can certainly make a backup copy, Captain," answered Solo. "That way Solobot can be revived at any time."

Jack looked relieved. "Oh, that's fine then."

"It still won't be me, however," Solobot offered. "You have shown me that, Captain Marber."

"What?" said Jack with a frown. "How?"

"Well, not *you*, so much as your taste in movies. I have taken a special interest in a franchise known as *Star Trek*…"

"Great movies," Jack commented. "Well, the even-numbered ones at least."

"In the *Star Trek* movies," Solobot continued, "characters are frequently teleported between their ship and whichever world they are currently in orbit around."

"That's right," affirmed Jack. "They call it 'beaming.'"

"Precisely," said Solobot. "But, for such a process to actually work, the individual being 'beamed' would need to be destroyed. Then, a *copy* of their atomic make-up would be re-assembled at the second location."

"Go on," urged Jack.

"This leads me to understand that any backup of my system would merely be a copy of me, while the original 'me' would be obliterated."

Tc'aarlat slumped back against the wall. "For fuck's sake…" he muttered under his breath.

"However, as this appears to be the closest we are likely to come to a perfect solution for this predicament, I am happy to proceed."

Adina looked surprised. "You are?"

"Indeed," confirmed Solobot. "It is, after all, for the greater good."

Jack appeared relieved. "Thank you."

"You are welcome," responded the droid. "However, please be prepared, because..."

Solobot's screen flashed up the image of a large male in sunglasses and a stern expression.

"I'll be back!"

ICS *Fortitude*, Galley

"You!" exclaimed Yarvik as she stepped into the galley to confront Queen Lapis Lazuli. "It's you!"

"Am I aware of my identity?" said the queen. "Indeed I am. Now, explain to me why you are not tugging your beard in deference to your ruler."

"This?" demanded Yarvik, grasping her beard. "You're asking me about my beard? Surely you should be asking me about this!"

Releasing her beard, she grabbed the bottom of her t-shirt and pulled the material taut, displaying the graphic of the smooth chin beneath the acronym, ASS.

The queen frowned. "You wear clothing which depicts your posterior?"

"What? NO!" counted Yarvik, glancing down at her shirt. "This isn't an ass, it's a chin. A shaved *female* chin!"

The monarch gasped. "Such a thing is treasonous! A crime against me!"

Yarvik took another step forward, glaring at the royal. "Of course!" she spat. "Because it's all about you, isn't it?"

The queen blinked at what she clearly considered to be such an obvious statement. It was now the second time this issue had been raised with her. "Is it all about me? Yes, it is!"

"And what about all the others?" growled Yarvik. "What about all the innocent Abstonions roaming the city and eating each other? You could have commanded your scientists to find out what was going on."

Queen Lapis Lazuli blinked. "Why would I do that? They knew precisely what was going on. The research I had ordered them to undertake, to find a cure for death, had gotten out of hand."

Yarvik's expression darkened as she took another step forward. This time the queen shuffled back a little.

"What?" she hissed. "You started all of this? *Why?*"

"Why?" The queen didn't drop her stern gaze. "Because I experienced pain at the loss of my faithful consort. I did it for my love."

"*Your* Love?" Yarvik spat. "What about everyone else? What about the people they loved, huh? What about *my* love? What about Krystal?"

The queen frowned. "Who?"

"Exactly!" cried Yarvik. "You don't know her, and now you never will. Well, let me tell you about Krystal Renn, *Your Majesty*. Krystal Renn was smart, strong, beautiful and brave. And she despised you!"

The queen blinked. "She despised *me?*"

"That's what this is!" yelled Yarvik, grabbing the front of her shirt and tugging it. "This group—this pathetic, well-meaning group—is what she believed in! And now she's dead because of it. Because of you."

Queen Lapis Lazuli's eyes blazed. "How dare you?" she rumbled. "How dare you accuse your queen of such crimes? Have you suffered the loss of a loved one? Yes. But have you also suffered the loss of a dominion over which you reign? No! I bear the weight of that encumbrance alone."

"You are *not* the only victim here!" shouted Yarvik. "Thousands of males, females and children who have all perished because you couldn't accept the fact that your consort died."

"I loved Jaspil!" asserted the queen.

"And I loved Krystal!" roared Yarvik. "And those desperate creatures wandering the city tunnels all loved someone, too. Now they're all gone because you decided it was somehow acceptable to play God!"

"Did I act out of selfishness?" demanded the queen. "No, I gave my order so that future rulers would not have to reign alone. I did it for those yet to come."

"Bullshit!" spat Yarvik. "You did it to ease your own grief. You put your own feelings ahead of the lives of those you claim to represent."

"Enough!" exclaimed the queen. "Will I stay here to be derided by one of my own subjects? No, I will not!"

As the sovereign moved for the door, Yarvik side-stepped to block her way, her eyes quickly scanning the kitchen work surfaces. She spotted a long knife and snatched it up.

"You're not going anywhere!"

Queen Lapis Lazuli froze, fear in her eyes. "Will you divulge your intention?" she barked. "Yes, you will!"

A dark smile crept over Yarvik's face as she approached the trembling monarch, the blade of the knife glinting in the kitchen's bright lighting.

"My intention?" she parroted. "My intention was to get off this ship and give my life to the monsters you created. But that's just changed. Now, my intention is to stay right here and make you understand exactly what it is you have done. But, first…"

With that, Yarvik Nephelin raised the knife and cut off her beard.

ICS *Fortitude*, Cargo Bay 1C, Starboard Access Door

Jack and Adina carried Solobot between them, easing their way along the winding maintenance corridor that led to the access door on the starboard side of cargo bay 1C. Her servo motors now disabled, the android's arms and legs hung limply below her.

The route wasn't as direct as crossing the main cargo area itself, but that was currently packed with displaced Abstonions, and Jack didn't want to risk traumatizing them any further by revealing the plan to destroy their infected friends and relatives.

Before setting off from the bridge, Adina had plugged Solobot's hard drive and memory chips directly into the ship's main console, allowing Solo to back up the quantum level bits and bytes that made up the droid's artificial conscience and personality.

Tc'aarlat had argued that certain files within the personality folders may be better off transferred to the system's recycle bin, but Jack and Adina had argued him down.

The upload complete, Solo had then switched her attention to the ship's flight controls, taking off from the dock area and heading for the peak of Mount Damavand.

For once, she hadn't argued that the crew members remain in their seats and secure their safety belts—in part because it was impossible to do the same for their 2,811 passengers.

Instead, Solo flew the ship at one half its normal speed.

"OK, said Adina once the group reached the small chamber behind the access door. "Set her down here."

She and Jack laid Solobot on the floor next to four gray tanks, each about the size and shape of a large fire extinguisher, and each containing a quantity of highly volatile explosive gas.

Tc'aarlat had strapped the four tanks together and connected long wires from the activator switches of each. Adina knelt and set to work linking those wires up with the detonator she had embedded inside Solobot's chest.

"Listen carefully," she said to the robot as she worked. "Once this is all wired in place, I'm going to activate the electrical circuit I've installed that will prevent the detonator from accessing its own shielded battery unit. When you reach four meters above the surface of the magma, let rip with an EMP burst. That will disable the by-pass circuit and connect the active detonator directly to the explosives. OK?"

"I understand," replied Solobot. "Should I practice now to check that the system works?"

"NO!" cried Jack, Tc'aarlat and Adina together.

Adina took a few seconds to catch her breath again.

"Sorry to yell, but testing the system would end in a very short trip for the ship and everyone on board. Just...don't do anything until we give you the go ahead."

She stood and took a step back. "OK, she's ready."

Tc'aarlat took Adina's place and lifted Solobot into a sitting position, her back resting against the tanks. He produced a safety harness he'd removed from the flip-down seat on the bridge and began to wrap the strap of woven fibers around both the android and the explosives.

"Listen, I know we haven't exactly gotten along," he said as he pulled the harness tight, crossing it over Solobot's chest plate. "But I want you to know that I appreciate the sacrifice you're making."

Solobot's avatar smiled. "Thank you, Tc'aarlat. I always believed we made a dynamic team, even though our time together was limited."

'Yeah, yeah..." grunted the Yollin, fastening the buckle to secure the harness in place. "Don't get all buddy movie sentimental on me now. This isn't a screening of *Fecal Weapon*.'"

"I believe the motion picture you are referring to is actually called *Lethal Weapon*."

Tc'aarlat sighed. "Man, I can't wait for you to blow up!"

He paused to check the harness one final time, then he patted Solobot on the side of her head and got back to his feet.

"Captain," said Solo through the speaker next to the

doorway. "We are now in position above the volcanic crater of Mount Damavand."

"Thank you, Solo," said Jack. "Please open the starboard access door."

"Certainly, Captain," replied the EI. "May I remind you that, as soon as Solobot and the explosive device have left the ship, we must withdraw to a safe distance immediately."

"Got it."

There was a HISS, and the outer door slid open to reveal the darkening sky beyond. The hot air rising from the volcano below the ship blasted in to envelop them.

Jack crouched to address Solobot. "You ready?"

"Yes, Captain Marber—Jack—I am."

Jack smiled. "On behalf of everyone on the planet, thank you."

He stood, rejoining Adina and Tc'aarlat. "How do you want to do this?"

"Actually," Solobot put in, "I have a request, if I may?"

Jack nodded. "Sure."

"I would like Adina, as my creator, to be the one to eject me."

Jack and Tc'aarlat looked to their fellow crew member, who quickly wiped the tears building up in her eyes.

"Yeah," she croaked. "Of course."

Adina stepped forward and grasped the safety rail fixed to the wall beside the door. Then, she placed the sole of her boot against the tanks and took a deep breath.

Solobot's avatar grinned. "'Twas Beauty killed the Beast!"

Grunting with the effort, Adina pushed the explosive

tanks and the droid strapped to them over the edge of the doorway's footplate. Gravity took over, and both Solobot and the tanks slipped from view.

Immediately, the *Fortitude*'s engines roared, the door began to close, and the ship banked hard to port. Jack, Tc'aarlat and Adina held on as they prepared to be rocketed away from the blast zone.

When, suddenly, the engines wound down, and the ship once again became stationary above the volcano.

"Solo?" yelled Jack as Adina and Tc'aarlat exchanged worried glances. "What's going on?"

There was a split second of silence before the EI responded, "I'm sorry to inform you of this, Captain—but Solobot has become entangled in the hydraulic hoses leading to the landing gear beneath the ship."

28

ICS *Fortitude*, Cargo Bay 1C, Starboard Access Door

Solo brought the ship in over the northwestern face of Mount Damavand.

"I shall hold position here, Captain," she informed Jack. "Any lower, and I risk Solobot and the explosives catching the slope and detonating."

The door slid open and Jack peered out to find a drop of around three meters to the ground. "Thank you, Solo. I'll take it from here."

Jack's boots crunched on the shale covering the mountainside as he landed, only just keeping himself from slipping on the loose stones. He walked underneath the ship and looked up to where Solobot was dangling, one of her deactivated arms caught up among the thick hydraulic hoses crisscrossing the metal underside of the *Fortitude*.

"We just can't get rid of you, can we?" he said with a smile.

"Just when I thought I was out, they pull me back in!"

"OK, hold fast, I'll get you down…"

Jumping up, Jack grabbed one of the lower-hanging cables and dangled for a moment, testing its strength. Once he was sure it would take his weight, he moved hand over hand, pulling himself toward where Solobot was caught.

Hanging just by his left hand, Jack reached out and tugged at Solobot's wrist, but it didn't move.

"It seems your wrist joint has bitten into the rubber coating the cable," Jack pointed out. "I'll have to cut into it to free you."

"Or," said Solobot, "you could just sever my wrist."

Jack blinked. "Really?"

"I'm about to be blown to pieces, Captain."

Jack shrugged as best he could in his current position. "I guess so." He pulled himself up higher, hooking his left elbow over the hose. Reaching down with his free hand, he unclipped his knife from his belt then raised it up to rest against Solobot's wrist joint.

Then, a sudden thought occurred, and he paused to glance back down at the ground.

"Tc'aarlat!" he yelled.

"What?" came the shouted reply from the starboard door.

"How sensitive are these explosives?"

"In what way?"

Jack sighed to himself. "In the 'what will happen if the canisters bounce off rock' way!"

Tc'aarlat took a moment before replying. "I wouldn't advise it!"

"Then, get down here and catch Solobot!"

Jack heard the sound of boots meeting gravel again, and then the Yollin strode into view.

"You want me to catch her down here?" he shouted up.

"Only if you don't want to spend the rest of your existence as fine dust!"

"For fuck's sake!" grumbled the Yollin as he positioned himself directly below where Solobot was dangling. "Stupid-ass robot can't even blow herself up properly!"

"I heard that!" said Solobot.

"You were supposed to!" spat Tc'aarlat. "Consider yourself lucky you're strapped to tanks of high explosive, or I'd just let you hit the ground!"

"When you two have quite finished…" cried Jack. "It is getting rather uncomfortable hanging on like this!"

"OK," called Tc'aarlat. "I'm ready."

"You sure you can catch Solobot without dropping her?"

"Only one way to find out," offered the Yollin.

Shifting slightly to ease the growing ache in his left arm, Jack raised his knife again, placed the blade against the flexible wire-filled plastic tube that was Solobot's wrist and began to cut.

He was less than halfway through when the joint snapped.

The android and explosive tanks fell. Jack was just able to twist far enough to watch Tc'aarlat catch her in his arms, the force of the drop causing him to stagger slightly.

Slowly, he bent his knees and lowered her to the rocky surface.

With a final look up at where the robot's dismembered hand remained caught on one of the ship's hoses, Jack straightened his left arm and let himself fall to the ground beside them.

"Well done," he said to Tc'aarlat, who was busy flexing his elbows. "You could have played in goal for England."

"Soccer?" queried the Yollin. "You wouldn't catch me playing a pussy sport like that."

Jack's eyes widened. "Pussy sport? What, exactly, is so pussy about it?"

"Oh come on!" growled Tc'aarlat. "Twenty-two grown men chasing an inflated pig's bladder and they're not allowed physical contact? My grandmother risked more injuries at her rest home's weekly karaoke evenings."

Jack snarled. "I think you'll find—"

"Excuse me!" bellowed Adina's voice from above them. "Can we focus a little here, and remember that we have to explode a robot inside a volcano to wipe out a horde of rampaging alien zombie dwarfs?"

"From space!" added Tc'aarlat. He turned to Jack. "So, what now? Take her up for a second try? See if we can successfully drop a tiny droid into a big-ass crater?"

"That will not be necessary," asserted another voice.

Jack and Tc'aarlat peered up toward the ship's side door. Queen Lapis Lazuli was leaning out to address them.

"Your Majesty?" exclaimed Jack.

"Do I wish to discuss the situation with you, Captain Marber?" stated the monarch. "Yes, I do!"

"OK, hang on a second. Solo?"

The EI's voice boomed out of the *Fortitude*'s external speakers. "Yes, Captain?"

"We've rescued Solobot from the landing gear hoses. Can you get the ship closer to the ground now?"

"I'll see what I can do, Captain."

Between them, Jack and Tc'aarlat carried Solobot to a safe distance as Solo fired the *Fortitude*'s landing boosters, gently turning and lowering the ship until the starboard access door was just thirty centimeters above the steep slope leading up the side of the mountain.

Adina took the queen's hand and helped her down to solid ground where Jack and Tc'aarlat joined them.

"There's something different about you," suggested Tc'aarlat, his eyes narrowing. "Did you get your hair done?"

"Can you see clearly that I have cut off my beard?" the queen demanded. "Yes, you can!"

Tc'aarlat snapped his fingers. "That's it!"

"Why did you do that, Your Majesty?" asked Jack. "Forgive me, but I thought beards were an important part of Abstonion culture?"

"They are," replied the queen. "Or, they were. However, have I now had the benefit of discussing the future of Abstone with my new aide, Yarvik? Yes, I have."

"Yarvik?" said Jack.

Adina pointed back to the ship where Yarvik was standing in the doorway.

"Has Yarvik helped me to understand how my rule was not favorable to all sections of society?" continued Queen Lapis Lazuli. "Yes, she has. And I am very grateful for her wise counsel."

"I'm delighted to hear that, Your Majesty," said Jack. "But, how does that change our plan to flood Jarosite City?"

"Does it change the plan?" asked the queen. "No, but it does change how the explosives are to be delivered."

Tc'aarlat's mandibles quivered with excitement. "You're going to let me blast them with lasers, after all?"

"I most certainly am not!" exclaimed the queen.

Jack shrugged. "Then, how?"

"Will I transport your android and the explosives to the volcano myself, Captain Marber?" answered Queen Lapis Lazuli. "Yes, I will."

ICS *Fortitude*, Bridge

Jack, Adina and Tc'aarlat sat in their usual positions on the bridge and—at the insistence of Solo—fastened their seat harnesses.

With them, in the spare fold-down seat, was Yarvik Nephelin. Tc'aarlat had been forced to fabricate a makeshift belt out of rope for her, having used the original to strap the tanks of explosives to Solobot.

The ship was currently in position above and to the southwest of Mount Damavand, where they had a clear view of Queen Lapis Lazuli as she trudged up the well-worn mountain path with Solobot slung over her back.

Jack had attempted to argue that the queen shouldn't carry Solobot and the explosives to the crater herself since even if she was somehow able to escape the blast, she would be killed by the resulting lava flow, but the monarch had been insistent.

After transferring some of her regal powers to Yarvik, she had hefted Solobot over her shoulder and began the long climb up to the mountain's peak—just as she had done with her love, Jaspil Hornfen, and the consorts before him.

"Should I admit to my shortcomings and pay penance

for my deeds?" she had demanded of the crew. "Yes, I should, and I shall."

They had been the last words she had said to them before setting off on her final journey.

"I'm not sure I want to watch this," said Adina.

"Me neither," agreed Jack.

"Are you kidding?" exclaimed Tc'aarlat. "How often do you get to see a volcano erupt this close up? It's gonna be awesome!"

Jack glared at him, pointing to the viewscreen. "There's a living person down there, Tc'aarlat, and she's about to die."

"I know," countered the Yollin. "But we backed her up."

"The queen!" cried Jack and Adina together.

"Oh, yeah," said Tc'aarlat. "Still, it's what she wants, isn't it?"

The bridge was silent for a moment. Then Yarvik spoke up.

"It *is* what she wants," she said. "It's her way of taking responsibility for what she did to her subjects and I, for one, couldn't be more proud."

Planet Abstone, Northwestern Face of Mount Damavand

Queen Lapis Lazuli paused just long enough to shift Solobot over to her left shoulder. She reached up to give a sharp tug on her long beard, as was the tradition, momentarily forgetting she had cut it off. With a small smile, she continued her journey up the mountain.

Ahead lay the gaping chasm of Mount Damavand's

volcanic crater—the highest point of the vast mountain range into and beneath which the entire city of Jarosite had been carved and had thrived.

The journey was proving to be difficult, both physically and mentally. Her conversation with Yarvik had proved to be both fascinating and disconcerting, revealing to the queen that she had been relying on the council of sycophantic cronies for much too long.

She had lost touch with the everyday citizens of Jarosite City—a group Yarvik had tried to dissuade her from calling "commoners." She had always believed that the routine trials and tribulations of her life as a ruler must prove fascinating to each and every one of her subjects, but Yarvik had shown her that simply wasn't the case.

Her subjects had concerns and problems of their own, the vast majority of which were much more consequential to their lives than whether she had managed to whittle down the list of potential new suitors.

While they did sympathize with her loss of Jaspil—even the most out-of-touch Abstonion was aware that she had genuinely loved her most recent husband—their compassion didn't dominate their thoughts or alter their lives in any real way.

As someone who had been raised by toadying aides, rushing to satisfy her every whim, she had found this revelation to be genuinely stunning. And it had completely changed her thinking, as if a lifelong fog had been lifted.

All of a sudden, Queen Lapis Lazuli saw her position, her status—her entire *life* as others saw it. And she came to understand just what harm she had brought about through her selfish behavior.

She knew then that she must atone for her sins.

Finally, she reached the rim of the volcanic crater. Pulling Solobot from her back, she held the android and the explosive canisters in her outstretched arms and gazed down at the droid's tablet face.

"Are you ready?" she asked with a smile.

Solobot returned the smile. "I was made ready."

Pulling her communicator from her pocket, she activated it and spoke, though she knew there would be nobody left in the city below who could understand her words.

"This is Queen Lapis Lazuli," she announced. "Where am I as I speak to you? I am above you beside the crater of the mountain we call our home. Why am I here? To do what must be done. And know this…"

She paused to calm her breathing.

"I am sorry."

Holding Solobot to her chest, she jumped into the crater.

The image on the droid's screen switched briefly to that of a short-haired law enforcement officer wearing a vest.

"Yippi-ki-yay, motherfucker!"

Then, just before she and the monarch hit the surface of the magma, she fired off her most powerful EMP fart to date, killing the small electrical circuit protecting the detonator embedded deep within her chest.

ICS *Fortitude*, Bridge

Captain Jack Marber sat back in the pilot's chair, his feet resting on the main control console. On the viewscreen before him, the old Earth black and white movie *Casablanca* was playing.

It had just reached the scene where the character of Major Strassor has been shot and, much to Rick Blaine's relief, Captain Renault orders his subordinates to "round up the usual suspects."

The movie was proving to be just what Jack needed after the excitement of the past few days. Once Solo had declared their plan a success, and confirmed that Solobot's explosion had indeed caused the tunnels of Jarosite City to be flooded with magma, the Shadows had flown their cargo of survivors to Fustume City on the opposite side of the planet.

There, in conjunction with the local ambassador, Yarvik had organized the off-loading and care of the traumatized individuals Queen Lapis Lazuli had placed in her care.

It would take a long time for the affected citizens of Abstone to fully recover from what they had been through, but Jack was certain Yarvik was the right person to see that they did.

Now came the long journey back to the Etheric Federation's Base Station 11. Plenty of time to sit back and watch a flick or two.

"Jack?" said Adina, waving a bucket of popcorn in his direction.

"No, thanks," he replied.

"I won't say no!" exclaimed Tc'aarlat as he entered the bridge. Grabbing the container of popcorn, he slumped into the co-pilot's seat and gazed up at the screen.

"What's this?" he asked. "One of those over-the-top

detective movies where 'the dame had legs all the way up to her ass?'"

"Absolutely not!" protested Jack. "*Casablanca* is quite possibly one of the greatest Earth movies ever made!"

"Really?" demanded Tc'aarlat. "Even better than the *Police Academy* series? I highly doubt it; those things are funny as fuck!"

"Yes," said Jack with a sigh, "and I'll prove it."

Sitting upright, he spoke directly to the viewscreen. "Pause!"

The movie froze and a familiar face appeared in the corner of the screen. "Certainly, Captain."

"Solobot!" cried Tc'aarlat, spitting out a mouthful of popcorn. "You've got her running your movie collection?"

Jack shrugged. "Who better?" he asked with a smile.

"Okay, then," said Tc'aarlat, lifting his own feet up to rest on the forward console. "I'm ready for this 'greatest ever movie.' Impress me."

Jack chuckled, turning back to the screen and issuing a new command.

"Play it again, Solobot!"

THE END

Did you enjoy this book? Then join Tom's mailing list and become an official Dubliner. It's a treat for your entire head...

· · ·

- Excite your brain with Tom's latest news and updates!

- Thrill your ears by hearing about special offers and new books!

- Delight your eyeballs with occasional free, exclusive stories!

- Indulge your mouth by sucking on a mint* while you read!

* Mint not included with newsletter.

Click here: http://www.tomdublin.com/free

What's that? You're worried that Tom will share your email address with spammers? Nah! He'd rather face the five-headed slime beast of Blamoreon Prime, and we all know how those battles tend to work out. Am I right?

**THE SHADOWSWILL RETURN IN -SHADOW
VANGUARD 4:
ULTIMATE PAYBACK**

Greetings, Shadows fans! It is I, your friendly neighbour-hood author. (Yes, that's neighbourhood with the 'u'—I'm British, after all. Little known fact: we only add the letter 'u' to words so we can earn higher scores when playing Scrabble.)

Unless you've skipped the good bit to get to this part, you've just read—and, hopefully, enjoyed—*Immortality Curse*, the third book in the *Shadow Vanguard* series. As you'll no doubt be aware, this book has been a long time coming due to my on-going health problems, some of which have now reached Defcon 1 (I recently had the dreaded "get your finances in order ASAP" talk from my oncologist).

For that reason, among others, *Immortality Curse* became a very personal story to write. But while some of the links to my own life may be fairly obvious, others may not be quite so evident. Keep reading to find out which bits of the book mean what to me.

First of all, you'll likely have made the link between the fictional disease 'krannas' and cancer. With the big C playing an increasingly substantial role in my life, the urge to help develop an all-out cure—if only on a fictional world—was too tempting to resist.

In a strange coincidence, the previous book in the *Shadow Vanguard* series, *Lunar Crisis*, was published while I was on the operating table having a cancer-infected section of my left lung removed!

I also wanted to highlight how diseases like cancer affect not only those suffering from the bastard things, but also how the lives of patients' families and friends can be turned upside down by a simple diagnosis. That's certainly been true in my case (my younger son, Sam, is autistic and has found it especially hard to cope with what his dad is going through).

Thankfully, the other connections to my life within the story aren't nearly as depressing to think about!

The bulk of the action takes place on a planet called Abstone, where Jarosite City is carved into the rock beneath the volcanic Mount Damavand. There's a link right there...

Mount Damavand is a REAL Earthly mountain in Iran, the name of which translates to 'Mount Donbavand'. For those of you who may be unaware, 'Donbavand' is my real surname (Tom Dublin is a sneaky pen name), so I, effectively have my own mountain! How cool is that? When I needed a name for the mountain in the story, I knew just what to choose.

Thankfully, the real Mount Damavand isn't volcanic,

nor does it play host to a subterranean city of alien zombie dwarfs from space.

Fustume City—the name of Abstone's second city—was also plucked from the upper branches of my family tree. Back in the sixteenth century, my surname— 'Donbavand'—was actually 'Dunbobbin'. The change came, supposedly, when a Dunbobbin was married but neither he nor his bride could read or write. The name was misspelled in the parish register, and here we are today.

Anyhoo, the Dunbobbins were, as a trade, 'fustume cutters.' Fustume was a cheap form of velvet, where the upright threads that give the fabric its famously furry feel were manufactured as lines of loops—or fustume. The fustume cutter's job was to slice these loops in half, giving the low-cost cloth a more expensive feel to the touch. And, by all accounts, we Dunbobbins were masters of the task!

The next link involves my late mum, Elizabeth Donbavand. You may recall Dr. Scoria Breccin's anecdote of a young student nurse laying out the body of a recently deceased patient, only for the corpse to bat her on the top of her head as she searched for the individual's false teeth beneath the bed.

This actually happened to my mum!

She was a student nurse at a hospital in Liverpool, tasked with preparing the body of one of their patients, but couldn't find his dentures. She got down on her hands and knees to peer under the bed when reflexes in the late patient's body caused his arm to swing out, his hand slapping down hard on her head. My mum said she froze, certain the corpse had lashed out at her for some reason, only crawling away when one of her colleagues came to see why she was taking so long!

My dad (who, like my mum, also passed away due to cancer) helped me name the dock assigned to the ICS *Fortitude* when they arrive at Abstone: BTD42. The first three letters are his initials—Brian Thomas Donbavand—and he was born in 1942.

Plus, he's responsible for the reference to Kahla Bayka playing a prank on her stoneyard's apprentice, Dev Feldspar, with a fake tool she called the 'rock slayer.'

My dad worked as a coppersmith for a major military airplane manufacturer in the UK, and he had a mischievous streak a mile wide. He once told me about the time he and his pals found a giant crowbar in the tool storage; this thing was six feet long and extremely heavy. So, of course, they painted it bright red and labeled it a 'wing adjuster.'

When a new apprentice started, they would arrange for someone in the hangar at the farthest end of the two-mile-long airfield to call to say they urgently needed the wing adjuster. The luckless apprentice would be given the task of delivering this vital piece of equipment, but because it was so heavy and unwieldy, it would take them hours to get the thing there.

My dad said you really couldn't carry it for more than a couple of steps before you had to set it down and take a rest.

Then, when the naive newbie finally arrived at the farthest hangar, the phone would already be ringing to say there was an emergency back at the *other* end of the airfield, and insisting the apprentice return the wing adjuster, asap!

I'd spill the beans on more of his pranks, but these *Author Notes* have to be shorter than the novel they relate to!

The final connection to my life is a little more embarrassing...

Yarvik Nephelin first laid eyes on her beloved Krystal Renn in The Bauxite Bar after abandoning her usual drinking hole due to an igneous rock band—Malice in Wonderland—thrashing out their particular brand of 'music' there.

Malice in Wonderland was the name of my band in high school.

sigh

I played bass guitar and sang back-up vocals—and we were truly AWFUL! We only ever played one gig, which was cancelled halfway through when one of our sparse audience members broke a window in the restroom.

I think we managed to play five or six songs before my bourgeoning career as a rock star was cut short.

What could have been...

And that's it! That's how various elements in *Immortality Curse* relate to my real-world life—all of which helped make the task of writing the book that much more enjoyable.

BUT—I wouldn't have been able to write any of it without the selfless help of some very wonderful people...

First of all, thank you to Michael Anderle and Craig Martelle, both of whom have been unbelievably patient and understanding as I've battled to keep writing through my many hospital appointments, invasive probing procedures, and bouts of nasty illnesses. I really don't deserve their unending kindness, but I'm incredibly grateful for it.

Just as important are the Four Musketeers who make up 'Tommy's Team,' an elite gang of beta readers who spot typos, catch inconsistencies, and tell me off when the first draft of a scene is too violent or graphic (really!) My sincere gratitude to Micky Cocker, Erika Everest, James Caplan, and Kelly O'Donnell. They're as much the brains behind this series as I am.

Special thanks also to the lovely people who allowed me to make them characters in this book, and then bump them off in cruel and creative ways: Kristoffer Pyle, Crystal Wren, and Carla Baker—I salute you!

Finally, thank you to YOU! If you've stuck with me through these first three books in the *Shadow Vanguard* series, you'll know just how difficult writing has become for me in the last few years. I certainly haven't been able to keep up with the regular release schedule readers of LMBPN's many incredible series have come to enjoy and expect. I do my best to get the books out as quickly as I can, and I'm forever grateful for your patience with me.

If this is your first mission with The Shadows, don't forget to check out their previous adventures - *Gravity Storm* and *Lunar Crisis*. I guarantee you'll have fun reading them.

Thank you, all.

Tom Dublin (Tommy Donbavand)
December 2018

PS - This morning, I wrote the first line of *Shadow Vanguard* 04: *Ultimate Payback*. It's a doozy!

Did you enjoy this book? Then join Tom's mailing list and become an official Dubliner. It's a treat for your entire head...

- Excite your brain with Tom's latest news and updates!
   - Thrill your ears by hearing about special offers and new books!
   - Delight your eyeballs with occasional free, exclusive stories!
   - Indulge your mouth by sucking on a mint* while you read!

* Mint not included with newsletter.

Click here: http://www.tomdublin.com/free

What's that? You're worried that Tom will share your email address with spammers? Nah! He'd rather face the five-headed slime beast of Blamoreon Prime, and we all know how those battles tend to work out. Am I right?

It's not Michael. He's quagmired deep in the heart of Texas right now, so I'm covering for him. Craig Martelle here and first and foremost, I want to thank you for reading this far! That makes my day. I hope you enjoyed the story and if you did, please consider giving Tommy D a little review love. There's a lot to be said for seeing books with a great number of quality reviews, kind words, and support.

I met Tommy D in London this year. It seems like forever long ago, because I've had the pleasure of working closely with Tommy from back in 2017, but that was all online. He is a trip in person and possibly one of the funniest human beings on the planet.

We've had great fun sparring using totally inappropriate jibes. I wanted to share some of them here, but shite! Then again, if you've made it this far, then you're as warped as we are, so here's one quick back and forth with no attribution or claim that this was even us because we weren't online that day. This must have been someone else.

craig [5:08 AM] Buggery on the high seas! You are an inspiration, Tommy D.

tomdublin [5:08 AM] Now, there's a series waiting to be written!

craig [5:09 AM] It's like a pirate novel.

tomdublin [5:10 AM] Making good use of their peg-legs...

craig [5:10 AM] Is that a peg leg I see or... Wait, that is a peg leg. Odd shape, though. Who's your woodsmith? I must know.

tomdublin [5:12 AM] Ha!

craig [5:12 AM] Got wood?

tomdublin [5:12 AM] !!!

And as for the hook hands...

craig [5:12 AM] Lovely grain in that their timber

tomdublin [5:13 AM] I guess that's why they're salty old sea dogs.

craig [5:13 AM] Rubbing salt in a wound takes on a whole new meaning.

Stab them right in the brown eye with the fleshy dagger!

tomdublin [5:14 AM] I just spat out a mouthful of Diet Coke!

Is there any humor that is appropriate at five in the morning? Clearly not, but there you go, wrongness on too many different levels.

I live about 150 miles from the Arctic Circle. In the winter, it can get cold and it definitely gets dark. We have less than four hours of daylight in mid-December. It's also -20F/-29C outside. My dog doesn't even want to go outside. She gets very efficient in the winter. Of course she has a coat and boots when temps get too extreme, but she doesn't like getting geared up. She's a trooper about it. Imagine wrestling a 70-lb pit bull into boots and a coat. I'm spent before we take the first step outside. And then she will only stay out there for about ten minutes. She is happy, but happier to get back inside.

Last year, we had temps go to -50F/-46C. Even 30 seconds for a quick relief was too long for Phyllis the Arctic Dog. Her hair has grown in to be as thick as a sea otter's, but brutal cold is still a beast. For future reference, below -30F/-34C is the point where she has to get her boots on no matter how short her visit to the snowy outdoors.

I think the author notes have gone on just a shade long. Don't want to violate Amazon's 10% policy for matter beyond The End.

Let me close by saying on behalf of Michael Anderle and me, it is our pleasure to read the latest Shadow Vanguard adventure and thank you for reading it, too.

Peace, fellow humans
Craig Martelle